METROPOLITAN MYSTERIES

A Casebook of
London's Detectives

edited by

MARTIN EDWARDS

BRITISH LIBRARY

This collection first published in 2024 by
The British Library
96 Euston Road
London NW1 2DB

Cataloguing in Publication Data
A catalogue record for this publication is available from the British Library

ISBN 978 0 7123 5551 3
e-ISBN 978 0 7123 6892 6

Original cover image: *By Tram to the Embankment* by Herbert K. Rooke,
1924. Image © London Metropolitan Archives (City of London).
Text design and typesetting by Tetragon, London
Printed in England by TJ Books, Padstow, Cornwall

CONTENTS

INTRODUCTION   7

A NOTE FROM THE PUBLISHER   11

The Vindictive Story of the Footsteps That Ran   13
   Dorothy L. Sayers

The Adventure of the Bruce-Partington Plans   35
   Arthur Conan Doyle

The Miser of Maida Vale   71
   Baroness Orczy

The Real Thing   105
   Henry Wade

These Artists!   123
   Henry Wade

The Case of the Faulty Drier   141
   Josephine Bell

Unsound Mind   153
   Anthony Berkeley

Man in Bond Street   173
   Anthony Gilbert

Death on Nelson's Column 185
   Eric Bennett

The Crime in Nobody's Room 207
   Carter Dickson

The Locked Room 229
   John Dickson Carr

Sergeant Dobbin Works It Out 249
   J. Jefferson Farjeon

Mum Knows Best 263
   Margery Allingham

Sergeant Pockle in Parliament 273
   William Fienburgh

Murder in St. James's 281
   Malcolm Gair

The Most Hated Man in London 289
   Patricia Moyes

The Dead Man Climbed Upstairs 295
   Raymond Postgate

Back in Five Years 305
   Michael Gilbert

INTRODUCTION

How sweet the morning air is! See how that one little cloud floats like a pink feather from some gigantic flamingo. Now the red rim of the sun pushes itself over the London cloud-bank. It shines on a good many folk, but on none, I dare bet, who are on a stranger errand than you and I. How small we feel with our petty ambitions and strivings in the presence of the great elemental forces of Nature!

ARTHUR CONAN DOYLE, *The Sign of Four*

Few if any cities anywhere in the world have supplied the scene of the crime for as many good mystery stories as London. Not only is the capital home to Scotland Yard, legendary headquarters of the Metropolitan Police, it is also the stamping-ground of some of the most notable private and amateur detectives who have ever appeared in the world of fiction, with Sherlock Holmes of 221b Baker Street, arguably the most memorable and influential fictional character yet created, leading the way.

In compiling *Metropolitan Mysteries*, my aim has been to create a casebook presenting a wide range of detectives, amateur and professional, at work in the city that prompted Holmes to the lyrical outburst quoted above (and this, as Sherlockian expert Leslie Klinger has pointed out, from a man who later had the nerve to tell Dr. Watson to "cut out the poetry"!).

The very first Crime Classic to be revived by the British Library was a London-based detective novel, *The Notting Hill Mystery*, by Charles

Felix (now believed to be the pseudonym of a writer and lawyer called Charles Warren Adams). This interesting book, sometimes claimed to be the first detective *novel*, was made available as a print-on-demand title in 2011, as part of a collection of nineteenth-century works. A positive review in the *New York Times* led to publication of a trade paperback edition, and a number of other Victorian crime novels followed before the British Library decided to focus the Crime Classics brand on twentieth century titles, starting with three titles by Mavis Doriel Hay—including the London Tube mystery *Murder Underground* (1934)—and then a couple by John Bude, the latter coinciding with the start of my involvement with the series.

The Crime Classics have—amongst many other things—provided a wonderful showcase for the extraordinary range of crime novels set in London. Ellen Wilkinson's *The Division Bell Mystery* (1932), written by a high-profile politician, is an "impossible crime" story set in the House of Commons. Michael Gilbert's *Smallbone Deceased* (1950) is set in a London solicitor's firm; he, like Wilkinson, was writing about a world that he knew inside out. John Dickson Carr's *The Lost Gallows* (1931) is a London novel written by an American who became a devotee of England and the English; his description of the disreputable Brimstone Club in the West End of the capital smoulders with youthful verve. *The Port of London Murders* (1938), in contrast, is much more realistic, much less exuberant: Josephine Bell drew on her experience of working as a doctor in the Greenwich area to create perhaps the most compelling mystery of her long career.

London and Londoners suffered grievously during the Second World War, and in particular during the Blitz. As the Crime Classics series has demonstrated time and again, detective novels from the past now often serve as fascinating social documents, even though their authors seldom envisaged that their work would enjoy such longevity. Today it is intriguing to read E. C. R. Lorac's *Murder by Matchlight* (1945), in which murder is committed in Regent's Park during the black-out, alongside *Murder's a Swine* (1943), a cheerful story by Nap Lombard (a pen-name for the husband and wife duo Pamela Hansford Johnson and Neil Stewart). In very different ways, both books give us a picture of what it was like to live through times of almost unbearable tension and anxiety.

In London, it seems, nowhere is safe from the machinations of malevolent murderers. One of the cleverest whodunits ever written, Anthony Berkeley's *The Poisoned Chocolates Case* (1929) starts with the delivery of a mysterious—and, as it turns out, deadly—box of chocolates to a highly respectable London club. In John Ferguson's bibliomystery *Death of Mr. Dodsley* (1937), death comes to a bookshop in Charing Cross Road, while in another Lorac novel, *These Names Make Clues* (1937), her detective Macdonald is invited to a "treasure hunt" at the home of a London publisher along with a group of writers, only for one of the authors to wind up dead. And the throat-clutching atmosphere of London's murky past is evocatively captured in Christianna Brand's *London Particular* aka *Fog of Doubt* (1952).

In my previous Crime Classic collection of London mysteries, *Capital Crimes* (2014), I gave a brief and selective account of the development of the London detective novel. The very positive response to that book has persuaded the British Library and me to return to the city for another selection of vintage mysteries which focuses on characters as well as the city.

It would seem a little odd to produce a book of London-based mysteries without including a Sherlock Holmes story, so the great consulting detective is represented here in one of the very best of his twentieth-century cases. Also making an appearance is Lord Peter Wimsey, in the first short story that ever featured him. In these pages you will also meet Albert Campion and Colonel March, two notable if very different characters whose investigations have featured in television series, starring those equally different actors Peter Davison and

Boris Karloff. But there are also several less renowned sleuths based in the capital who feature in this anthology; examples include Anthony Gilbert's Inspector Field, Malcolm Gair's Mark Raeburn, and Eric Bennett's Superintendent Aldgate.

Similarly, alongside eminent authors such as Arthur Conan Doyle, Dorothy L. Sayers, and Margery Allingham are to be found deeply obscure names such as Malcolm Gair and Eric Bennett, as well as several talented writers who may not be entirely forgotten, but are by no means as well-known as they deserve to be, such as Henry Wade and Patricia Moyes. The other contributors include a Hungarian baroness, an American specialist in the "impossible crime", and a Labour MP who died tragically young. One thing they all had in common was a fascination with London.

The city offers wonderful variety in terms of settings for mystery stories, and so we have close encounters with crime on Nelson's Column, in Bond Street, in Maida Vale, in a West End beauty parlour—and in a flat based on Dorothy L. Sayers' own home in Great James Street.

Producing a book of this nature is a collective effort. In seeking out stories that are particularly elusive, and information about authors that is hard to come by, I'm regularly assisted by a variety of supportive crime enthusiasts, notably Nigel Moss, John Cooper, and Phil Stephensen-Payne. In compiling this particular anthology, Jamie Sturgeon has gone beyond the call of duty, sharing with me copies of stories that previously I never even knew existed, including a very rare short story by Raymond Postgate. Thanks to Jamie's researches, and those of John Herrington, I've been able to piece together a short account of the life and criminal doings of Eric Bennett. I'd also like to thank the team at the publications department of the British Library for the work they have done in putting this book together.

MARTIN EDWARDS
www.martinedwardsbooks.com

A NOTE FROM THE PUBLISHER

1928

Lord Peter Wimsey in

THE VINDICTIVE STORY OF THE
FOOTSTEPS THAT RAN

Dorothy L. Sayers

Dorothy Leigh Sayers (1893–1957) was born in Oxford and raised in East Anglia. In 1920 she was gifted but unemployed and bruised by the end of a love affair. She decided to settle in London and took an unfurnished room at the top of a women's club at 36 St. George's Square, Pimlico; later, her engaging character Miss Climpson, assistant to Lord Peter Wimsey, occupied a top-floor flat in the same square. She moved to 44 Mecklenburgh Square (the time she spent there has been documented by Francesca Wade in her interesting book *Square Haunting*) and took a job teaching in Clapham. She was leading a rather hand-to-mouth existence and cheered herself up by inventing Wimsey, a detective to whom money was no object. During this time, she worked on her first novel about Wimsey, *Whose Body?*, which was ultimately published in 1923.

In December 1921, she left Mecklenburgh Square and moved to a flat in 24 Great James Street, which was to remain her London address for the rest of her life, although after her marriage she made her principal home in Witham, Essex. The layout of the kitchen described in this story, which may have been the first short story that she wrote about Wimsey, was—according to Barbara Reynolds' authoritative biography—modelled on that of the kitchen in her flat. A blue plaque now records Sayers' association with the property. Although probably written in 1922, as far as I know this story was first published in *Lord Peter Views the Body* (1928).

M R. BUNTER WITHDREW HIS HEAD FROM BENEATH THE FOCUS-ing cloth.

"I fancy that will be quite adequate, sir," he said deferentially, "unless there are any further patients, if I may call them so, which you would wish put on record."

"Not today," replied the doctor. He took the last stricken rat gently from the table, and replaced it in its cage with an air of satisfaction. "Perhaps on Wednesday, if Lord Peter can kindly spare your services once again—"

"What's that?" murmured his lordship, withdrawing his long nose from the investigation of a number of unattractive-looking glass jars. "Nice old dog," he added vaguely. "Wags his tail when you mention his name, what? Are these monkey-glands, Hartman, or a south-west elevation of Cleopatra's duodenum?"

"You don't know anything, do you?" said the young physician, laughing. "No use playing your bally-fool-with-an-eyeglass tricks on me, Wimsey. I'm up to them. I was saying to Bunter that I'd be no end grateful if you'd let him turn up again three days hence to register the progress of the specimens—always supposing they do progress, that is."

"Why ask, dear old thing?" said his lordship. "Always a pleasure to assist a fellow-sleuth, don't you know. Trackin' down murderers—all in the same way of business and all that. All finished? Good egg! By the way, if you don't have that cage mended you'll lose one of your patients—Number 5. The last wire but one is workin' loose—assisted by the intelligent occupant. Jolly little beasts, ain't they? No need of dentists—wish I was a rat—wire much better for the nerves than that fizzlin' drill."

Dr. Hartman uttered a little exclamation.

"How in the world did you notice that, Wimsey? I didn't think you'd even looked at the cage."

"Built noticin'—improved by practice," said Lord Peter quietly. "Anythin' wrong leaves a kind of impression on the eye; brain trots along afterwards with the warnin'. I saw that when we came in. Only just grasped it. Can't say my mind was glued on the matter. Shows the victim's improvin', anyhow. All serene, Bunter?"

"Everything perfectly satisfactory, I trust, my lord," replied the manservant. He had packed up his camera and plates, and was quietly restoring order in the little laboratory, whose fittings—compact as those of an ocean liner—had been disarranged for the experiment.

"Well," said the doctor, "I am enormously obliged to you, Lord Peter, and to Bunter too. I am hoping for a great result from these experiments, and you cannot imagine how valuable an assistance it will be to me to have a really good series of photographs. I can't afford this sort of thing—yet," he added, his rather haggard young face wistful as he looked at the great camera, "and I can't do the work at the hospital. There's no time; I've got to be here. A struggling G.P. can't afford to let his practice go, even in Bloomsbury. There are times when even a half-crown visit makes all the difference between making both ends meet and having an ugly hiatus."

"As Mr. Micawber said," replied Wimsey, "'Income twenty pounds, expenditure nineteen, nineteen, six—result: happiness; expenditure twenty pounds, ought, six—result: misery.' Don't prostrate yourself in gratitude, old bean; nothin' Bunter loves like messin' round with pyro and hyposulphite. Keeps his hand in. All kinds of practice welcome. Fingerprints and process plates spell seventh what-you-may-call-it of bliss, but focal-plane work on scurvy-ridden rodents (good phrase!)

acceptable if no crime forthcoming. Crimes have been rather short lately. Been eatin' our heads off, haven't we, Bunter? Don't know what's come over London. I've taken to prying into my neighbour's affairs to keep from goin' stale. Frightened the postman into a fit the other day by askin' him how his young lady at Croydon was. He's a married man, livin' in Great Ormond Street."

"How did you know?"

"Well, I didn't really. But he lives just opposite to a friend of mine—Inspector Parker; and his wife—not Parker's; he's unmarried; the postman's, I mean—asked Parker the other day whether the flyin' shows at Croydon went on all night. Parker, bein' flummoxed, said 'No,' without thinkin'. Bit of a giveaway, what? Thought I'd give the poor devil a word in season, don't you know. Uncommonly thought-less of Parker."

The doctor laughed. "You'll stay to lunch, won't you?" he said. "Only cold meat and salad, I'm afraid. My woman won't come Sundays. Have to answer my own door. Deuced unprofessional, I'm afraid, but it can't be helped."

"Pleasure," said Wimsey, as they emerged from the laboratory and entered the dark little flat by the back door. "Did you build this place on?"

"No," said Hartman; "the last tenant did that. He was an artist. That's why I took the place. It comes in very useful, ramshackle as it is, though this glass roof is a bit sweltering on a hot day like this. Still, I had to have something on the ground floor, cheap, and it'll do till times get better."

"Till your vitamin experiments make you famous, eh?" said Peter cheerfully. "You're goin' to be the comin' man, you know. Feel it in my bones. Uncommonly neat little kitchen you've got, anyhow."

"It does," said the doctor. "The lab makes it a bit gloomy, but the woman's only here in the daytime."

He led the way into a narrow little dining-room, where the table was laid for a cold lunch. The one window at the end farthest from the kitchen looked out into Great James Street. The room was little more than a passage, and full of doors—the kitchen door, a door in the adjacent wall leading into the entrance-hall, and a third on the opposite side, through which his visitor caught a glimpse of a moderate-sized consulting-room.

Lord Peter Wimsey and his host sat down to table, and the doctor expressed a hope that Mr. Bunter would sit down with them. That correct person, however, deprecated any such suggestion.

"If I might venture to indicate my own preference, sir," he said, "it would be to wait upon you and his lordship in the usual manner."

"It's no use," said Wimsey. "Bunter likes me to know my place. Terrorisin' sort of man, Bunter. Can't call my soul my own. Carry on, Bunter; we wouldn't presume for the world."

Mr. Bunter handed the salad, and poured out the water with a grave decency appropriate to a crusted old tawny port.

It was a Sunday afternoon in that halcyon summer of 1921. The sordid little street was almost empty. The ice-cream man alone seemed thriving and active. He leaned luxuriously on the green post at the corner, in the intervals of driving a busy trade. Bloomsbury's swarm of able-bodied and able-voiced infants was still; presumably within-doors, eating steamy Sunday dinners inappropriate to the tropical weather. The only disturbing sounds came from the flat above, where heavy footsteps passed rapidly to and fro.

"Who's the merry-and-bright bloke above?" enquired Lord Peter presently. "Not an early riser, I take it. Not that anybody is on a Sunday mornin'. Why an inscrutable Providence ever inflicted such a ghastly day on people livin' in town I can't imagine. I ought to be in the country, but I've got to meet a friend at Victoria this afternoon. Such a day to choose... Who's the lady? Wife or accomplished friend? Gather she takes a properly submissive view of woman's duties in the home, either way. That's the bedroom overhead, I take it."

Hartman looked at Lord Peter in some surprise.

"'Scuse my beastly inquisitiveness, old thing," said Wimsey. "Bad habit. Not my business."

"How did you—?"

"Guesswork," said Lord Peter, with disarming frankness. "I heard the squawk of an iron bedstead on the ceiling and a heavy fellow get out with a bump, but it may quite well be a couch or something. Anyway, he's been potterin' about in his stocking feet over these few feet of floor for the last half-hour, while the woman has been clatterin' to and fro, in and out of the kitchen and away into the sittin'-room, with her high heels on, ever since we've been here. Hence deduction as to domestic habits of the first-floor tenants."

"I thought," said the doctor, with an aggrieved expression, "you'd been listening to my valuable exposition of the beneficial effects of Vitamin B, and Lind's treatment of scurvy with fresh lemons in 1755."

"I was listenin'," agreed Lord Peter hastily, "but I heard the footsteps as well. Fellow's toddled into the kitchen—only wanted the matches, though; he's gone off into the sittin'-room and left her to carry on the good work. What was I sayin'? Oh, yes! You see, as I was sayin' before, one hears a thing or sees it without knowin' or thinkin' about it. Then afterwards one starts meditatin', and it all comes back, and one sorts out one's impressions. Like those plates of Bunter's. Picture all there, l—la—what's the word I want, Bunter?"

"Latent, my lord."

"That's it. My right-hand man, Bunter; couldn't do a thing without him. The picture's latent till you put the developer on. Same with the brain. No mystery. Little grey books all my respected grandmother! Little grey matter's all you want to remember things with. As a matter of curiosity, was I right about those people above?"

"Perfectly. The man's a gas-company's inspector. A bit surly, but devoted (after his own fashion) to his wife. I mean, he doesn't mind hulking in bed on a Sunday morning and letting her do the chores, but he spends all the money he can spare on giving her pretty hats and fur coats and what not. They've only been married about six months. I was called in to her when she had a touch of flu in the spring, and he was almost off his head with anxiety. She's a lovely little woman, I must say—Italian. He picked her up in some eating-place in Soho, I believe. Glorious dark hair and eyes: Venus sort of figure; proper contours in all the right places; good skin—all that sort of thing. She was a bit of a draw to that restaurant while she was there, I fancy. Lively. She had an old admirer round here one day—awkward little Italian fellow, with a knife—active as a monkey. Might have been unpleasant, but I happened to be on the spot, and her husband came along. People are always laying one another out in these streets. Good for business, of course, but one gets tired of tying up broken heads and slits in the jugular. Still, I suppose the girl can't help being attractive, though I don't say she's what you might call stand-offish in her manner. She's sincerely fond of Brotherton, I think, though—that's his name."

Wimsey nodded inattentively. "I suppose life is a bit monotonous here," he said.

"Professionally, yes. Births and drunks and wife-beatings are pretty common. And all the usual ailments, of course. Just at present I'm living on infant diarrhoea chiefly—bound to, this hot weather, you know. With the autumn, flu and bronchitis set in. I may get an occasional pneumonia. Legs, of course, and varicose veins—God!" cried the doctor explosively, "if only I could get away, and do my experiments!"

"Ah!" said Peter, "where's that eccentric old millionaire with a mysterious disease, who always figures in the novels? A lightning diagnosis—a miraculous cure—'God bless you, doctor, here are five thousand pounds'—Harley Street—"

"That sort doesn't live in Bloomsbury," said the doctor.

"It must be fascinatin', diagnosin' things," said Peter thoughtfully. "How d'you do it? I mean, is there a regular set of symptoms for each disease, like callin' a club to show you want your partner to go no trumps? You don't just say: 'This fellow's got a pimple on his nose, therefore he has fatty degeneration of the heart—'"

"I hope not," said the doctor dryly.

"Or is it more like gettin' a clue to a crime?" went on Peter. "You see somethin'—a room, or a body, say, all knocked about anyhow, and there's a damn sight of symptoms of somethin' wrong, and you've got just to pick out the ones which tell the story?"

"That's more like it," said Dr. Hartman. "Some symptoms significant in themselves—like the condition of the gums in scurvy, let us say—others in conjunction with—"

He broke off, and both sprang to their feet as a shrill scream sounded suddenly from the flat above, followed by a heavy thud. A man's voice cried out lamentably; feet ran violently to and fro; then, as the doctor and his guests stood frozen in consternation, came the man himself—falling down the stairs in his haste, hammering at Hartman's door.

"Help! Help! Let me in! My wife! He's murdered her!"

They ran hastily to the door and let him in. He was a big, fair man, in his shirt-sleeves and stockings. His hair stood up, and his face was set in bewildered misery.

"She is dead—dead. He was her lover," he groaned. "Come and look—take her away—Doctor! I have lost my wife! My Maddalena—" He paused, looked wildly for a moment, and then said hoarsely, "Someone's been in—somehow—stabbed her—murdered her. I'll have the law on him, doctor. Come quickly—she was cooking the chicken for my dinner—Ah-h-h!"

He gave a long, hysterical shriek, which ended in a hiccupping laugh. The doctor took him roughly by the arm and shook him. "Pull yourself together, Mr. Brotherton," he said sharply. "Perhaps she is only hurt. Stand out of the way!"

"Only hurt?" said the man, sitting heavily down on the nearest chair. "No—no—she is dead—little Maddalena—Oh, my God!"

Dr. Hartman had snatched a roll of bandages and a few surgical appliances from the consulting-room, and he ran upstairs, followed closely by Lord Peter. Bunter remained for a few moments to combat hysterics with cold water. Then he stepped across to the dining-room window and shouted.

"Well, wot is it?" cried a voice from the street.

"Would you be so kind as to step in here a minute, officer?" said Bunter. "There's been murder done."

When Brotherton and Bunter arrived upstairs with the constable, they found Dr. Hartman and Lord Peter in the little kitchen. The doctor was kneeling beside the woman's body. At their entrance he looked up, and shook his head.

"Death instantaneous," he said. "Clean through the heart. Poor child. She cannot have suffered at all. Oh, constable, it is very fortunate you are here. Murder appears to have been done—though I'm afraid the man has escaped. Probably Mr. Brotherton can give us some help. He was in the flat at the time."

The man had sunk down on a chair, and was gazing at the body with a face from which all meaning seemed to have been struck out. The policeman produced a notebook.

"Now, sir," he said, "don't let's waste any time. Sooner we can get to work the more likely we are to catch our man. Now, you was 'ere at the time, was you?"

Brotherton stared a moment, then, making a violent effort, he answered steadily:

"I was in the sitting-room, smoking and reading the paper. My—*she*—was getting the dinner ready in here. I heard her give a scream, and I rushed in and found her lying on the floor. She didn't have time to say anything. When I found she was dead, I rushed to the window, and saw the fellow scrambling away over the glass roof there. I yelled at him, but he disappeared. Then I ran down—"

"'Arf a mo'," said the policeman. "Now, see, 'ere, sir, didn't you think to go after 'im at once?"

"My first thought was for her," said the man. "I thought maybe she wasn't dead. I tried to bring her round—" His speech ended in a groan.

"You say he came in through the window," said the policeman.

"I beg your pardon, officer," interrupted Lord Peter, who had been apparently making a mental inventory of the contents of the kitchen. "Mr. Brotherton suggested that the man went *out* through the window. It's better to be accurate."

"It's the same thing," said the doctor. "It's the only way he could have come in. These flats are all alike. The staircase door leads into the sitting-room, and Mr. Brotherton was there, so the man couldn't have come that way."

"And," said Peter, "he didn't get in through the bedroom window, or we should have seen him. We were in the room below. Unless, indeed, he let himself down from the roof. Was the door between the bedroom and the sitting-room open?" he asked suddenly, turning to Brotherton.

The man hesitated a moment. "Yes," he said finally. "Yes, I'm sure it was."

"Could you have seen the man if he had come through the bedroom window?"

"I couldn't have helped seeing him."

"Come, come, sir," said the policeman, with some irritation, "better let *me* ask the questions. Stands to reason the fellow wouldn't get in through the bedroom window in full view of the street."

"How clever of you to think of that," said Wimsey. "Of course not. Never occurred to me. Then it must have been this window, as you say."

"And, what's more, here's his marks on the window-sill," said the constable triumphantly, pointing to some blurred traces among the London soot. "That's right. Down he goes by that drain-pipe, over the glass roof down there—what's that the roof of?"

"My laboratory," said the doctor. "Heavens! to think that while we were there at dinner this murdering villain—"

"Quite so, sir," agreed the constable. "Well, he'd get away over the wall into the court be'ind. 'E'll 'ave been seen there, no fear; you needn't anticipate much trouble in layin' 'ands on 'im, sir. I'll go round there in 'arf a tick. Now then, sir"—turning to Brotherton—"'ave you any idea wot this party might have looked like?"

Brotherton lifted a wild face, and the doctor interposed.

"I think you ought to know, constable," he said, "that there was—well, not a murderous attack, but what might have been one, made on this woman before—about eight weeks ago—by a man named Marincetti—an Italian waiter—with a knife."

"Ah!" The policeman licked his pencil eagerly. "Do you know this party as 'as been mentioned?" he enquired of Brotherton.

"That's the man," said Brotherton, with concentrated fury. "Coming here after my wife—God curse him! I wish to God I had him dead here beside her!"

"Quite so," said the policeman. "Now, sir"—to the doctor—"'ave you got the weapon wot the crime was committed with?"

"No," said Hartman, "there was no weapon in the body when I arrived."

"Did *you* take it out?" pursued the constable, to Brotherton.

"No," said Brotherton, "he took it with him."

"Took it with 'im," the constable entered the fact in his notes. "Phew! Wonderful 'ot it is in 'ere, ain't it, sir?" he added, mopping his brow.

"It's the gas-oven, I think," said Peter mildly. "Uncommon hot thing, a gas-oven, in the middle of July. D'you mind if I turn it out? There's the chicken inside, but I don't suppose you want—"

Brotherton groaned, and the constable said: "Quite right, sir. A man wouldn't 'ardly fancy 'is dinner after a thing like this. Thank you, sir. Well now, doctor, wot kind of weapon do you take this to 'ave been?"

"It was a long, narrow weapon—something like an Italian stiletto, I imagine," said the doctor, "about six inches long. It was thrust in with great force under the fifth rib, and I should say it had pierced the heart centrally. As you see, there has been practically no bleeding. Such a wound would cause instant death. Was she lying just as she is now when you first saw her, Mr. Brotherton?"

"On her back, just as she is," replied the husband.

"Well, that seems clear enough," said the policeman. "This 'ere Marinetti, or wotever 'is name is, 'as a grudge against the poor young lady—"

"I believe he was an admirer," put in the doctor.

"Quite so," agreed the constable. "Of course, these foreigners are like that—even the decentest of 'em. Stabbin' and such-like seems to come nateral to them, as you might say. Well, this 'ere Marinetti climbs in 'ere, sees the poor young lady standin' 'ere by the table all alone, gettin' the dinner ready; 'e comes in be'ind, catches 'er round the waist, stabs 'er—easy job, you see; no corsets nor nothink—she shrieks out, 'e pulls 'is stiletty out of 'er an' makes tracks. Well, now we've got to find 'im, and by your leave, sir, I'll be gettin' along. We'll 'ave 'im by the 'eels before long, sir, don't you worry. I'll 'ave to put a man in charge 'ere, sir, to keep folks out, but that needn't worry you. Good mornin', gentlemen."

"May we move the poor girl now?" asked the doctor.

"Certainly. Like me to 'elp you, sir?"

"No. Don't lose any time. We can manage." Dr. Hartman turned
to Peter as the constable clattered downstairs. "Will you help me,
Lord Peter?"

"Bunter's better at that sort of thing," said Wimsey, with a hard
mouth.

The doctor looked at him in some surprise, but said nothing, and
he and Bunter carried the still form away. Brotherton did not follow
them. He sat in a grief-stricken heap, with his head buried in his hands.
Lord Peter walked about the little kitchen, turning over the various
knives and kitchen utensils, peering into the sink bucket, and apparently
taking an inventory of the bread, butter, condiments, vegetables, and so
forth which lay about in preparation for the Sunday meal. There were
potatoes in the sink, half peeled, a pathetic witness to the quiet domestic
life which had been so horribly interrupted. The colander was filled
with green peas. Lord Peter turned these things over with an inquisitive
finger, gazed into the smooth surface of a bowl of dripping as though
it were a divining-crystal, ran his hands several times right through a
bowl of flour—then drew his pipe from his pocket and filled it slowly.

The doctor returned, and put his hand on Brotherton's shoulder.

"Come," he said gently, "we have laid her in the other bedroom. She
looks very peaceful. You must remember that, except for that moment
of terror when she saw the knife, she suffered nothing. It is terrible for
you, but you must try not to give way. The police—"

"The police can't bring her back to life," said the man savagely.
"She's dead. Leave me alone, curse you! Leave me alone, I say!"

He stood up, with a violent gesture.

"You must not sit here," said Hartman firmly. "I will give you something to take, and you must try to keep calm. Then we will leave you,
but if you don't control yourself—"

After some further persuasion, Brotherton allowed himself to be
led away.

"Bunter," said Lord Peter, as the kitchen door closed behind them, "do you know why I am doubtful about the success of those rat experiments?"

"Meaning Dr. Hartman's, my lord?"

"Yes. Dr. Hartman has a theory. In any investigation, my Bunter, it is most damnably dangerous to have a theory."

"I have heard you say so, my lord."

"Confound you—you know it as well as I do! What is wrong with the doctor's theories, Bunter?"

"You wish me to reply, my lord, that he only sees the facts which fit into the theory."

"Thought-reader!" exclaimed Lord Peter bitterly.

"And that he supplies them to the police, my lord."

"Hush!" said Peter, as the doctor returned.

"I have got him to lie down," said Dr. Hartman, "and I think the best thing we can do is to leave him to himself."

"D'you know," said Wimsey, "I don't cotton to that idea, somehow."

"Why? Do you think he's likely to destroy himself?"

"That's as good a reason to give as any other, I suppose," said Wimsey, "when you haven't got any reason which can be put into words. But my advice is, don't leave him for a moment."

"But why? Frequently, with a deep grief like this, the presence of other people is merely an irritant. He begged me to leave him."

"Then for God's sake go back to him," said Peter.

"Really, Lord Peter," said the doctor, "I think I ought to know what is best for my patient."

"Doctor," said Wimsey, "this is not a question of your patient. A crime has been committed."

"But there is no mystery."

"There are twenty mysteries. For one thing, when was the window-cleaner here last?"

"The window-cleaner?"

"Who shall fathom the ebony-black enigma of the window-cleaner?" pursued Peter lightly, putting a match to his pipe. "You are quietly in your bath, in a state of more or less innocent nature, when an intrusive head appears at the window, like the ghost of Hamilton Tighe, and a gruff voice, suspended between earth and heaven, says 'Good morning, sir.' Where do window-cleaners go between visits? Do they hibernate, like busy bees? Do they—?"

"Really, Lord Peter," said the doctor, "don't you think you're going a bit beyond the limit?"

"Sorry you feel like that," said Peter, "but I really want to know about the window-cleaner. Look how clear these panes are."

"He came yesterday, if you want to know," said Dr. Hartman, rather stiffly.

"You are sure?"

"He did mine at the same time."

"I thought as much," said Lord Peter. "In the words of the song:

> "I thought as much,
> It was a little—window-cleaner.

In that case," he added, "it is absolutely imperative that Brotherton should not be left alone for a moment. Bunter! Confound it all, where's that fellow got to?"

The door into the bedroom opened.

"My lord?" Mr. Bunter unobtrusively appeared, as he had unobtrusively stolen out to keep an unobtrusive eye upon the patient.

"Good," said Wimsey. "Stay where you are." His lackadaisical manner had gone, and he looked at the doctor as four years previously he might have looked at a refractory subaltern.

"Dr. Hartman," he said, "something is wrong. Cast your mind back.

We were talking about symptoms. Then came the scream. Then came the sound of feet running. *Which direction did they run in?*"

"I'm sure I don't know."

"Don't you? Symptomatic, though, doctor. They have been troubling me all the time, subconsciously. Now I know why. They ran *from the kitchen*."

"Well?"

"Well! And now the window-cleaner—"

"What about him?"

"Could you swear that it wasn't the window-cleaner who made those marks on the sill?"

"And the man Brotherton saw—?"

"Have we examined your laboratory roof for his footsteps?"

"But the weapon? Wimsey, this is madness! Someone took the weapon."

"I know. But did you think the edge of the wound was clean enough to have been made by a smooth stiletto? It looked ragged to me."

"Wimsey, what are you driving at?"

"There's a clue here in the flat—and I'm damned if I can remember it. I've seen it—I know I've seen it. It'll come to me presently. Meanwhile, don't let Brotherton—"

"What?"

"Do whatever it is he's going to do."

"But what is it?"

"If I could tell you that I could show you the clue. Why couldn't he make up his mind whether the bedroom door was open or shut? Very good story, but not quite thought out. Anyhow—I say, doctor, make some excuse, and strip him, and bring me his clothes. And send Bunter to me."

The doctor stared at him, puzzled. Then he made a gesture of acquiescence and passed into the bedroom. Lord Peter followed him, casting a ruminating glance at Brotherton as he went. Once in the sitting-room, Lord Peter sat down on a red velvet armchair, fixed his eyes on a gilt-framed oleograph, and became wrapped in contemplation.

Presently Bunter came in, with his arms full of clothing. Wimsey took it, and began to search it, methodically enough, but listlessly. Suddenly he dropped the garments, and turned to the manservant.

"No," he said, "this is a precaution, Bunter mine, but I'm on the wrong tack. It wasn't here I saw—whatever I did see. It was in the kitchen. Now, what was it?"

"I could not say, my lord, but I entertain a conviction that I was also, in a manner of speaking, conscious—not consciously conscious, my lord, if you understand me, but still conscious of an incongruity."

"Hurray!" said Wimsey suddenly. "Cheer-oh! for the subconscious what's-his-name! Now let's remember the kitchen. I cleared out of it because I was gettin' obfuscated. Now then. Begin at the door. Fryin'-pans and saucepans on the wall. Gas-stove—oven goin'—chicken inside. Racks of wooden spoons on the wall, gas-lighter, pan-lifter. Stop me when I'm gettin' hot. Mantelpiece. Spice-boxes and stuff. Anything wrong with them? No. Dresser. Plates. Knives and forks,—all clean; flour dredger—milk-jug—sieve on the wall—nutmeg-grater. Three-tier steamer. Looked inside—no grisly secrets in the steamer."

"Did you look in all the dresser drawers, my lord?"

"No. That could be done. But the point is, I *did* notice somethin'. What did I notice? That's the point. Never mind. On with the dance— let joy be unconfined! Knife-board. Knife-powder. Kitchen table. Did you speak?"

"No," said Bunter, who had moved from his attitude of wooden deference.

"Table stirs a chord. Very good. On table. Choppin'-board. Remains of ham and herb stuffin'. Packet of suet. Another sieve. Several plates. Butter in a glass dish. Bowl of drippin'—"

"Ah!"

"Drippin'—! Yes, there was—"

"Something unsatisfactory, my lord—"

"About the drippin'! Oh, my head! What's that they say in *Dear Brutus*, Bunter? 'Hold on to the workbox.' That's right. Hold on to the drippin'. Beastly slimy stuff to hold on to—Wait!"

There was a pause.

"When I was a kid," said Wimsey, "I used to love to go down into the kitchen and talk to old cookie. Good old soul she was, too. I can see her now, gettin' chicken ready, with me danglin' my legs on the table. *She* used to pluck an' draw 'em herself. I revelled in it. Little beasts boys are, ain't they, Bunter? Pluck it, draw it, wash it, stuff it, tuck its little tail through its little what-you-may-call-it, truss it, grease the dish—Bunter?"

"My lord!"

"Hold on to the dripping!"

"The bowl, my lord—"

"The bowl—visualise it—what was wrong?"

"It was full, my lord!"

"Got it—got it—*got* it! The bowl was full—smooth surface. Golly! I knew there was something queer about it. Now why shouldn't it be full? Hold on to the—"

"The bird was in the oven."

"Without dripping!"

"Very careless cookery my lord."

"The bird—in the oven—no dripping. Bunter! Suppose it was never put in till after she was dead? Thrust in hurriedly by someone who had something to hide—horrible!"

"But with what object, my lord?"

"Yes, why? That's the point. One more mental association with the bird. It's just coming. Wait a moment. Pluck, draw, wash, stuff, tuck up, truss—By God!"

"My lord?"

"Come on, Bunter. Thank Heaven we turned off the gas!"

He dashed through the bedroom, disregarding the doctor and the patient, who sat up with a smothered shriek. He flung open the oven door and snatched out the baking-tin. The skin of the bird had just begun to discolour. With a little gasp of triumph, Wimsey caught the iron ring that protruded from the wing, and jerked out—the six-inch spiral skewer.

The doctor was struggling with the excited Brotherton in the doorway. Wimsey caught the man as he broke away, and shook him into the corner with a jiu-jitsu twist.

"Here is the weapon," he said.

"Prove it, blast you!" said Brotherton savagely.

"I will," said Wimsey. "Bunter, call in the policeman whom you will find at the door. Doctor, we shall need your microscope."

In the laboratory the doctor bent over the microscope. A thin layer of blood from the skewer had been spread upon the slide.

"Well?" said Wimsey impatiently.

"It's all right," said Hartman. "The roasting didn't get anywhere near the middle. My God, Wimsey, yes, you're right—round corpuscles, diameter $\frac{1}{3621}$ —mammalian blood—probably human—"

"Her blood," said Wimsey.

"It was very clever, Bunter," said Lord Peter, as the taxi trundled along on the way to his flat in Piccadilly. "If that fowl had gone on roasting a bit longer the blood-corpuscles might easily have been destroyed beyond all hope of recognition. It all goes to show that the unpremeditated crime is usually the safest."

"And what does your lordship take the man's motive to have been?"

"In my youth," said Wimsey meditatively, "they used to make me read the Bible. Trouble was, the only books I ever took to naturally were the ones they weren't over and above keen on. But I got to know the Song of Songs pretty well by heart. Look it up, Bunter; at your age it won't hurt you; it talks sense about jealousy."

"I have perused the work in question, your lordship," replied Mr. Bunter, with a sallow blush. "It says, if I remember rightly: *'Jealousy is cruel as the grave.'*"

Sherlock Holmes in

THE ADVENTURE OF THE BRUCE-PARTINGTON PLANS

Arthur Conan Doyle

Arthur Conan Doyle (1859–1930) was a Scot who, after qualifying in medicine, practised in Plymouth and Portsmouth prior to studying ophthalmology in Vienna with a view to becoming an eye surgeon. He opened an office and consulting rooms in 2 Upper Wimpole Street, London, a short walk from 23 Montague Place in Bloomsbury, where he lived with his wife and young daughter. By this time, he had already published (to relatively little fanfare) two long stories about Sherlock Holmes. But shortly after returning to London, he wrote the first Holmes short story; he recalled that he did so at Wimpole Street, because he had no patients to see. The success of that story, "A Scandal in Bohemia", changed his life. He gave up medicine and embarked on a career as a full-time author.

In the brilliant story "The Red-Headed League", Holmes said: "It is a hobby of mine to have an exact knowledge of London", a city which Dr. Watson had described in *A Study in Scarlet* as "that great cesspool into which all the loungers and idlers of the Empire are irresistibly drained." Doyle's gift for conjuring up the atmosphere of the gas-lit London streets was one of the great strengths of the stories about Holmes, whose rooms were at 221b Baker Street, the most famous address in detective fiction. This particular story, one of Doyle's personal favourites, was first published in the *Strand Magazine* in December 1908.

IN THE THIRD WEEK OF NOVEMBER, IN THE YEAR 1895, A DENSE yellow fog settled down upon London. From the Monday to the Thursday I doubt whether it was ever possible from our windows in Baker Street to see the loom of the opposite houses. The first day Holmes had spent in cross-indexing his huge book of references. The second and third had been patiently occupied upon a subject which he had recently made his hobby—the music of the Middle Ages. But when, for the fourth time, after pushing back our chairs from breakfast we saw the greasy, heavy brown swirl still drifting past us and condensing in oily drops upon the window-panes, my comrade's impatient and active nature could endure this drab existence no longer. He paced restlessly about our sitting-room in a fever of suppressed energy, biting his nails, tapping the furniture, and chafing against inaction.

"Nothing of interest in the paper, Watson?" he said.

I was aware that by anything of interest, Holmes meant anything of criminal interest. There was the news of a revolution, of a possible war, and of an impending change of government; but these did not come within the horizon of my companion. I could see nothing recorded in the shape of crime which was not commonplace and futile. Holmes groaned and resumed his restless meanderings.

"The London criminal is certainly a dull fellow," said he in the querulous voice of the sportsman whose game has failed him. "Look out this window, Watson. See how the figures loom up, are dimly seen, and then blend once more into the cloud-bank. The thief or the murderer could roam London on such a day as the tiger does the jungle, unseen until he pounces, and then evident only to his victim."

"There have," said I, "been numerous petty thefts."

Holmes snorted his contempt.

"This great and sombre stage is set for something more worthy than that," said he. "It is fortunate for this community that I am not a criminal."

"It is, indeed!" said I heartily.

"Suppose that I were Brooks or Woodhouse, or any of the fifty men who have good reason for taking my life, how long could I survive against my own pursuit? A summons, a bogus appointment, and all would be over. It is well they don't have days of fog in the Latin countries—the countries of assassination. By Jove! here comes something at last to break our dead monotony."

It was the maid with a telegram. Holmes tore it open and burst out laughing.

"Well, well! What next?" said he. "Brother Mycroft is coming round."

"Why not?" I asked.

"Why not? It is as if you met a tram-car coming down a country lane. Mycroft has his rails and he runs on them. His Pall Mall lodgings, the Diogenes Club, Whitehall—that is his cycle. Once, and only once, he has been here. What upheaval can possibly have derailed him?"

"Does he not explain?"

Holmes handed me his brother's telegram.

"Must see you over Cadogan West. Coming at once."

MYCROFT

"Cadogan West? I have heard the name."

"It recalls nothing to my mind. But that Mycroft should break out in this erratic fashion! A planet might as well leave its orbit. By the way, do you know what Mycroft is?"

I had some vague recollection of an explanation at the time of the Adventure of the Greek Interpreter.

"You told me that he had some small office under the British government."

Holmes chuckled.

"I did not know you quite so well in those days. One has to be discreet when one talks of high matters of state. You are right in thinking that he is under the British government. You would also be right in a sense if you said that occasionally he *is* the British government."

"My dear Holmes!"

"I thought I might surprise you. Mycroft draws four hundred and fifty pounds a year, remains a subordinate, has no ambitions of any kind, will receive neither honour nor title, but remains the most indispensable man in the country."

"But how?"

"Well, his position is unique. He has made it for himself. There has never been anything like it before, nor will be again. He has the tidiest and most orderly brain, with the greatest capacity for storing facts, of any man living. The same great powers which I have turned to the detection of crime he has used for this particular business. The conclusions of every department are passed to him, and he is the central exchange, the clearinghouse, which makes out the balance. All other men are specialists, but his specialism is omniscience. We will suppose that a minister needs information as to a point which involves the Navy, India, Canada and the bimetallic question; he could get his separate advices from various departments upon each, but only Mycroft can focus them all, and say offhand how each factor would affect the other. They began by using him as a short-cut, a convenience; now he has made himself an essential. In that great brain of his everything is pigeon-holed and can be handed out in an instant. Again and again his word has decided the national policy. He lives in it. He thinks of nothing else save when, as an intellectual exercise, he unbends if I call upon him and ask him to advise me on one of my little problems. But Jupiter is descending today. What on earth can it mean? Who is Cadogan West, and what is he to Mycroft?"

"I have it," I cried, and plunged among the litter of papers upon the sofa. "Yes, yes, here he is, sure enough! Cadogan West was the young man who was found dead on the Underground on Tuesday morning."

Holmes sat up at attention, his pipe halfway to his lips.

"This must be serious, Watson. A death which has caused my brother to alter his habits can be no ordinary one. What in the world can he have to do with it? The case was featureless as I remember it. The young man had apparently fallen out of the train and killed himself. He had not been robbed, and there was no particular reason to suspect violence. Is that not so?"

"There has been an inquest," said I, "and a good many fresh facts have come out. Looked at more closely, I should certainly say that it was a curious case."

"Judging by its effect upon my brother, I should think it must be a most extraordinary one." He snuggled down in his armchair. "Now, Watson, let us have the facts."

"The man's name was Arthur Cadogan West. He was twenty-seven years of age, unmarried, and a clerk at Woolwich Arsenal."

"Government employ. Behold the link with Brother Mycroft!"

"He left Woolwich suddenly on Monday night. Was last seen by his fiancée, Miss Violet Westbury, whom he left abruptly in the fog about 7:30 that evening. There was no quarrel between them and she can give no motive for his action. The next thing heard of him was when his dead body was discovered by a plate-layer named Mason, just outside Aldgate Station on the Underground system in London."

"When?"

"The body was found at six on Tuesday morning. It was lying wide of the metals upon the left hand of the track as one goes eastward, at a point close to the station, where the line emerges from the tunnel in which it runs. The head was badly crushed—an injury which might well have been caused by a fall from the train. The body could only have come on the line in that way. Had it been carried down from any neighbouring street, it must have passed the station barriers, where a collector is always standing. This point seems absolutely certain."

"Very good. The case is definite enough. The man, dead or alive, either fell or was precipitated from a train. So much is clear to me. Continue."

"The trains which traverse the lines of rail beside which the body was found are those which run from west to east, some being purely Metropolitan, and some from Willesden and outlying junctions. It can be stated for certain that this young man, when he met his death, was travelling in this direction at some late hour of the night, but at what point he entered the train it is impossible to state."

"His ticket, of course, would show that."

"There was no ticket in his pockets."

"No ticket! Dear me, Watson, this is really very singular. According to my experience it is not possible to reach the platform of a Metropolitan train without exhibiting one's ticket. Presumably, then, the young man had one. Was it taken from him in order to conceal the station from which he came? It is possible. Or did he drop it in the carriage? That is also possible. But the point is of curious interest. I understand that there was no sign of robbery?"

"Apparently not. There is a list here of his possessions. His purse contained two pounds fifteen. He had also a cheque-book on the Woolwich branch of the Capital and Counties Bank. Through this his identity was established. There were also two dress-circle tickets for the Woolwich Theatre, dated for that very evening. Also a small packet of technical papers."

Holmes gave an exclamation of satisfaction.

"There we have it at last, Watson! British government—Woolwich. Arsenal—technical papers—Brother Mycroft, the chain is complete. But here he comes, if I am not mistaken, to speak for himself."

A moment later the tall and portly form of Mycroft Holmes was ushered into the room. Heavily built and massive, there was a suggestion of uncouth physical inertia in the figure, but above this unwieldy frame there was perched a head so masterful in its brow, so alert in its steel-grey, deep-set eyes, so firm in its lips, and so subtle in its play of expression, that after the first glance one forgot the gross body and remembered only the dominant mind.

At his heels came our old friend Lestrade, of Scotland Yard—thin and austere. The gravity of both their faces foretold some weighty quest. The detective shook hands without a word. Mycroft Holmes struggled out of his overcoat and subsided into an armchair.

"A most annoying business, Sherlock," said he. "I extremely dislike altering my habits, but the powers that be would take no denial. In the present state of Siam it is most awkward that I should be away from the office. But it is a real crisis. I have never seen the Prime Minister so upset. As to the Admiralty—it is buzzing like an overturned bee-hive. Have you read up the case?"

"We have just done so. What were the technical papers?"

"Ah, there's the point! Fortunately, it has not come out. The press would be furious if it did. The papers which this wretched youth had in his pocket were the plans of the Bruce-Partington submarine."

Mycroft Holmes spoke with a solemnity which showed his sense of the importance of the subject. His brother and I sat expectant.

"Surely you have heard of it? I thought everyone had heard of it."

"Only as a name."

"Its importance can hardly be exaggerated. It has been the most jealously guarded of all government secrets. You may take it from me that naval warfare becomes impossible within the radius of a Bruce-Partington's operation. Two years ago a very large sum was smuggled through the Estimates and was expended in acquiring a monopoly of the invention. Every effort has been made to keep the secret. The plans, which are exceedingly intricate, comprising some thirty separate patents, each essential to the working of the whole, are kept in an elaborate safe in a confidential office adjoining the arsenal, with burglar-proof doors and windows. Under no conceivable circumstances were the plans to be taken from the office. If the chief constructor of the Navy desired to consult them, even he was forced to go to the Woolwich office for the purpose. And yet here we find them in the pocket of a dead junior clerk in the heart of London. From an official point of view it's simply awful."

"But you have recovered them?"

"No, Sherlock, no! That's the pinch. We have not. Ten papers were taken from Woolwich. There were seven in the pocket of Cadogan West. The three most essential are gone—stolen, vanished. You must drop everything, Sherlock. Never mind your usual petty puzzles of the police-court. It's a vital international problem that you have to solve. Why did Cadogan West take the papers, where are the missing ones, how did he die, how came his body where it was found, how can the evil be set right? Find an answer to all these questions, and you will have done good service for your country."

"Why do you not solve it yourself, Mycroft? You can see as far as I."

"Possibly, Sherlock. But it is a question of getting details. Give me your details, and from an armchair I will return you an excellent expert opinion. But to run here and run there, to cross-question railway guards, and lie on my face with a lens to my eye—it is not my métier.

No, you are the one man who can clear the matter up. If you have a fancy to see your name in the next honours list—"

My friend smiled and shook his head.

"I play the game for the game's own sake," said he. "But the problem certainly presents some points of interest, and I shall be very pleased to look into it. Some more facts, please."

"I have jotted down the more essential ones upon this sheet of paper, together with a few addresses which you will find of service. The actual official guardian of the papers is the famous government expert, Sir James Walter, whose decorations and sub-titles fill two lines of a book of reference. He has grown grey in the service, is a gentleman, a favoured guest in the most exalted houses, and, above all, a man whose patriotism is beyond suspicion. He is one of two who have a key of the safe. I may add that the papers were undoubtedly in the office during working hours on Monday, and that Sir James left for London about three o'clock taking his key with him. He was at the house of Admiral Sinclair at Barclay Square during the whole of the evening when this incident occurred."

"Has the fact been verified?"

"Yes; his brother, Colonel Valentine Walter, has testified to his departure from Woolwich, and Admiral Sinclair to his arrival in London; so Sir James is no longer a direct factor in the problem."

"Who was the other man with a key?"

"The senior clerk and draughtsman, Mr. Sidney Johnson. He is a man of forty, married, with five children. He is a silent, morose man, but he has, on the whole, an excellent record in the public service. He is unpopular with his colleagues, but a hard worker. According to his own account, corroborated only by the word of his wife, he was at home the whole of Monday evening after office hours, and his key has never left the watch-chain upon which it hangs."

"Tell us about Cadogan West."

"He has been ten years in the service and has done good work. He has the reputation of being hot-headed and imperious, but a straight, honest man. We have nothing against him. He was next Sidney Johnson in the office. His duties brought him into daily, personal contact with the plans. No one else had the handling of them."

"Who locked up the plans that night?"

"Mr. Sidney Johnson, the senior clerk."

"Well, it is surely perfectly clear who took them away. They are actually found upon the person of this junior clerk, Cadogan West. That seems final, does it not?"

"It does, Sherlock, and yet it leaves so much unexplained. In the first place, why did he take them?"

"I presume they were of value?"

"He could have got several thousands for them very easily."

"Can you suggest any possible motive for taking the papers to London except to sell them?"

"No, I cannot."

"Then we must take that as our working hypothesis. Young West took the papers. Now this could only be done by having a false key—"

"Several false keys. He had to open the building and the room."

"He had, then, several false keys. He took the papers to London to sell the secret, intending, no doubt, to have the plans themselves back in the safe next morning before they were missed. While in London on this treasonable mission he met his end."

"How?"

"We will suppose that he was travelling back to Woolwich when he was killed and thrown out of the compartment."

"Aldgate, where the body was found, is considerably past the station London Bridge, which would be his route to Woolwich."

"Many circumstances could be imagined under which he would pass London Bridge. There was someone in the carriage, for example, with whom he was having an absorbing interview. This interview led to a violent scene in which he lost his life. Possibly he tried to leave the carriage, fell out on the line, and so met his end. The other closed the door. There was a thick fog, and nothing could be seen."

"No better explanation can be given with our present knowledge; and yet consider, Sherlock, how much you leave untouched. We will suppose, for argument's sake, that young Cadogan West *had* determined to convey these papers to London. He would naturally have made an appointment with the foreign agent and kept his evening clear. Instead of that he took two tickets for the theatre, escorted his fiancée halfway there, and then suddenly disappeared."

"A blind," said Lestrade, who had sat listening with some impatience to the conversation.

"A very singular one. That is objection No. 1. Objection No. 2: We will suppose that he reaches London and sees the foreign agent. He must bring back the papers before morning or the loss will be discovered. He took away ten. Only seven were in his pocket. What had become of the other three? He certainly would not leave them of his own free will. Then, again, where is the price of his treason? One would have expected to find a large sum of money in his pocket."

"It seems to me perfectly clear," said Lestrade. "I have no doubt at all as to what occurred. He took the papers to sell them. He saw the agent. They could not agree as to price. He started home again, but the agent went with him. In the train the agent murdered him, took the more essential papers, and threw his body from the carriage. That would account for everything, would it not?"

"Why had he no ticket?"

"The ticket would have shown which station was nearest the agent's house. Therefore he took it from the murdered man's pocket."

"Good, Lestrade, very good," said Holmes. "Your theory holds together. But if this is true, then the case is at an end. On the one hand, the traitor is dead. On the other, the plans of the Bruce-Partington submarine are presumably already on the Continent. What is there for us to do?"

"To act, Sherlock—to act!" cried Mycroft, springing to his feet. "All my instincts are against this explanation. Use your powers! Go to the scene of the crime! See the people concerned! Leave no stone unturned! In all your career you have never had so great a chance of serving your country."

"Well, well!" said Holmes, shrugging his shoulders. "Come, Watson! And you, Lestrade, could you favour us with your company for an hour or two? We will begin our investigation by a visit to Aldgate Station. Goodbye, Mycroft. I shall let you have a report before evening, but I warn you in advance that you have little to expect."

An hour later Holmes, Lestrade and I stood upon the Underground railroad at the point where it emerges from the tunnel immediately before Aldgate Station. A courteous red-faced old gentleman represented the railway company.

"This is where the young man's body lay," said he, indicating a spot about three feet from the metals. "It could not have fallen from above, for these, as you see, are all blank walls. Therefore, it could only have come from a train, and that train, so far as we can trace it, must have passed about midnight on Monday."

"Have the carriages been examined for any sign of violence?"

"There are no such signs, and no ticket has been found."

"No record of a door being found open?"

"None."

"We have had some fresh evidence this morning," said Lestrade. "A passenger who passed Aldgate in an ordinary Metropolitan train about 11:40 on Monday night declares that he heard a heavy thud, as of a body striking the line, just before the train reached the station. There was dense fog, however, and nothing could be seen. He made no report of it at the time. Why, whatever is the matter with Mr. Holmes?"

My friend was standing with an expression of strained intensity upon his face, staring at the railway metals where they curved out of the tunnel. Aldgate is a junction, and there was a network of points. On these his eager, questioning eyes were fixed, and I saw on his keen, alert face that tightening of the lips, that quiver of the nostrils, and concentration of the heavy, tufted brows which I knew so well.

"Points," he muttered; "the points."

"What of it? What do you mean?"

"I suppose there are no great number of points on a system such as this?"

"No; they are very few."

"And a curve, too. Points, and a curve. By Jove! if it were only so."

"What is it, Mr. Holmes? Have you a clue?"

"An idea—an indication, no more. But the case certainly grows in interest. Unique, perfectly unique, and yet why not? I do not see any indications of bleeding on the line."

"There were hardly any."

"But I understand that there was a considerable wound."

"The bone was crushed, but there was no great external injury."

"And yet one would have expected some bleeding. Would it be possible for me to inspect the train which contained the passenger who heard the thud of a fall in the fog?"

"I fear not, Mr. Holmes. The train has been broken up before now, and the carriages redistributed."

"I can assure you, Mr. Holmes," said Lestrade, "that every carriage has been carefully examined. I saw to it myself."

It was one of my friend's most obvious weaknesses that he was impatient with less alert intelligences than his own.

"Very likely," said he, turning away. "As it happens, it was not the carriages which I desired to examine. Watson, we have done all we can here. We need not trouble you any further, Mr. Lestrade. I think our investigations must now carry us to Woolwich."

At London Bridge, Holmes wrote a telegram to his brother, which he handed to me before dispatching it. It ran thus:

See some light in the darkness, but it may possibly flicker out. Meanwhile, please send by messenger, to await return at Baker Street, a complete list of all foreign spies or international agents known to be in England, with full address.—SHERLOCK.

"That should be helpful, Watson," he remarked as we took our seats in the Woolwich train. "We certainly owe Brother Mycroft a debt for having introduced us to what promises to be a really very remarkable case."

His eager face still wore that expression of intense and high-strung energy, which showed me that some novel and suggestive circumstance had opened up a stimulating line of thought. See the foxhound with hanging ears and drooping tail as it lolls about the kennels, and compare it with the same hound as, with gleaming eyes and straining muscles, it runs upon a breast-high scent—such was the change in Holmes since the morning. He was a different man from the limp and lounging figure in the mouse-coloured dressing-gown who had prowled so restlessly only a few hours before round the fog-girt room.

"There is material here. There is scope," said he. "I am dull indeed not to have understood its possibilities."

"Even now they are dark to me."

"The end is dark to me also, but I have hold of one idea which may lead us far. The man met his death elsewhere, and his body was on the *roof* of a carriage."

"On the roof!"

"Remarkable, is it not? But consider the facts. Is it a coincidence that it is found at the very point where the train pitches and sways as it comes round on the points? Is not that the place where an object upon the roof might be expected to fall off? The points would affect no object inside the train. Either the body fell from the roof, or a very curious coincidence has occurred. But now consider the question of the blood. Of course, there was no bleeding on the line if the body had bled elsewhere. Each fact is suggestive in itself. Together they have a cumulative force."

"And the ticket, too!" I cried.

"Exactly. We could not explain the absence of a ticket. This would explain it. Everything fits together."

"But suppose it were so, we are still as far as ever from unravelling the mystery of his death. Indeed, it becomes not simpler but stranger."

"Perhaps," said Holmes, thoughtfully, "perhaps." He relapsed into a silent reverie, which lasted until the slow train drew up at last in Woolwich Station. There he called a cab and drew Mycroft's paper from his pocket.

"We have quite a little round of afternoon calls to make," said he. "I think that Sir James Walter claims our first attention."

The house of the famous official was a fine villa with green lawns stretching down to the Thames. As we reached it the fog was lifting, and a thin, watery sunshine was breaking through. A butler answered our ring.

"Sir James, sir!" said he with solemn face. "Sir James died this morning."

"Good heavens!" cried Holmes in amazement. "How did he die?"

"Perhaps you would care to step in, sir, and see his brother, Colonel Valentine?"

"Yes, we had best do so."

We were ushered into a dim-lit drawing-room, where an instant later we were joined by a very tall, handsome, light-bearded man of fifty, the younger brother of the dead scientist. His wild eyes, stained cheeks, and unkempt hair all spoke of the sudden blow which had fallen upon the household. He was hardly articulate as he spoke of it.

"It was this horrible scandal," said he. "My brother, Sir James, was a man of very sensitive honour, and he could not survive such an affair. It broke his heart. He was always so proud of the efficiency of his department, and this was a crushing blow."

"We had hoped that he might have given us some indications which would have helped us to clear the matter up."

"I assure you that it was all a mystery to him as it is to you and to all of us. He had already put all his knowledge at the disposal of the police. Naturally he had no doubt that Cadogan West was guilty. But all the rest was inconceivable."

"You cannot throw any new light upon the affair?"

"I know nothing myself save what I have read or heard. I have no desire to be discourteous, but you can understand, Mr. Holmes, that we are much disturbed at present, and I must ask you to hasten this interview to an end."

"This is indeed an unexpected development," said my friend when we had regained the cab. "I wonder if the death was natural, or whether the poor old fellow killed himself! If the latter, may it be taken as some sign of self-reproach for duty neglected? We must leave that question to the future. Now we shall turn to the Cadogan Wests."

A small but well-kept house in the outskirts of the town sheltered the bereaved mother. The old lady was too dazed with grief to be of any use to us, but at her side was a white-faced young lady, who introduced herself as Miss Violet Westbury, the fiancée of the dead man, and the last to see him upon that fatal night.

"I cannot explain it, Mr. Holmes," she said. "I have not shut an eye since the tragedy, thinking, thinking, thinking, night and day, what the true meaning of it can be. Arthur was the most single-minded, chivalrous, patriotic man upon earth. He would have cut his right hand off before he would sell a State secret confided to his keeping. It is absurd, impossible, preposterous to anyone who knew him."

"But the facts, Miss Westbury?"

"Yes, yes; I admit I cannot explain them."

"Was he in any want of money?"

"No; his needs were very simple and his salary ample. He had saved a few hundreds, and we were to marry at the New Year."

"No signs of any mental excitement? Come, Miss Westbury, be absolutely frank with us."

The quick eye of my companion had noted some change in her manner. She coloured and hesitated.

"Yes," she said at last, "I had a feeling that there was something on his mind."

"For long?"

"Only for the last week or so. He was thoughtful and worried. Once I pressed him about it. He admitted that there was something, and that it was concerned with his official life. 'It is too serious for me to speak about, even to you,' said he. I could get nothing more."

Holmes looked grave.

"Go on, Miss Westbury. Even if it seems to tell against him, go on. We cannot say what it may lead to."

"Indeed, I have nothing more to tell. Once or twice it seemed to me that he was on the point of telling me something. He spoke one evening of the importance of the secret, and I have some recollection that he said that no doubt foreign spies would pay a great deal to have it."

My friend's face grew graver still.

"Anything else?"

"He said that we were slack about such matters—that it would be easy for a traitor to get the plans."

"Was it only recently that he made such remarks?"

"Yes, quite recently."

"Now tell us of that last evening."

"We were to go to the theatre. The fog was so thick that a cab was useless. We walked, and our way took us close to the office. Suddenly he darted away into the fog."

"Without a word?"

"He gave an exclamation; that was all. I waited but he never returned. Then I walked home. Next morning, after the office opened, they came to inquire. About twelve o'clock we heard the terrible news. Oh, Mr. Holmes, if you could only, only save his honour! It was so much to him."

Holmes shook his head sadly.

"Come, Watson," said he, "our ways lie elsewhere. Our next station must be the office from which the papers were taken.

"It was black enough before against this young man, but our inquiries make it blacker," he remarked as the cab lumbered off. "His coming marriage gives a motive for the crime. He naturally wanted money. The idea was in his head, since he spoke about it. He nearly made the girl an accomplice in the treason by telling her his plans. It is all very bad."

"But surely, Holmes, character goes for something? Then, again, why should he leave the girl in the street and dart away to commit a felony?"

"Exactly! There are certainly objections. But it is a formidable case which they have to meet."

Mr. Sidney Johnson, the senior clerk, met us at the office and received us with that respect which my companion's card always commanded. He was a thin, gruff, bespectacled man of middle age, his cheeks haggard, and his hands twitching from the nervous strain to which he had been subjected.

"It is bad, Mr. Holmes, very bad! Have you heard of the death of the chief?"

"We have just come from his house."

"The place is disorganised. The chief dead, Cadogan West dead, our papers stolen. And yet, when we closed our door on Monday evening, we were as efficient an office as any in the government service. Good God, it's dreadful to think of! That West, of all men, should have done such a thing!"

"You are sure of his guilt, then?"

"I can see no other way out of it. And yet I would have trusted him as I trust myself."

"At what hour was the office closed on Monday?"

"At five."

"Did you close it?"

"I am always the last man out."

"Where were the plans?"

"In that safe. I put them there myself."

"Is there no watchman to the building?"

"There is, but he has other departments to look after as well. He is an old soldier and a most trustworthy man. He saw nothing that evening. Of course the fog was very thick."

"Suppose that Cadogan West wished to make his way into the building after hours; he would need three keys, would he not, before he could reach the papers?"

"Yes, he would. The key of the outer door, the key of the office, and the key of the safe."

"Only Sir James Walter and you had those keys?"

"I had no keys of the doors—only of the safe."

"Was Sir James a man who was orderly in his habits?"

"Yes, I think he was. I know that so far as those three keys are concerned he kept them on the same ring. I have often seen them there."

"And that ring went with him to London?"

"He said so."

"And your key never left your possession?"

"Never."

"Then West, if he is the culprit, must have had a duplicate. And yet none was found upon his body. One other point: if a clerk in this office desired to sell the plans, would it not be simpler to copy the plans for himself than to take the originals, as was actually done?"

"It would take considerable technical knowledge to copy the plans in an effective way."

"But I suppose either Sir James, or you, or West has that technical knowledge?"

"No doubt we had, but I beg you won't try to drag me into the matter, Mr. Holmes. What is the use of our speculating in this way when the original plans were actually found on West?"

"Well, it is certainly singular that he should run the risk of taking originals if he could safely have taken copies, which would have equally served his turn."

"Singular, no doubt—and yet he did so."

"Every inquiry in this case reveals something inexplicable. Now there are three papers still missing. They are, as I understand, the vital ones."

"Yes, that is so."

"Do you mean to say that anyone holding these three papers, and without the seven others, could construct a Bruce-Partington submarine?"

"I reported to that effect to the Admiralty. But today I have been over the drawings again, and I am not so sure of it. The double valves with the automatic self-adjusting slots are drawn in one of the papers which have been returned. Until the foreigners had invented that for themselves they could not make the boat. Of course they might soon get over the difficulty."

"But the three missing drawings are the most important?"

"Undoubtedly."

"I think, with your permission, I will now take a stroll round the premises. I do not recall any other question which I desired to ask."

He examined the lock of the safe, the door of the room, and finally the iron shutters of the window. It was only when we were on the lawn outside that his interest was strongly excited. There was a laurel bush outside the window, and several of the branches bore signs of having been twisted or snapped. He examined them carefully with his lens, and then some dim and vague marks upon the earth beneath. Finally he asked the chief clerk to close the iron shutters, and he pointed out to me that they hardly met in the centre, and that it would be possible for anyone outside to see what was going on within the room.

"The indications are ruined by three days' delay. They may mean something or nothing. Well, Watson, I do not think that Woolwich can help us further. It is a small crop which we have gathered. Let us see if we can do better in London."

Yet we added one more sheaf to our harvest before we left Woolwich Station. The clerk in the ticket office was able to say with confidence that he saw Cadogan West—whom he knew well by sight—upon the Monday night, and that he went to London by the 8:15 to London Bridge. He was alone and took a single third-class ticket. The clerk was struck at the time by his excited and nervous manner. So shaky was he that he could hardly pick up his change, and the clerk had helped him with it. A reference to the time-table showed that the 8:15 was the first train which it was possible for West to take after he had left the lady about 7:30.

"Let us reconstruct, Watson," said Holmes after half an hour of silence. "I am not aware that in all our joint researches we have ever had a case which was more difficult to get at. Every fresh advance which we make only reveals a fresh ridge beyond. And yet we have surely made some appreciable progress.

"The effect of our inquiries at Woolwich has in the main been against young Cadogan West; but the indications at the window would lend themselves to a more favourable hypothesis. Let us suppose, for example, that he had been approached by some foreign agent. It might have been done under such pledges as would have prevented him from speaking of it, and yet would have affected his thoughts in the direction indicated by his remarks to his fiancée. Very good. We will now suppose that as he went to the theatre with the young lady he suddenly, in the fog, caught a glimpse of this same agent going in the direction of the office. He was an impetuous man, quick in his decisions. Everything gave way to his duty. He followed the man, reached the window, saw the abstraction of the documents, and pursued the thief. In this way we get over the objection that no one would take originals when he could make copies. This outsider had to take originals. So far it holds together."

"What is the next step?"

"Then we come into difficulties. One would imagine that under such circumstances the first act of young Cadogan West would be to seize the villain and raise the alarm. Why did he not do so? Could it have been an official superior who took the papers? That would explain West's conduct. Or could the chief have given West the slip in the fog, and West started at once to London to head him off from his own rooms, presuming that he knew where the rooms were? The call must have been very pressing, since he left his girl standing in the fog and made no effort to communicate with her. Our scent runs cold here, and there is a vast gap between either hypothesis and the laying of West's body, with seven papers in his pocket, on the roof of a Metropolitan train. My instinct now is to work from the other end. If Mycroft has given us the list of addresses we may be able to pick our man and follow two tracks instead of one."

Surely enough, a note awaited us at Baker Street. A government messenger had brought it post-haste. Holmes glanced at it and threw it over to me.

> There are numerous small fry, but few who would handle so big an affair. The only men worth considering are Adolph Mayer, of 13, Great George Street, Westminster; Louis La Rothière, of Campden Mansions, Notting Hill; and Hugo Oberstein, 13, Caulfield Gardens, Kensington. The latter was known to be in town on Monday and is now reported as having left. Glad to hear you have seen some light. The Cabinet awaits your final report with the utmost anxiety. Urgent representations have arrived from the very highest quarter. The whole force of the State is at your back if you should need it.—MYCROFT.

"I'm afraid," said Holmes, smiling, "that all the Queen's horses and all the Queen's men cannot avail in this matter." He had spread out his big map of London and leaned eagerly over it. "Well, well," said he presently with an exclamation of satisfaction, "things are turning a little in our direction at last. Why, Watson, I do honestly believe that we are going to pull it off, after all." He slapped me on the shoulder with a sudden burst of hilarity. "I am going out now. It is only a reconnaissance. I will do nothing serious without my trusted comrade and biographer at my elbow. Do you stay here, and the odds are that you will see me again in an hour or two. If time hangs heavy get foolscap and a pen, and begin your narrative of how we saved the State."

I felt some reflection of his elation in my own mind, for I knew well that he would not depart so far from his usual austerity of demeanour unless there was good cause for exultation. All the long November evening I waited, filled with impatience for his return. At last, shortly after nine o'clock, there arrived a messenger with a note:

> Am dining at Goldini's Restaurant, Gloucester Road, Kensington. Please come at once and join me there. Bring with you a jemmy, a dark lantern, a chisel, and a revolver.—S.H.

It was a nice equipment for a respectable citizen to carry through the dim, fog-draped streets. I stowed them all discreetly away in my overcoat and drove straight to the address given. There sat my friend at a little round table near the door of the garish Italian restaurant.

"Have you had something to eat? Then join me in a coffee and curaçao. Try one of the proprietor's cigars. They are less poisonous than one would expect. Have you the tools?"

"They are here, in my overcoat."

"Excellent. Let me give you a short sketch of what I have done, with some indication of what we are about to do. Now it must be evident to you, Watson, that this young man's body was *placed* on the roof of the train. That was clear from the instant that I determined the fact that it was from the roof, and not from a carriage, that he had fallen."

"Could it not have been dropped from a bridge?"

"I should say it was impossible. If you examine the roofs you will find that they are slightly rounded, and there is no railing round them. Therefore, we can say for certain that young Cadogan West was placed on it."

"How could he be placed there?"

"That was the question which we had to answer. There is only one possible way. You are aware that the Underground runs clear of tunnels at some points in the West End. I had a vague memory that as I have travelled by it I have occasionally seen windows just above my head.

Now, suppose that a train halted under such a window, would there be any difficulty in laying a body upon the roof?"

"It seems most improbable."

"We must fall back upon the old axiom that when all other contingencies fail, whatever remains, however improbable, must be the truth. Here all other contingencies *have* failed. When I found that the leading international agent, who had just left London, lived in a row of houses which abutted upon the Underground, I was so pleased that you were a little astonished at my sudden frivolity."

"Oh, that was it, was it?"

"Yes, that was it. Mr. Hugo Oberstein, of 13, Caulfield Gardens, had become my objective. I began my operations at Gloucester Road Station, where a very helpful official walked with me along the track and allowed me to satisfy myself not only that the back-stair windows of Caulfield Gardens open on the line but the even more essential fact that, owing to the intersection of one of the larger railways, the Underground trains are frequently held motionless for some minutes at that very spot."

"Splendid, Holmes! You have got it!"

"So far—so far, Watson. We advance, but the goal is afar. Well, having seen the back of Caulfield Gardens, I visited the front and satisfied myself that the bird was indeed flown. It is a considerable house, unfurnished, so far as I could judge, in the upper rooms. Oberstein lived there with a single valet, who was probably a confederate entirely in his confidence. We must bear in mind that Oberstein has gone to the Continent to dispose of his booty, but not with any idea of flight; for he had no reason to fear a warrant, and the idea of an amateur domiciliary visit would certainly never occur to him. Yet that is precisely what we are about to make."

"Could we not get a warrant and legalise it?"

"Hardly on the evidence."

"What can we hope to do?"

"We cannot tell what correspondence may be there."

"I don't like it, Holmes."

"My dear fellow, you shall keep watch in the street. I'll do the criminal part. It's not a time to stick at trifles. Think of Mycroft's note, of the Admiralty, the Cabinet, the exalted person who waits for news. We are bound to go."

My answer was to rise from the table.

"You are right, Holmes. We are bound to go."

He sprang up and shook me by the hand.

"I knew you would not shrink at the last," said he, and for a moment I saw something in his eyes which was nearer to tenderness than I had ever seen. The next instant he was his masterful, practical self once more.

"It is nearly half a mile, but there is no hurry. Let us walk," said he. "Don't drop the instruments, I beg. Your arrest as a suspicious character would be a most unfortunate complication."

Caulfield Gardens was one of those lines of flat-faced pillared, and porticoed houses which are so prominent a product of the middle Victorian epoch in the West End of London. Next door there appeared to be a children's party, for the merry buzz of young voices and the clatter of a piano resounded through the night. The fog still hung about and screened us with its friendly shade. Holmes had lit his lantern and flashed it upon the massive door.

"This is a serious proposition," said he. "It is certainly bolted as well as locked. We would do better in the area. There is an excellent archway down yonder in case a too zealous policeman should intrude. Give me a hand, Watson, and I'll do the same for you."

A minute later we were both in the area. Hardly had we reached the dark shadows before the step of the policeman was heard in the fog above. As its soft rhythm died away, Holmes set to work upon the lower door. I saw him stoop and strain until with a sharp crash it flew open. We sprang through into the dark passage, closing the area door behind us. Holmes led the way up the curving, uncarpeted stair. His little fan of yellow light shone upon a low window.

"Here we are, Watson—this must be the one." He threw it open, and as he did so there was a low, harsh murmur, growing steadily into a loud roar as a train dashed past us in the darkness. Holmes swept his light along the window-sill. It was thickly coated with soot from the passing engines, but the black surface was blurred and rubbed in places.

"You can see where they rested the body. Halloa, Watson! what is this? There can be no doubt that it is a blood mark." He was pointing to faint discolorations along the woodwork of the window. "Here it is on the stone of the stair also. The demonstration is complete. Let us stay here until a train stops."

We had not long to wait. The very next train roared from the tunnel as before, but slowed in the open, and then, with a creaking of brakes, pulled up immediately beneath us. It was not four feet from the window-ledge to the roof of the carriages. Holmes softly closed the window.

"So far we are justified," said he. "What do you think of it, Watson?"

"A masterpiece. You have never risen to a greater height."

"I cannot agree with you there. From the moment that I conceived the idea of the body being upon the roof, which surely was not a very abstruse one, all the rest was inevitable. If it were not for the grave interests involved the affair up to this point would be insignificant. Our difficulties are still before us. But perhaps we may find something here which may help us."

We had ascended the kitchen stair and entered the suite of rooms upon the first floor. One was a dining-room, severely furnished and containing nothing of interest. A second was a bedroom, which also drew blank. The remaining room appeared more promising, and my companion settled down to a systematic examination. It was littered with books and papers, and was evidently used as a study. Swiftly and methodically Holmes turned over the contents of drawer after drawer and cupboard after cupboard, but no gleam of success came to brighten his austere face. At the end of an hour he was no further than when he started.

"The cunning dog has covered his tracks," said he. "He has left nothing to incriminate him. His dangerous correspondence has been destroyed or removed. This is our last chance."

It was a small tin cash-box which stood upon the writing-desk. Holmes pried it open with his chisel. Several rolls of paper were within, covered with figures and calculations, without any note to show to what they referred. The recurring words, "water pressure" and "pressure to the square inch" suggested some possible relation to a submarine. Holmes tossed them all impatiently aside. There only remained an envelope with some small newspaper slips inside it. He shook them out on the table, and at once I saw by his eager face that his hopes had been raised.

"What's this, Watson? Eh? What's this? Record of a series of messages in the advertisements of a paper. *Daily Telegraph* agony column by the print and paper. Right-hand top corner of a page. No dates—but messages arrange themselves. This must be the first:

"Hoped to hear sooner. Terms agreed to. Write fully to address given on card.—PIERROT.

"Next comes:

"Too complex for description. Must have full report. Stuff awaits you when goods delivered.—PIERROT.

"Then comes:

> "Matter presses. Must withdraw offer unless contract completed. Make appointment by letter. Will confirm by advertisement.—PIERROT.

"Finally:

> "Monday night after nine. Two taps. Only ourselves. Do not be so suspicious. Payment in hard cash when goods delivered.—PIERROT.

"A fairly complete record, Watson! If we could only get at the man at the other end!" He sat lost in thought, tapping his fingers on the table. Finally he sprang to his feet.

"Well, perhaps it won't be so difficult, after all. There is nothing more to be done here, Watson. I think we might drive round to the offices of the *Daily Telegraph*, and so bring a good day's work to a conclusion."

Mycroft Holmes and Lestrade had come round by appointment after breakfast next day and Sherlock Holmes had recounted to them our proceedings of the day before. The professional shook his head over our confessed burglary.

"We can't do these things in the force, Mr. Holmes," said he. "No wonder you get results that are beyond us. But some of these days you'll go too far, and you'll find yourself and your friend in trouble."

"For England, home and beauty—eh, Watson? Martyrs on the altar of our country. But what do you think of it, Mycroft?"

"Excellent, Sherlock! Admirable! But what use will you make of it?"

Holmes picked up the *Daily Telegraph* which lay upon the table.

"Have you seen Pierrot's advertisement today?"

"What? Another one?"

"Yes, here it is:

"Tonight. Same hour. Same place. Two taps. Most vitally important. Your own safety at stake.—PIERROT."

"By George!" cried Lestrade. "If he answers that we've got him!"

"That was my idea when I put it in. I think if you could both make it convenient to come with us about eight o'clock to Caulfield Gardens we might possibly get a little nearer to a solution."

One of the most remarkable characteristics of Sherlock Holmes was his power of throwing his brain out of action and switching all his thoughts on to lighter things whenever he had convinced himself that he could no longer work to advantage. I remember that during the whole of that memorable day he lost himself in a monograph which he had undertaken upon the Polyphonic Motets of Lassus. For my own part I had none of this power of detachment, and the day, in consequence, appeared to be interminable. The great national importance of the issue, the suspense in high quarters, the direct nature of the experiment which we were trying—all combined to work upon my nerve. It was a relief to me when at last, after a light dinner, we set out upon our expedition. Lestrade and Mycroft met us by appointment at the outside of Gloucester Road Station. The area door of Oberstein's house had been left open the night before, and it was necessary for me, as Mycroft Holmes absolutely and indignantly declined to climb the railings, to pass in and open the hall door. By nine o'clock we were all seated in the study, waiting patiently for our man.

An hour passed and yet another. When eleven struck, the measured beat of the great church clock seemed to sound the dirge of our hopes. Lestrade and Mycroft were fidgeting in their seats and looking twice a minute at their watches. Holmes sat silent and composed, his eyelids half shut, but every sense on the alert. He raised his head with a sudden jerk.

"He is coming," said he.

There had been a furtive step past the door. Now it returned. We heard a shuffling sound outside, and then two sharp taps with the knocker. Holmes rose, motioning us to remain seated. The gas in the hall was a mere point of light. He opened the outer door, and then as a dark figure slipped past him he closed and fastened it. "This way!" we heard him say, and a moment later our man stood before us. Holmes had followed him closely, and as the man turned with a cry of surprise and alarm he caught him by the collar and threw him back into the room. Before our prisoner had recovered his balance the door was shut and Holmes standing with his back against it. The man glared round him, staggered, and fell senseless upon the floor. With the shock, his broad-brimmed hat flew from his head, his cravat slipped down from his lips, and there were the long light beard and the soft, handsome delicate features of Colonel Valentine Walter.

Holmes gave a whistle of surprise.

"You can write me down an ass this time, Watson," said he. "This was not the bird that I was looking for."

"Who is he?" asked Mycroft eagerly.

"The younger brother of the late Sir James Walter, the head of the Submarine Department. Yes, yes; I see the fall of the cards. He is coming to. I think that you had best leave his examination to me."

We had carried the prostrate body to the sofa. Now our prisoner sat up, looked round him with a horror-stricken face, and passed his hand over his forehead, like one who cannot believe his own senses.

"What is this?" he asked. "I came here to visit Mr. Oberstein."

"Everything is known, Colonel Walter," said Holmes. "How an English gentleman could behave in such a manner is beyond my comprehension. But your whole correspondence and relations with Oberstein are within our knowledge. So also are the circumstances connected with the death of young Cadogan West. Let me advise you to gain at least the small credit for repentance and confession, since there are still some details which we can only learn from your lips."

The man groaned and sank his face in his hands. We waited, but he was silent.

"I can assure you," said Holmes, "that every essential is already known. We know that you were pressed for money; that you took an impress of the keys which your brother held; and that you entered into a correspondence with Oberstein, who answered your letters through the advertisement columns of the *Daily Telegraph*. We are aware that you went down to the office in the fog on Monday night, but that you were seen and followed by young Cadogan West, who had probably some previous reason to suspect you. He saw your theft, but could not give the alarm, as it was just possible that you were taking the papers to your brother in London. Leaving all his private concerns, like the good citizen that he was, he followed you closely in the fog and kept at your heels until you reached this very house. There he intervened, and then it was, Colonel Walter, that to treason you added the more terrible crime of murder."

"I did not! I did not! Before God I swear that I did not!" cried our wretched prisoner.

"Tell us, then, how Cadogan West met his end before you laid him upon the roof of a railway carriage."

"I will. I swear to you that I will. I did the rest. I confess it. It was just as you say. A Stock Exchange debt had to be paid. I needed the money badly. Oberstein offered me five thousand. It was to save myself from ruin. But as to murder, I am as innocent as you."

"What happened, then?"

"He had his suspicions before, and he followed me as you describe. I never knew it until I was at the very door. It was thick fog, and one could not see three yards. I had given two taps and Oberstein had come to the door. The young man rushed up and demanded to know what we were about to do with the papers. Oberstein had a short life-preserver. He always carried it with him. As West forced his way after us into the house Oberstein struck him on the head. The blow was a fatal one. He was dead within five minutes. There he lay in the hall, and we were at our wits' end what to do. Then Oberstein had this idea about the trains which halted under his back window. But first he examined the papers which I had brought. He said that three of them were essential, and that he must keep them. 'You cannot keep them,' said I. 'There will be a dreadful row at Woolwich if they are not returned.' 'I must keep them,' said he, 'for they are so technical that it is impossible in the time to make copies.' 'Then they must all go back together tonight,' said I. He thought for a little, and then he cried out that he had it. 'Three I will keep,' said he. 'The others we will stuff into the pocket of this young man. When he is found the whole business will assuredly be put to his account.' I could see no other way out of it, so we did as he suggested. We waited half an hour at the window before a train stopped. It was so thick that nothing could be seen, and we had no difficulty in lowering West's body on to the train. That was the end of the matter so far as I was concerned."

"And your brother?"

"He said nothing, but he had caught me once with his keys, and I think that he suspected. I read in his eyes that he suspected. As you know, he never held up his head again."

There was silence in the room. It was broken by Mycroft Holmes.

"Can you not make reparation? It would ease your conscience, and possibly your punishment."

"What reparation can I make?"

"Where is Oberstein with the papers?"

"I do not know."

"Did he give you no address?"

"He said that letters to the Hôtel du Louvre, Paris, would eventually reach him."

"Then reparation is still within your power," said Sherlock Holmes.

"I will do anything I can. I owe this fellow no particular good-will. He has been my ruin and my downfall."

"Here are paper and pen. Sit at this desk and write to my dictation. Direct the envelope to the address given. That is right. Now the letter:

"DEAR SIR:

"With regard to our transaction, you will no doubt have observed by now that one essential detail is missing. I have a tracing which will make it complete. This has involved me in extra trouble, however, and I must ask you for a further advance of five hundred pounds. I will not trust it to the post, nor will I take anything but gold or notes. I would come to you abroad, but it would excite remark if I left the country at present. Therefore I shall expect to meet you in the smoking-room of the Charing Cross Hotel at noon on Saturday. Remember that only English notes, or gold, will be taken.

"That will do very well. I shall be very much surprised if it does not fetch our man."

And it did! It is a matter of history—that secret history of a nation which is often so much more intimate and interesting than its public chronicles—that Oberstein, eager to complete the coup of his lifetime, came to the lure and was safely engulfed for fifteen years in a British prison. In his trunk were found the invaluable Bruce-Partington plans, which he had put up for auction in all the naval centres of Europe.

Colonel Walter died in prison towards the end of the second year of his sentence. As to Holmes, he returned refreshed to his monograph upon the Polyphonic Motets of Lassus, which has since been printed for private circulation, and is said by experts to be the last word upon the subject. Some weeks afterwards I learned incidentally that my friend spent a day at Windsor, whence he returned with a remarkably fine emerald tie-pin. When I asked him if he had bought it, he answered that it was a present from a certain gracious lady in whose interests he had once been fortunate enough to carry out a small commission. He said no more; but I fancy that I could guess at that lady's august name, and I have little doubt that the emerald pin will forever recall to my friend's memory the adventure of the Bruce-Partington plans.

1925

"The Old Man in the Corner" in

THE MISER OF MAIDA VALE

Baroness Orczy

Emma Magdalena Rozália Mária Jozefa Borbála Orczy de Orci (1865–1947) is much better-known as Emmuska, or Baroness Orczy. She was born into a wealthy Hungarian family, but her parents left their estate because they were afraid of a peasants' revolt. When Emmuska was fourteen, they moved to 162 Great Portland Street, London, where they lodged with a countryman. Emma subsequently attended West London School of Art and married a Yorkshire-born illustrator, Henry Barstow. They supplemented their income with writing and Emmuska published short stories in magazines before coming up (while travelling on the London underground) with the idea of a story about a British aristocrat who rescues members of the French nobility from the threat of the guillotine during the French Revolution. She and her husband turned the concept into a play, *The Scarlet Pimpernel*, which became a West End hit and ran for over two thousand performances.

Her most notable stories in the crime genre feature "the Old Man in the Corner", who is generally to be found in the corner of an ABC teashop in London, in conversation with a woman journalist. The first six stories were called "Mysteries of London" and published in the *Royal Magazine* in 1901. This story first appeared in *Hutchinson's Magazine* in February 1925, prior to being collected in book form in *Unravelled Knots* in the same year.

I

"ONE OF THE MOST PUZZLING CASES I EVER REMEMBER WATCH-ing," the Old Man in the Corner said to me that day, "was the one known to the public as that of 'The Miser of Maida Vale.' It presented certain altogether novel features, and for once I was willing to admit that, though the police had a very hard nut to crack in the elucidation of the mystery, and in the end failed to find a solution, they were at one time very near putting their finger on the key of the puzzle. If they had only possessed some of that instinct for true facts with which Nature did so kindly endow me, there is no doubt that they would have brought that clever criminal to book."

I wish it were in my power to convey something of that air of ludi-crous complacency with which he said this. I could almost hear him purring to himself, like a lean, shabby old cat. He had his inevitable bit of string in his hand, and had been in rapturous contemplation of a series of knots which he had been fashioning until the moment when I sat down beside him and he began to speak. But as soon as he embarked upon his beloved topic he turned his rapturous contempla-tion on himself. He just sat there and admired himself, and now and again blinked at me, with such an air of self-satisfaction that I longed to say something terribly rude first, and then to flounce out of the place, leaving him to admire himself at his leisure.

But, of course, this could not be. To use the funny creature's own verbiage, Nature had endowed me with the journalistic instinct. I had to listen to him; I had to pick his brains and to get copy out of him. The irresistible desire to learn something new, something that would thrill my editor, as well as my public, compelled me to swallow my impatience, to smile at him—somewhat wryly, perhaps—and then to beg him to proceed.

I was all attention.

"Well," he said, still wearing an irritating air of condescension, "do you remember the case of the old miser of Maida Vale?"

"Only vaguely," I was willing to admit.

"It presented some very interesting features," he went on, blandly, "and assuming that you really only remember them vaguely, I will put them before you as clearly as possible, in order that you may follow my argument more easily later on.

"The victim of the mysterious tragedy was, as no doubt you remember, an eccentric old invalid named Thornton Ashley, the well-known naval constructor, who had made a considerable fortune during the war and then retired, chiefly, it was said, owing to ill-health. He had two sons, one of whom, Charles, was a misshapen, undersized creature, singularly unprepossessing both in appearance and in manner, whilst the other, Philip, was a tall, good-looking fellow, very agreeable and popular wherever he went. Both these young men were bachelors, a fact which, it appears, had been for some time a bone of contention between them and their father. Old Ashley was passionately fond of children, and the one desire of his declining years was to see the grandchildren who would ultimately enjoy the fortune which he had accumulated. Whilst he was ready to admit that Charles, with his many afflictions, did not stand much chance with the fair sex, there was no reason at all why Philip should not marry, and there had been more than one heated quarrel between father and son on that one subject.

"So much so, indeed, that presently Philip cut his stick and went to live in rooms in Jermyn Street. He had a few hundreds a year of his own, left to him by a godmother. He had been to Rugby and to Cambridge, and had been a temporary officer in the war: pending his obtaining some kind of job he settled down to live the life of a smart young bachelor in town, whilst his brother Charles was left to look after the old man, who became more and more eccentric as his health gradually broke up. He sold his fine house in Hyde Park Gardens, his motor, and the bulk of his furniture, and moved into a cheap flat in Maida Vale, where he promptly took to his bed, which he never left again. His eccentricities became more and more pronounced and his temper more and more irascible. He took a violent dislike to strangers, refused to see anybody except his sons and two old friends, Mr. Oldwall, the well-known solicitor, and Dr. Fanshawe-Bigg, who visited him from time to time and whose orders he obstinately refused to obey. Worst of all, as far as the unfortunate Charles was concerned, he became desperately mean, denying himself (and, incidentally, his son) every luxury, subsisting on the barest necessities, and keeping no servant to wait on him except a daily 'char.'

"Soon his miserliness degenerated into a regular mania.

"'Charles and I are saving money for the grandchildren you are going to give me one day,' he would say with a chuckle whenever Philip tried to reason with him on the subject of this self-denying ordinance. 'When you have an establishment of your own, you can invite us to come and live with you. There will be plenty then for housekeeping, I promise you!'

"At which the handsome Philip would laugh and shrug his shoulders and go back to his comfortable rooms in Jermyn Street. But no one knew what Charles thought about it all. To an outsider his case must always have appeared singularly pathetic. He had no money of his own and his delicate health had made it impossible for him to take up any profession: he could not cut his stick like his brother Philip had done, but, truth to tell, he did not appear to wish to do so. Perhaps it was real fondness for his father that made him seem contented with his lot. Certain it is that as time went on he became a regular slave to the old man, waiting on him hand and foot, more hard-worked than the daily 'char,' who put on her bonnet and walked out of the flat every day at six o'clock when her work was done, and who had all her Sundays to herself.

"All the relaxation that Charles ever had were alternate weekends, when his brother Philip would come over and spend Saturday to Monday in the flat taking charge of the invalid. On those occasions Charles would get on an old bicycle, and with just a few shillings in his pocket which he had saved during the past fortnight out of the meagre housekeeping allowance which he handled, he would go off for the day somewhere into the country, nobody ever knew where. Then on Monday morning he would return to the flat in Maida Vale, ready to take up his slave's yoke, to all appearances with a light heart.

"'Charles Ashley is wise,' the gossiping acquaintances would say, 'he sticks to the old miser. Thornton Ashley can't live for ever, and Oldwall says that he is worth close on a quarter of a million.'

"Philip, on the other hand, could have had no illusions with regard to his father's testamentary intentions. The bone of contention— Philip's celibacy—was still there, making bad blood between father and son; more than once the old miser had said to him with a sardonic grin: 'Let me see you married soon, my boy, and with a growing family around you, or I tell you that my money shall go to that fool Charles, or to the founding of an orphan asylum or the establishment of a matrimonial agency.'

"Mr. Oldwall, the solicitor, a very old friend of the Ashleys, and who had seen the two boys grow up, threw out as broad a hint to Philip on that same subject as professional honour allowed.

"'Your father,' he said to him one day, 'has got that mania for saving money, but otherwise he is perfectly sane, you know. He'll never forgive you if you don't gratify his wish to see you married. Hang it all, man, there are plenty of nice girls about. And what on earth would poor old Charles do with a quarter of a million, I'd like to know.'

"But for a long time Philip remained obstinate and his friends knew well enough the cause of this obstinacy; it had its root in a pre-war romance. Philip Ashley had been in love—some say that he had actually been engaged to her—with a beautiful girl, Muriel Balleine, the daughter of the eminent surgeon, Sir Arnold Balleine. The two young people were thought to be devoted to one another. But the lovely Muriel had, as it turned out, another admirer in Sir Wilfred Peet-Jackson, the wealthy shipowner, who worshipped her in secret. Philip Ashley and Wilfred Peet-Jackson were great friends; they had been at school and 'Varsity together. In 1915 they both obtained a com-mission in the Coldstreams and in 1916 Peet-Jackson was very severely wounded. He was sent home to be nursed by the beautiful Muriel in her father's hospital in Grosvenor Square. His case had already been pronounced hopeless, and Sir Arnold himself, as well as other equally eminent surgeons, gave it as their opinion that the unfortunate young man could not live more than a few months—if that.

"We must then take it that pity and romance played their part in the events that ensued. Certain it is that London society was one day thrilled to read in its *Times* that Miss Muriel Balleine had been mar-ried the previous morning to Sir Wilfred Peet-Jackson, the wealthy shipowner and owner of lovely Deverill Castle in Northamptonshire. Her friends at once put it about that Muriel had only yielded to a dying man's wish, and that there was nothing mercenary or calculating in this unexpected marriage; she probably would be a widow within a very short time and free to return to her original love and to marry Philip Ashley. But in this case, like in so many others in life, the unexpected occurred. Sir Wilfred Peet-Jackson did not die—not just then. He lived six years after the doctors had said that he must die in six months. He remained an invalid and he and his beautiful wife spent their winters in the Canaries and their summers in Switzerland, but Muriel did not become a widow until 1922, and Philip Ashley all that time never looked at another girl; he was even willing to allow a fortune to slip away from him, because he always hoped that the woman whom he had never ceased to worship would be his wife one day.

"Probably old Ashley knew all that; probably he hated the idea that this one woman should spoil his son's life for always; probably he thought that threat of disinheritance would bring Philip back out of the realms of romance to the realities of life. All this we shall never know. The old man spoke to no one about that, not even to Mr. Oldwall, possibly not even to Charles. By the time that Sir Wilfred Peet-Jackson had died and Philip had announced his engagement to the beautiful widow, Thornton Ashley was practically a dying man. However, he did have the satisfaction before he died of hearing the good news. Philip told him of his engagement one Saturday in May when he came for his usual fortnightly weekend visit. Strangely enough, although the old man must have been delighted at this tardy realisation of his life's desire, he did not after that make any difference in his mode of life. He remained just as irascible, just as difficult, and every bit as mean as he had always been; he never asked to see his future daughter-in-law, whom he had known in the past, though she did come once or twice to see him; nor did he encourage Philip to come and see him any more frequently than he had done before. The only indication he ever gave that he was pleased with the engagement was an obvious impatience to see the wedding-day fixed as soon as possible, and one day he worked himself up into a state of violent passion because Philip told him that Lady Peet-Jackson was bound to let a full year lapse before she married again, out of respect for poor Wilfred's memory.

2

"Of course a good deal of gossip was concentrated on all these events. Although Thornton Ashley had, for the past three years, cut himself adrift from all social intercourse, past friends and acquaintances had not altogether forgotten him, whilst Philip Ashley and Lady Peet-Jackson had always been well-known figures in a certain set in London. It was not likely, therefore, that their affairs would not be discussed and commented on at tea-parties and in the clubs. Philip Ashley was exalted to the position of a hero. By his marriage he would at last grasp the fortune which he had so obstinately and romantically evaded: true love was obtaining its just reward, and so on. Lady Peet-Jackson, on the other hand, was not quite so leniently dealt with by the gossips. It was now generally averred that she had originally thrown Philip Ashley over only because Peet-Jackson was a very rich man and had a handle to his name, and that she was only returning to her former lover now because Thornton Ashley had already one foot in the grave, and was reputed to be worth a quarter of a million.

"I have a photograph here," the Old Man in the Corner went on, and threw a bundle of newspaper cuttings down before me, "of Lady Peet-Jackson. As no doubt you will admit, she is very beautiful, but the face is hard; looking at it one feels instinctively that she is not a woman who would stand by a man in case of trouble or disgrace. But it is difficult to judge from these smudgy reproductions, and there is no doubt that Philip Ashley was madly in love with her. That she had enemies, especially amongst those of her own sex, was only natural in view of the fact that she was exceptionally beautiful, had made one brilliant marriage, and was on the point of making another.

"But the two romantic lovers were not the sole food of the gossip-mongers. There was the position of Charles Ashley to be discussed and talked over. What was going to become of him? How would he take this change in his fortune? If rumour, chiefly based on Mr. Oldwall's indiscretions, was correct, he would be losing that reputed quarter of a million if Philip's marriage came off. But in this case gossip had to rest satisfied with conjectures. No one ever saw Charles, and Philip, when questioned about him, had apparently very little to say.

"'Charles is a queer fish,' he would reply. 'I don't profess to know what goes on inside him. He seems delighted at the prospect of my marriage, but he doesn't say much. He is very shy and very sensitive about his deformity, and he won't see any one now, not even Muriel.'

"And thus the stage was set," the funny creature continued with a fatuous grin, "for the mysterious tragedy which has puzzled the public and the police as much as the friends of the chief actors in the drama. It was set for the scene of Philip Ashley's marriage to Muriel Lady Peet-Jackson, which was to take place very quietly at St. Saviour's, Warwick Road, early in the following year.

"On the twenty-seventh of August old Thornton Ashley died, that is to say he was found dead in his bed by his son Charles, who had returned that morning from his fortnightly weekend holiday. The cause of death was not in question at first, though Dr. Fanshawe-Bigg was out of town at the moment, his *locum tenens* knew all about the case, and had seen the invalid on the Thursday preceding his death. In accordance with the amazing laws of this country, he gave the necessary certificate without taking a last look at the dead man, and Thornton Ashley would no doubt have been buried then and there, without either fuss or ceremony, but for the amazing events which thereupon followed one another in quick succession.

"The funeral had been fixed for Thursday, the thirtieth, but within twenty-four hours of the old miser's death it had already transpired that he had indeed left a considerable fortune, which included one or two substantial life insurances, and that the provisions of his will were very much as Philip Ashley and his friends had surmised. After sundry legacies to various charitable institutions concerned with the care of children, Thornton Ashley had left the residue of his personalty to whichever of his sons was first married within a year from the time of the testator's death, the other son receiving an annuity of three hundred pounds. This clearly was aimed at Philip, as poor misshapen Charles had always been thought to be out of the running. Moreover, a further clause in the will directed that in the event of both the testator's sons being still unmarried within that given time, then the whole of the residue was to go to Charles, with an annuity of one hundred pounds to Philip and a sum of ten thousand pounds for the endowment of an orphan asylum at the discretion of the Charity Organisation Society.

"There were a few conjectures as to whether Charles Ashley, who, by his brother's impending marriage, would be left with a paltry three hundred pounds a year, would contest his father's will on the grounds of *non compos mentis*, but, as you know, it is always very difficult in this country to upset a will, and the provisions of this particular one were so entirely in accord with the wishes expressed by the deceased on every possible occasion, that the plea that he was of unsound mind when he made it would never have been upheld, quite apart from the fact that Mr. Oldwall, who drew up the will and signed it as one of the witnesses, would have repudiated any suggestion that his client was anything but absolutely sane at the time.

"Everything then appeared quite smooth and above board when suddenly, like a bolt from the blue, came the demand from the Insurance Company in which the late Mr. Thornton Ashley had a life policy for forty thousand pounds for a *post-mortem* examination, the company not being satisfied that the deceased had died a natural death. Naturally, Dr. Percy Jutt, who had signed the death certificate, was furious, but he was overruled by the demands of the Insurance Company, backed by no less a person than Charles Ashley. Indeed, it soon transpired that it was in consequence of certain statements made by Mr. Triscott, a local solicitor, on behalf of Charles Ashley to the general manager of the company, that the latter took action in the matter.

"Philip Ashley, through his solicitor, Mr. Oldwall, and backed by Dr. Jutt, might perhaps have opposed the proceedings, but quite apart from the fact that opposition from that quarter would have been impolitic, it probably also would have been unsuccessful. Anyway, the sensation-mongers had quite a titbit to offer to the public that afternoon; the evening papers came out before midday with flaring headlines: 'The mystery miser of Maida Vale.' Also, 'Sensational developments,' and 'Sinister Rumours.'

"By four o'clock in the afternoon some of the papers had it that a *post-mortem* examination of the body of the late Mr. Thornton Ashley had been conducted by Dr. Dawson, the divisional surgeon, and that it had revealed the fact that the old miser had not died a natural death, traces of violence having been discovered on the body. It was understood that the police were already in possession of certain facts and that the coroner of the district would hold an inquest on Thursday, the thirtieth, the very day on which the funeral was to have taken place.

3

"Now I have attended many an inquest in my day," the Old Man in the Corner continued after a brief pause, during which his claw-like fingers worked away with feverish energy at his bit of string, "but seldom have I been present at a more interesting one. There were so many surprises, such an unexpected turn of events, that one was kept on tenterhooks the whole time as to what would happen next.

"Even to those who were in the know, the witnesses in themselves were a surprise. Of course, every one knew Mr. Oldwall, the solicitor and life-long friend of old Thornton Ashley, and the divisional surgeon, whose evidence would be interesting; then there was poor Charles Ashley and his handsome brother, Philip, now the owner of a magnificent fortune, whose romantic history had more than once been paragraphed in the Press. But what in the world had Mr. Triscott, a local lawyer whom nobody knew, and Mrs. Trapp, a slatternly old 'char,' to do with the case? And there was also Dr. Percy Jutt, who had not come out of the case with flying professional colours, and who must have cursed the day when he undertook the position of *locum tenens* for Dr. Fanshawe-Bigg.

"The proceedings began with the sensational evidence of Dr. Dawson, the divisional surgeon, who had conducted the *post-mortem*. He stated that the deceased had been in an advanced state of uræmia, but this had not actually been the cause of death. Death was due to heart failure, caused by fright and shock, following on violent aggression and an attempt at strangulation. There were marks round the throat, and evidences of a severe blow having been dealt on the face and cranium causing concussion. In the patient's weak state of health, shock and fright had affected the heart's action with fatal results.

"All the while that the divisional surgeon gave evidence, going into technical details which the layman could not understand, Dr. Percy Jutt had obvious difficulty to control himself. He had a fidgety, nervous way with him and was constantly biting his nails. When he, in his turn, entered the witness-box, he was as white as a sheet and tried to hide his nervousness behind a dictatorial, blustering manner. In answer to the coroner, he explained that he had been acting as *locum tenens* for Dr. Fanshawe-Bigg, who was away on his holiday. He had visited the deceased once or twice during the past fortnight, and had last seen him on the Thursday preceding his death. Dr. Fanshawe-Bigg had left him a few notes on the case.

"'I found,' he went on to explain, 'the deceased in an advanced stage of uræmia, and there was very little that I could do, more especially as I was made to understand that my visits were not particularly wanted. On the Thursday, deceased was in a very drowsy state, this being one of the best-known symptoms of the disease, and I didn't think that he

could live much longer. I told Mr. Charles Ashley so; at the same time,
I did not think that the end would come quite so soon. However, I was
not particularly surprised when on the Monday morning I received a
visit from Mr. Charles Ashley who told me that his father was dead.
I found him very difficult to understand,' Dr. Jutt continued, in reply
to a question from the coroner, 'emotion had, I thought, addled his
speech a little. He may have tried to tell me something in connection
with his father's death, but I was so rushed with work that morning,
and, as I say, I was fully prepared for the event, that all I could do was
to promise to come round some time during the day, and, in the meanwhile, in order to facilitate arrangements for the funeral, I gave the
necessary certificate. I was entirely within my rights,' he concluded,
with somewhat aggressive emphasis, 'and, as far as I can recollect, Mr.
Charles Ashley said nothing that in any way led me to think that there
was anything wrong.'

"Mr. Oldwall, the solicitor, was the next witness called, and his
testimony was unimportant to the main issue. He had drafted the late
Mr. Thornton Ashley's will in 1919, and had last seen him alive before
starting on a short holiday some time in June. Deceased had just heard
then of his son's engagement and witness thought him looking wonderfully better and brighter than he had been for a long time.

"'Mr. Ashley,' the coroner asked, 'didn't say anything to you then
about any alteration to his will?'

"'Most emphatically, no!' the witness replied.

"'Or at any time?'

"'At no time,' Mr. Oldwall asserted.

"These questions put by the coroner in quick succession had, figu-
ratively speaking, made every one sit up. Up to now the general public
had not been greatly interested, one had made up one's mind that the
old miser had kept certain sums of money, after the fashion of his kind,
underneath his mattress; that some evil-doer had got wind of this and

entered the flat when no one was about, giving poor Thornton Ashley
a fright that had cost him his life.

"But with this reference to some possible alteration in the will the
case at once appeared more interesting. Suddenly one felt on the alert,
excitement was in the air, and when the next witness, a middle-aged,
dapper little man, wearing spectacles, a grey suit and white spats, stood
up to answer questions put to him by the coroner, a suppressed gasp
of anticipatory delight went round the circle of spectators.

"The witness gave his name as James Triscott, solicitor, of Warwick
Avenue. He said that he had known the deceased slightly, having seen
him on business in connection with the lease of 73, Malvine Mansions,
the landlord being a client of his. On the previous Friday, that is, the
twenty-fourth, witness received a note written in a crabbed hand and
signed, 'A. Thornton Ashley,' asking him to call at Malvine Mansions
any time during the day. This Mr. Triscott did that same afternoon. The
door was opened by Mr. Charles Ashley whom he had also met once
or twice before, who showed him into the room where the deceased
lay in bed, obviously very ill, but perfectly conscious and reasonable.

"'After some preliminary talk,' the witness went on, 'the deceased
explained to me that he was troubled in his mind about a will which
he had made some four years previously, and which had struck him
of late as being both harsh and unjust. He desired to make a new will,
revoking the previous one. I naturally told him that I was entirely at
his service, and he then dictated his wishes to me. I made notes and
promised to have the will ready for his signature by Monday. The
thought of this delay annoyed him considerably, and he pressed me
hard to have everything ready for him by the next day. Unfortunately,
I couldn't do that. I was obliged to go off into the country that evening
on business for another client, and couldn't possibly be back before
midday Saturday, when my clerk and typist would both be gone. All I
could do was to promise faithfully to call again on Monday at eleven

o'clock with the will quite ready for signature. I said I would bring my clerk with me, who could then sign as a witness.

"'I quite saw the urgency of the business,' Mr. Triscott went on in his brisk, rather consequential way, 'as the poor old gentleman certainly looked very ill. Before I left he asked me to let him at least have a copy of my notes before I went away this evening. This I was able to promise him. I got my clerk to copy the notes and to take them round to the flat later on in the day.'

"I can assure you," the Old Man in the Corner said, "that while that dapper little man was talking, you might have heard the proverbial pin drop amongst the public. You see, this was the first that any one had ever heard of any alteration in old Ashley's will, and Mr. Triscott's evidence opened up a vista of exciting situations that was positively dazzling. When he ceased speaking, you might almost have heard the sensation-mongers licking their chops like a lot of cats after a first bite at a succulent meal; glances were exchanged, but not a word spoken, and presently a sigh of eagerness went round when the coroner put the question which every one had been anticipating:

"'Have you got the notes, Mr. Triscott, which you took from the late Mr. Thornton Ashley's dictation?'

"At which suggestion Mr. Oldwall jumped up, objecting that such evidence was inadmissible. There was some legal argument between him and the coroner, during which Mr. Triscott, still standing in the witness-box, beamed at his colleague and at the public generally through his spectacles. In the end the jury decided the point by insisting on having the notes read out to them.

"Briefly, by the provisions of the new will, which was destined never to be signed, the miser left his entire fortune, with the exception of the same trifling legacies and of an annuity of a thousand pounds a year to Philip, to his son Charles absolutely, in grateful recognition for years of unflagging devotion to an eccentric and crabbed invalid.

Mr. Triscott explained that on the Monday morning he had the document quite ready by eleven o'clock, and that he walked round with it to Malvine Mansions, accompanied by his clerk. Great was his distress when he was met at the door by Charles Ashley, who told him that old Mr. Thornton Ashley was dead.

"That was the substance of Mr. Triscott's evidence, and I can assure you that even I was surprised at the turn which events had taken. You know what the sensation-mongers are; within an hour of the completion of Mr. Triscott's evidence, it was all over London that Mr. Philip Ashley had murdered his father in order to prevent his signing a will that would deprive him—Philip—of a fortune. That is the way of the world," the funny creature added with a cynical smile. "Philip's popularity went down like a sail when the wind suddenly drops, and in a moment public sympathy was all on the side of Charles, who had been done out of a fortune by a grasping and unscrupulous brother.

"But there was more to come.

"The next witness called was Mrs. Triscott, the wife of the dapper little solicitor, and her presence here in connection with the death of old Thornton Ashley seemed as surprising at first as that of her husband had been. She looked a hard, rather common, but capable woman, and after she had replied to the coroner's preliminary questions, she plunged into her story in a quiet, self-assured manner. She began by explaining that she was a trained nurse, but had given up her profession since her marriage. Now and again, however, either in an emergency or to oblige a friend, she had taken care of a patient.

"'On Friday evening last,' she continued, 'Mr. Triscott, who was just going off into the country on business, said to me that he had a client in the neighbourhood who was very ill, and about whom, for certain reasons, he felt rather anxious. He went on to say that he was chiefly sorry for the son, a delicate man, who was sadly deformed. Would I, like a good Samaritan, go and look after the sick man during the weekend? It seems that the doctor had ordered absolute rest, and Mr. Triscott feared that there might be some trouble with another son because, as a matter of fact, the old man had decided to alter his will.

"'I knew nothing about Mr. Thornton Ashley's family affairs,' the witness said, in reply to a question put to her by the coroner, and calmly ignoring the sensation which her statement was causing, 'beyond what I have just told you that Mr. Triscott said to me, but I agreed to go to Malvine Mansions and see if I could be of any use. I arrived at the flat on Friday evening and saw at once what the invalid was suffering from. I had nursed cases of uræmia before, and I could see that the poor old man had not many more days to live. Still I did not think that the end was imminent. Mr. Charles Ashley, who had welcomed me most effusively, looked to need careful nursing almost as much as his father did. He told me that he had not slept for three nights, so I just packed him off to bed and spent the night in an armchair in the patient's room.

"'The next morning Mr. Philip Ashley arrived and I was told of the arrangement whereby Mr. Charles got a weekend holiday once a fortnight. I welcomed the idea for his sake, and as he seemed very anxious about his father, and remembering what my husband had told me, I promised that I would stay on in the flat until his return on the Monday. Thus only was I able to persuade him to go off on his much-needed holiday. Directly he had gone, however, I thought it my duty to explain to Mr. Philip Ashley that really his father was very ill. He was only conscious intermittently and that in such cases the only thing that could be done was to keep the patient absolutely quiet. It was the only way, I added, to prolong life and to ensure a painless and peaceful death.

"'Mr. Philip Ashley,' the witness continued, 'appeared more annoyed than distressed, when I told him this, and asked me by whose authority I was here, keeping him out of his father's room, and so on. He also asked me several peremptory questions as to who had visited his father lately, and when I told him that I was the wife of a well-known solicitor in the neighbourhood, he looked for a moment as if he would give way to a violent fit of rage. However, I suppose he thought better of it, and presently I took him into the patient's room, who was asleep just then, begging him on no account to disturb the sufferer.

"'After he had seen his father, Mr. Ashley appeared more ready to admit that I was acting for the best. However, he asked me—rather rudely, I thought, considering that the patient was nothing to me and I was not getting paid for my services—how long I proposed staying in the flat. I told him that I would wait here until his brother's return, which I was afraid would not be before ten o'clock on Monday morning. Whereupon he picked up his hat, gave me a curt good-day, and walked out of the flat.

"'To my astonishment,' the witness now said amidst literally breathless silence on the part of the spectators, 'it had only just gone eight on the Monday morning, when Mr. Philip Ashley turned up once more. I must say that I was rather pleased to see him. I was expecting Mr. Triscott home and had a lot to do in my own house. The patient, who had rallied wonderfully the last two days, had just gone off into a comfortable sleep, and as I knew that Mr. Charles would be back soon, I felt quite justified in going off duty and leaving Mr. Philip in charge, with strict injunctions that he was on no account to disturb the patient. If he woke, he might be given a little barley-water first and then some beef-tea, all of which I had prepared and put ready. My intention was directly I got home to telephone to Dr. Jutt and ask him to look in at Malvine Mansions some time during the morning. Unfortunately, when I got home I had such a lot to do, that, frankly, I forgot to telephone to the doctor, and before the morning was over Mr. Triscott had come home with the news that old Mr. Thornton Ashley was dead.'

"This," the Old Man in the Corner continued, "was the gist of Mrs. Triscott's evidence at that memorable inquest. Of course, there were some dramatic incidents during the course of her examination; glances exchanged between Philip Ashley and Mr. Oldwall, and between him and the dapper little Mr. Triscott. The latter, I must tell you, still beamed on everybody; he looked inordinately proud of his capable, business-like wife, and very pleased with the prominence which he had attained through this mysterious and intricate case.

4

"The luncheon interval gave us all a respite from the tension that had kept our nerves strung up all morning. I don't think that Philip Ashley, for one, ate much lunch that day. I noticed, by the way, that he and Mr. Oldwall went off together, whilst Mr. and Mrs. Triscott took kindly charge of poor Charles. I caught sight of the three of them subsequently in a blameless teashop. Charles was indeed a pathetic picture to look upon; he looked the sort of man who lives on his nerves, with no flesh on his poor, misshapen bones, and a hungry, craving expression in his eyes, as in those of an under-fed dog.

"We had his evidence directly after luncheon. But, as a matter of fact, he had not much to say. He had last seen his father alive on the Saturday morning when he went off on his fortnightly weekend holiday. He had bicycled to Dorking and spent his time there at the Running Footman, as he had often done before. He was well known in the place. On Monday morning he made an early start and got to Malvine Mansions soon after ten and let himself into the flat with his latch-key. He expected to find his brother or Mrs. Triscott there, but there was no one. He then went into his father's room, and at first thought that the old man was only asleep. The blinds were down and the room very dark. He drew up the blind and went back to his father's bedside. Then only did he realise that the old man was dead. Though he was very ignorant in such matters, he thought that there was something strange about the dead man, and he tried to explain this to Dr. Jutt. But the latter seemed too busy to attend to him, so when Mr. Triscott came to call later on, he told him of this strange feeling that troubled him. Mr. Triscott then thought that as Dr. Jutt seemed so indifferent about the matter, it might be best to see the police.

"'But this,' Charles Ashley explained, 'I refused to do, and then Mr. Triscott asked me if I knew whether my dear father had any life insurances, and if so, in what company. I was able to satisfy him on that point, as I had heard him speak with Mr. Oldwall about a life policy he had in the Empire of India Life Insurance Company. Mr. Triscott then told me to leave the matter to him, which I was only too glad to do.'

"Witness was asked if he knew anything of his father's intentions with regard to altering his will, and to this he gave an emphatic 'No!' He explained that he had taken a note from his father to Mr. Triscott on the Friday and that he had seen Mr. Triscott when the latter called at the flat that afternoon, but when the coroner asked him whether he knew what passed between his father and the lawyer on that occasion, he again gave an emphatic 'No!'

"He had accepted gratefully Mr. Triscott's suggestion that Mrs. Triscott should come over for the weekend to take charge of the invalid; but he declared that this arrangement was in no way a reflection upon his brother. On the whole, then, Charles Ashley made a favourable impression upon the public and jury for his clear and straightforward evidence. The only time when he hesitated—and did so very obviously—was when the coroner asked him whether he knew of any recent disagreement between his father and his brother Philip, a disagreement which might have led to Mr. Thornton Ashley's decision to alter his will. Charles Ashley did hesitate at this point, and, though he was hard-pressed by the coroner, he only gave ambiguous replies, and when he had completed his evidence, he left one under the impression that he might have said something if he would, and that but for his many afflictions the coroner would probably have pressed him much harder.

"This impression was confirmed by the evidence of the next witness, a Mrs. Trapp, who had been the daily 'char' at Malvine Mansions. She began by explaining to the coroner that she had done the work at the flat for the past two years. At first she used to come every morning for a couple of hours with the exception of Sundays, but for the last two months or so she came on the Sundays, but stayed away on the Mondays; on Wednesdays she stayed the whole day, until about six, as Mr. Charles always did a lot of shopping those afternoons.

"Asked whether she remembered what happened at the flat on the Wednesday preceding Mr. Thornton Ashley's death, she said that she did remember quite well Mr. Philip Ashley called; he did do that sometimes on a Wednesday, when his brother was out. He stayed about an hour and, in Mrs. Trapp's picturesque language, he and his father 'carried on awful!'

"'I couldn't 'ear what they said,' Mrs. Trapp explained, with eager volubility, 'but I could 'ear the ole gentleman screaming. I 'ad 'eard 'im storm like that at Mr. Philip once before—about a month ago. But Lor' bless you, Mr. Philip 'e didn't seem to care, and on Wednesday, when I let 'im out of the flat 'e just looked quite cheerful like. But the ole gentleman 'e was angry. I 'ad to give 'im a nip o' brandy, 'e was sort o' shaken after Mr. Philip went.'

"You see then, don't you?" the Old Man in the Corner said with a grim chuckle, "how gradually a network of sinister evidence was being woven around Philip Ashley. He himself was conscious of it, and he was conscious also of the wave of hostility that was rising up against him. He looked now, not only grave, but decidedly anxious, and he held his arms tightly crossed over his chest, as if in the act of making a physical effort to keep his nerves under control.

"He gave me the impression of a man who would hate any kind of publicity, and the curious, eager looks that were cast upon him, especially by the women, must have been positive torture to a sensitive man. However, he looked a handsome and manly figure as he stood up to answer the questions put to him by the coroner. He said that he had arrived at the flat on the Saturday at about midday, explaining to the jury that he always came once a fortnight to be with his father, whilst his brother Charles enjoyed a couple of days in the country. On this occasion, however, he was told that his father was too ill to see him. Charles, however, went off on his bicycle as usual, but contrary to precedent, a lady had apparently been left in charge of the invalid. Witness understood that this was Mrs. Triscott, the wife of a neighbour, who had kindly volunteered to stay over the week-end. She was an experienced nurse and would know what to do in case the patient required anything. For the moment he was asleep and must not be disturbed.

"'I naturally felt very vexed,' the witness continued, 'at being kept out of my father's room, and I may have spoken rather sharply at the moment, but I flatly deny that I was rude to Mrs. Triscott, or that I was in a violent rage. I did get a glimpse of my father, as he lay in bed, and I must say that I did not think that he looked any worse than he had been all along. However, I was not going to argue the point. I preferred to wait until the Monday morning when my brother would be home, and I could tackle him on the subject.'

"At this point the coroner desired to know why, in that case, when the witness was told that his brother would not be at the flat before ten o'clock, he turned up there as early as half-past eight.

"'Because,' the witness replied, 'I was naturally rather anxious to know how things were, and because I hoped to get a day on the river with a friend, and to make an early start if possible. However, when I got to the flat, Mrs. Triscott wanted to get away, and so I agreed to stay there and wait until ten o'clock, when, so Mrs. Triscott assured me, my brother would certainly be home. As a matter of fact he always used to get home at that hour with clockwork regularity on the Monday mornings after his holiday. My father was asleep, and Mrs. Triscott left me instructions what to do in case he required anything. At half-past nine he woke. I heard him stirring and I went into his room and gave him some barley-water and sat with him for a little while. He seemed quite cheerful and good-tempered, and, honestly, I did not think that he was any worse than he had been for weeks. Just before ten o'clock he dropped off to sleep again. I knew that my brother would be in within the next half hour and, as this would not be the first time that my father had been left alone in the flat, I did not think that I should be doing anything wrong by leaving him. I went back to my chambers and was busy making arrangements for the day when I had a telephone message from my brother that our father was dead.'

"Questioned by the coroner as to the disagreement which he had had with his father on the previous Wednesday, Mr. Philip Ashley indignantly repudiated the idea that there was any quarrel.

"'My father,' he said, 'had a very violent temper and a very harsh, penetrating voice. He certainly did get periodically angry with me whenever I explained to him that my marriage to Lady Peet-Jackson could not, in all decency, take place for at least another six months. He would storm and shriek for a little while,' the witness went on, 'but we invariably parted the best of friends.'"

The Old Man in the Corner paused for a little while, leaving me both interested and puzzled. I was trying to piece together what I remembered of the case with what he had just told me, and I was longing to hear his explanation of the events which followed that memorable inquest. After a little while the funny creature resumed:

"I told you," he said, "that a wave of hostility had risen in the public mind against Philip Ashley. It came from a sense of sympathy for the other son, who, deformed and afflicted, had been done out of a fortune.

True that it would not have been of much use to him, and that in the original will ample provision had been made for his modest wants, but it now seemed as if, at the eleventh hour, the old miser had thought to make reparation toward the son who had given up his whole life to him, whilst the other had led one of leisure, independence, and gaiety. What had caused old Thornton Ashley thus to change his mind was never conclusively proved; there were some rumours already current that Philip Ashley was in debt and had appealed to his father for money, a fatal thing to do with a miser. But this also was never actually proved. The only persons who could have enlightened the jury on the subject were Philip Ashley himself and his brother, Charles, but each of them, for reasons of his own, chose to remain silent.

"And now you will no doubt recall the fact which finally determined the jury to bring in their sensational verdict, in consequence of which Philip Ashley was arrested on the coroner's warrant on a charge of attempted murder. It seemed horrible, ununderstandable, unbelievable, but, nevertheless, a jury of twelve men did arrive at that momentous decision after deliberation lasting less than half an hour. What I believe weighed with them in the end was the fact that the assistant who came with the divisional surgeon to conduct the *post-mortem* found underneath the bed of the deceased, a walking-stick with a crook-handle, and the crumpled and torn copy of the notes for the new will which Mr. Triscott had prepared. Philip Ashley when confronted with the stick admitted that it was his. He had missed it on the Saturday when he was leaving the flat, as he was under the impression that he had brought one with him; however, he did not want to spend any more time looking for it, as he was obviously so very much in the way.

"Now, both the charwoman and Mrs. Triscott swore that the patient's room had been cleaned and tidied on the Sunday, and that there was no sign of a walking-stick in the room then.

5

"And so," the Old Man in the Corner went on, with a cynical shrug of his lean shoulders, "Philip Ashley went through the terrible ordeal of being hauled up before the magistrate on the charge of having attempted to murder his father, an old man with one foot in the grave. He pleaded 'Not Guilty,' and reserved his defence. The whole of the evidence was gone through all over again, of course, but nothing new had transpired. The case was universally thought to look very black against the accused, and no one was surprised when he was eventually committed for trial.

"Public feeling remained distinctly hostile to him. It was a crime so horrible and so unique you would have thought that no one would have believed that a well-known, well-educated man could possibly have been guilty of it. Probably, if the event had occurred before the war, public opinion would have repudiated the possibility, but so many horrible crimes have occurred in every country these past few years that one was just inclined to shrug one's shoulders and murmur: 'Perhaps, one never knows!' One thing remained beyond a doubt: old Mr. Thornton Ashley died of shock or fright following a violent and dastardly assault, finger-marks were discovered round his throat, and there were evidences on his face and head that he had been repeatedly struck with what might easily have been the walking-stick which was found under his bed. Add to this the weight of evidence of the new will, about to be signed, and of the quarrel between father and son on the previous Wednesday, and you have as good a motive for the murder as any prosecuting counsel might wish for. Philip Ashley would not, of course, hang for murder, but it was even betting that he would get twenty years.

"Anyway, I don't think that, as things were, any one blamed Lady Peet-Jackson for her decision. A week before Philip Ashley's trial came on she announced her engagement to Lord Francis Firmour, son of the Marquis of Ettridge, whom she subsequently married.

"But Philip Ashley was acquitted—you remember that? He was acquitted because Sir Arthur Inglewood was his counsel, and Sir Arthur is the finest criminal lawyer we possess; and, because the evidence against him was entirely circumstantial, it was demolished by his counsel with masterly skill. Whatever might be said on the subject of 'motive,' there was nothing whatever to prove that the accused knew anything of his father's intentions with regard to a new will; and there was only a charwoman's word to say that he had quarrelled with his father on that memorable Wednesday.

"On the other hand, there was Mr. Oldwall and Dr. Fanshawe-Bigg, old friends of the deceased, both swearing positively that Thornton Ashley had a peculiarly shrill and loud voice, that he would often get into passions about nothing at all, when he would scream and storm, and yet mean nothing by it. The only evidence of any tangible value was the walking-stick but even that was not enough to blast a man's life with such a monstrous suspicion.

"Philip Ashley was acquitted, but there are not many people who followed that case closely who believed him altogether innocent at the time. What Lady Peet-Jackson thought about it no one knows. It was for her sake that the unfortunate man threw up the chances of a fortune, and when it came within his grasp it still seemed destined to evade him to the end. In losing the woman for whom he had been prepared to make so many sacrifices, poor Philip lost the fortune a second time, because, as he was not married within the prescribed time-limit, it was Charles who inherited under the terms of the original will. But I think you will agree with me that any sensitive man is well out of a union with a hard and mercenary woman.

"And now there has been another revolution in the wheel of Fate. Charles Ashley died the other day in a nursing home of heart failure, following an operation. He died intestate, and his brother is his sole heir. Funny, isn't it, that Philip Ashley should get his father's fortune in the end? But Fate does have a way sometimes of dealing out compensations, after she has knocked a man about beyond his deserts. Philip Ashley is a rich man now, and there is a rumour, I am told, current in the society papers, that Lady Francis Firmour has filed a petition for divorce, and that the proceedings will be undefended. But can you imagine any man marrying such a woman after all that she made him suffer?"

Then, as the funny creature paused and appeared entirely engrossed in the fashioning of complicated knots in his beloved bit of string, I felt that it was my turn to keep the ball rolling.

"Then you, for one," I said, "are quite convinced that Philip Ashley did not know that his father intended to make a new will, and did not try to murder him?"

"Aren't you?" he retorted.

"Well," I rejoined, somewhat lamely, "some one did assault the old miser, didn't they? If it was not Philip Ashley then it must have been just an ordinary burglar, who thought that the old man had some money hidden away under his mattress."

"Can't you theorise more intelligently than that?" the tiresome creature asked in his very rude and cynical manner. I would gladly have slapped his face, only—I did want to know.

"Your own theory," I retorted, choosing to ignore his impertinence, "seek him first whom the crime benefits."

"Well, and whom did that particular crime benefit the most?"

"Philip Ashley, of course," I replied, "but you said yourself—"

"Philip Ashley did not benefit by the crime," the old scarecrow broke in, with a dry cackle. "No, no, but for the fact that a merciful Providence removed Charles Ashley so very unexpectedly out of this wicked world, Philip would still be living on a few hundreds a year, most of which he would owe to the munificence of his brother."

"That," I argued, "was only because that Peet-Jackson woman threw him over, otherwise—"

"And why did she throw him over? Because old Thornton Ashley died under mysterious circumstances, and Philip Ashley was under a cloud because of it. Any one could have foreseen that that particular woman would throw him over the very moment that suspicion fell upon him."

"But Charles—" I began.

"Exactly," he broke in, excitedly, "it was Charles who benefited by the crime. It was he who inherited the fortune."

"But, by the new will he would have inherited anyhow. Then, why in the world—"

"You surely don't believe in that new will, do you? The way in which I marshalled the facts before you ought to have paved the way for more intelligent reasoning."

"But Mr. Triscott—" I argued.

"Ah, yes," he said, "Mr. Triscott—exactly. The whole thing could only be done in partnership, I admit. But does not everything point to a partnership in what, to my mind, is one of the ugliest crimes in our records? You ought to be able to follow the workings of Charles Ashley's mind, a mind as tortuous as the body that held it. Let me put the facts once more briefly before you. While Philip obstinately remained a bachelor, all was well. Charles stuck to the old miser, carefully watching over his interests lest they become jeopardised. But presently, Lady Peet-Jackson became a widow and Philip gaily announced his engagement. From that hour Charles, of course, must have seen the fortune on which he had already counted slipping away irretrievably from his grasp. Can you not see in your mind's eye that queer, misshapen creature setting his crooked brain to devise a way out of the difficulty? Can you not see the plan taking shape gradually, forming itself slowly into a resolve—a resolve to stop his brother's marriage at all costs? But how? Philip, passionately in love with Muriel Peet-Jackson, having won her after years of waiting, was not likely to give her up. No, but *she* might give *him* up. She had done it once for the sake of ambition, she might do it again if… if… well, Charles Ashley, obscure, poor, misshapen, was not likely to find a rival who would supplant his handsome brother in any woman's affections. Certainly not! But there remained the other possibility, the possibility that Philip, poor—or, better still, disgraced—might cease to be a prize in the matrimonial market. Disgraced! But how? By publicity? By crime? Yes, by crime! Now, can you see the plan taking shape?

"Can you see Charles cudgelling his wits as to what crime could most easily be fastened on a man of Philip's personality and social position? Probably a chance word dropped by his father put the finishing touch to his scheme, a chance word on the subject of a will. And there was the whole plan ready. The unsigned will, the assault on the dying man, and quarrels there always were plenty between the peppery old miser and his somewhat impatient son. As for Triscott, the dapper little local lawyer, I suppose it took some time for Charles Ashley's crooked schemes to appear as feasible and profitable to him. Of course, without him nothing could have been done, and the whole of my theory rests upon the fact that the two men were partners in the crime.

"Where they first met, and how they became friends, I don't profess to know. If I had had anything to do with the official investigation of that crime I should first of all have examined the servant in the Triscott household, and found out whether or no Mr. Charles Ashley had ever been a visitor there. In any case, I should have found out something about Triscott's friends and Triscott's haunts. I am sure that it would then have come to light that Charles Ashley and Mr. Triscott had constant intercourse together.

"I cannot bring myself to believe in that unsigned will. There was nothing whatever that led up to it, except the supposed quarrel on the Wednesday. But, if that old miser did want to alter his will, why should he have sent for a man whom he hardly knew and whom, mind you, he would have to pay for his services, rather than for his friend, Oldwall, who would have done the work for nothing? The man was a miser, remember. His meanness, we are told, amounted to a mania; a miser never pays for something he can get for nothing. There was also another little point that struck me during the inquest as significant. If Triscott was an entire stranger to Charles Ashley, why should he have taken such a personal interest in him and in the old man to the extent of sending his wife to spend two whole days and nights in charge of an invalid who was nothing to him? Why should Mrs. Triscott have undertaken such a thankless task in the house of a miser, where she would get no comforts and hardly anything to eat? Why, I say, should the Triscotts have done all that if they had not some vital self-interest at stake?

"And I contend that that self-interest demanded that one of them should be there, in the flat, on the watch, to see that no third person was present whilst Philip spent his time by his father's bedside—a witness, such as Lady Peet-Jackson, perhaps, or some friend—whose testimony might demolish the whole edifice of lies, which had been so carefully built up. And, did you notice another point? The charwoman, by a new arrangement, was never at the flat on a Monday morning, and that arrangement had only obtained for the past two months. Now why? Charwomen stay away, I believe, on Sundays always, but, I ask you, have you ever heard of a charwoman having a holiday on a Monday?"

I was bound to admit that it was unusual, whereupon the old scare-crow went on, with excitement that grew as rapidly as did the feverish energy of his fingers manipulating his bit of string.

"And now propel your mind back to that same Monday morning, when, the coast being clear, Charles Ashley, back at the flat and alone with the old man, was able at last to put the finishing touch to his work of infamy. One pressure of the fingers, one blow with the walking-stick, and the curtain was rung down finally on the hideous drama which he had so skilfully invented. Think of it all carefully and intelligently," the Old Man in the Corner concluded, as he stuffed his beloved bit of string into the capacious pocket of his checked ulster, "and you will admit that there is not a single flaw in my argument—"

"The walking-stick," I broke in, quickly.

"Exactly," he retorted, "the walking-stick. Charles was quick enough to grasp the significance of that, and on Saturday, while his brother's back was turned, he carefully hid the walking-stick, knowing that it would be a useful piece of evidence presently. Do you, for a moment, suppose," he added, dryly, "that any man would have been such a fool as to throw his walking-stick and the crumpled notes of the will underneath his victim's bed? They could not have been left there, remember, they could not have rolled under the bed, as the walking-stick had a crook-handle; they must deliberately have been thrown there.

"No, no!" he said, in conclusion, "there is no flaw. It is all as clear as daylight to any receptive intelligence, and though human justice did err at first, and it looked, at one time, as if the innocent alone would suffer and the guilty enjoy the fruits of his crime, a higher justice interposed in the end. Charles has gone, and Philip is in possession of the fortune which his father desired him to have. I only hope that his eyes are opened at last to the true value of the beautiful Muriel's love, and that it will be some other worthier woman who will share his fortune and help him forget all that he endured in the past."

"And what about the Triscotts?" I asked.

"Ah!" he said, with a sigh, "they are the wicked who prosper, and higher justice has apparently forgotten them, as it often does forget the evil-doer, for a time. We must take it that they were well paid for their share in the crime, and, if the unfortunate Charles had lived, he probably would have been blackmailed by them and bled white. As it is, they have gone scot-free. I made a few enquiries in the neighbourhood lately and I discovered that Mr. Triscott is selling his practice and retiring from business. Presently we'll hear that he has bought himself a cottage in the country. Then, perhaps, your last doubt will vanish and you will be ready to admit that I have found the true solution of the mystery that surrounded the death of the miser of Maida Vale."

The next moment he was gone, and I just caught sight of the corner of his checked ulster disappearing through the swing doors.

Inspector Poole in

THE REAL THING

Henry Wade

Henry Wade was the pseudonym under which Henry Lancelot Aubrey-Fletcher wrote detective fiction. Wade—to use that name—spent most of his life in Buckinghamshire, where he was appointed High Sheriff in 1925; he played minor counties cricket for the county and relished rural pursuits. Yet he knew London well and the capital was the setting for several of his excellent novels, including his accomplished debut, *The Verdict of You All* (1926), and *The Duke of York's Steps* (1929), which introduced his principal detective, Inspector John Poole; the latter title refers to the steps that connect The Duke of York Column with the Mall. Wade's masterpiece, *Lonely Magdalen* (1940), opens with the discovery of the body of a woman on Hampstead Heath, and the London scenes are, as usual, described with as much authority as the methods of police work.

Poole features in seven of the stories in *Policeman's Lot* (1933), including this one. Like many of the best authors of Golden Age detective fiction, Wade often seemed more comfortable using the greater length of a novel to weave intricate puzzles, but in a thoughtful review of the collection in the *Sunday Times*, Dorothy L. Sayers said: "*Policeman's Lot* is as good a collection of detective yarns as can be looked for under present conditions—a hundred times better worth reading than many a tale that has been blown up artificially to novel length in an effort to circumvent the prejudice against short stories."

ALBERT BIDDING, TICKET-COLLECTOR, SANK WITH A SIGH OF relief on to his stool. His post was at the top of the moving-staircase which brought passengers from the North London tube to the surface at Islington Park Station. It was not a station that was much used except during the rush hours at the beginning and end of the business day, and would probably not have had a moving-staircase if it had not been on a new extension of the line. It was now past seven in the evening, and for the last two hours the ticket-collector had been continuously on his feet, "passing through" the stream of returning workers: clerks, shop-girls, artisans, and a sprinkling of the old-fashioned business men who still liked to live close to their work.

From where he sat, ten yards back from the crest, Bidding could not see down the stairway, but he could see the ten-foot strip at the top where the moving platform flattened out and disappeared under the floor. The unceasing flow of the metal stream fascinated him, with its sense of perpetual motion, and now that he was tired, he sat and watched it with a half-mesmerised stare. The rush of traffic was slowing sensibly, trains following each other at longer intervals, but at any moment, he knew, another gush of passengers would call him back on to his feet. On the down stair there was practically no traffic; few people went south from Islington Park at this hour, and fewer north.

It was nearly two minutes now since the last passenger came up, and Bidding was almost nodding into a doze when a dark object heaved itself into view at the top of the stairs, rolled over once, and lay still. It was the body of a man.

For a moment Bidding stared at it with dropped jaw and distended eyes, then sprang to his feet and hurried towards it. He was about to put his hands under the man's arms, when he started back with a gasp of horror. From the centre of the black-coated back there protruded the handle of a knife, and oozing through on to the stone floor was a dark trickle of blood.

"Gosh a'mighty, he's been stuck!" gasped the ticket-collector, then dashed back to his barrier and rang the emergency bell which connected with the stationmaster's office on the street-level just above him. In a few seconds his superior was at his side, listening to the little that Bidding could tell him of the startling event. The sound of voices at the bottom of the stairs told of another batch of passengers; with quick decision Mr. Staples jerked over the emergency switch, flung two short orders over his shoulder to Bidding and a porter who had come with him, and dashed down the now stationary staircase.

"I'm sorry, gentlemen," he exclaimed to the startled passengers; "there's been an accident—someone killed—murdered, I'm afraid. Would you kindly go down and up by the other stairway—and I'm afraid I must ask you to wait on the landing till the police have questioned you—in case anyone's seen anything."

The stream deflected, Mr. Staples summoned another porter from the platforms and posted him at the bottom of the up-staircase.

"There's been a murder on the stairs, Cork," he said; "man knifed; you seen anything odd?"

"Nothing, sir—I'm on the up line—nothing doing there."

Inquiries of other members of the staff on the platform level were equally fruitless, and realising that the situation was now beyond his sphere, the stationmaster returned to the top landing, where a police-sergeant and two constables were already dealing with the little group of curious or indignant passengers.

"Evening, stationmaster," said the sergeant, when the last had gone. "Odd job, this; Mr. Evan Holkett, Inner Temple, according to his card-case and papers. Job for the Yard, this—I've just 'phoned them. None of those passengers knew anything; couldn't have done—their train must have come in after the body reached the landing, from what Bidding tells me."

In duty bound, Sergeant Bale questioned each member of the station staff, though he knew that the C.I.D. man would do it all over again. Within a quarter of an hour Detective-Inspector Poole appeared, and after introducing himself to Sergeant Bale and the stationmaster, began his own investigation.

Bidding, the ticket-collector, told him of the body's appearance and of the approximate length of time before the arrival of the stationmaster and the next lot of passengers—one minute and three minutes respectively. Mr. Staples described his stopping of the stairway, his deflection and holding up of the passengers, his vain questioning of the platform staff.

Inspector Poole, however, was evidently of the opinion that though the platform staff had seen nothing that struck them as unusual, they must indeed hold the key to the riddle. Sergeant Bale had already reported that nobody had used the emergency stairs and that a search of the station (closed now to traffic, by arrangement with headquarters) revealed no stranger. It followed, therefore, that the murderer must have left by train. Before proceeding to a detailed examination of the platform staff, however, Poole arranged for the guards and conductors of trains which had stopped at Islington Park just before and just after the approximate time of the murder to be questioned, and their names, with any information they had to give, submitted to him.

The next thing to be done was to fix the exact time of the murder. Bidding and Mr. Staples between them agreed that the body must have reached the top of the staircase somewhere between 7.10 and 7.15 p.m., and this was further confirmed by Sergeant Bale and the platform staff by deducting the lapse of time from their own first acquaintance with the tragedy. But that in itself was no definite evidence of the time at which the blow was actually struck—the body might have been pushed on to the escalator some time after the murder. A second search of the station revealed no trace of blood on the platform level, but when the staircase was restarted a section soon appeared that was smothered in blood; the inference was that the blow had actually been struck on the stairs themselves, or at any rate within a few feet of them.

This was an important piece of information, and, fixing 7.10 as the approximate time of the murder, Poole proceeded to a detailed examination of the platform staff.

George Tukes, porter on the down line, thought he remembered seeing the dead man leave the train which had come in soon after seven; he had not noticed anything particular about him or about any other passenger; of course, there was a large number of them and he was busy hurrying them off. Questioned about the succeeding down train, he thought that there were three passengers on the platform waiting to board it, one of whom—a man wearing a raincoat and trilby hat—had come on just as the train was drawing in; he had noticed nothing more particular about him and very much doubted if he would recognise him again.

Frederick Lottup, the other porter on duty on the down line, had noticed nothing, either as to the "off" or the "on" passengers—from his appearance Poole judged that he would have noticed nothing if Mr. Holkett had emerged with the knife already in his back. Thomas Cork, on the up line, had had one old lady "off" and three middle-aged ones "on" during the last half-hour; none of the latter appeared to have committed a murder recently.

With but one crumb of information, Poole returned to the top of the stairs, where he found the divisional surgeon waiting impatiently to be released.

"Sorry, sir," said Poole. "I had to see the station staff first in case there was anything immediate to be done in catching the fellow. I've hardly looked at the body. Anything to help, sir?"

"Knife blade has penetrated the heart. Blow struck from behind and to the left by a right-handed man, I should say, and with very great force. It's an odd weapon."

Gingerly Poole took the knife and turned it round between his fingers. The handle was of rough wood into which had been forced a blade of some unpolished metal, coarse and irregular, but with an extremely sharp point.

"Home made, isn't it?" asked the detective, turning to Sergeant Bale.

The sergeant inspected it carefully.

"Must be, sir," he said. "Harder to trace, I suppose the idea was, but it's a mighty rough job at that."

"Well, that's all we can do here, I think," said Poole. "We'll have the body sent along for your P.-M., doctor; no doubt you'll let us have a report as soon as possible."

Sergeant Bale was able to give Poole some information about the dead man, though he did not know him personally. Mr. Evan Holkett was a barrister of about fifty-five who had recently come to live in Islington with a spinster sister. It was probable that he had travelled by that line long enough to have become known by sight at any rate to some of the passengers who had travelled with him. There was nothing of special significance known to the local police about him.

At 35, Lavender Hill, Poole sent in his card and was presently engaged in the painful task of breaking the news of her brother's death to Miss Griselda Holkett, a little grey-haired woman, probably five years older than her brother. After the first shock, Miss Holkett showed astonishing courage and control, but was able to throw no light upon the mystery.

"My brother was the quietest of men, inspector," she said. "I can't believe that he had an enemy in the world or that anyone had anything to gain by his death—unless you would count me—I believe he has left whatever he has saved to me."

For further information Miss Holkett could only refer Poole to her brother's clerk, Purcell, who lived, she happened to know, at an address in Battersea. Half an hour later the detective was apologising to a little dry stick of a man for interrupting his supper. Mr. Bulwer Purcell was far more visibly distressed by the tragic fate of his employer than had been the dead man's sister. It was ten minutes before Poole could get anything coherent out of him, and then nothing helpful appeared likely to emerge. Purcell had been with Mr. Holkett for fifteen years, and during that time had never known him to have a quarrel with any man. Company law was his speciality, and though no doubt he had earned dislike from unsuccessful litigants, the subject hardly seemed to be a fruitful breeding ground for murderous hate.

"*Blatchlands* v. *Kenworth Company* was his most famous case," concluded Mr. Purcell. "Blatchlands expected a walkover, and I'm told that Oliver Blatchland was furious when Mr. Holkett turned him inside out in the box, but that was twelve years ago, and Mr. Blatchland's Sir Oliver now, and it hardly seems likely. Oh, oh, wait a minute, inspector! I remember now that Mr. Holkett told me that he had once done criminal work, but had given it up because it distressed him so much. It's just possible, perhaps—"

"Have you got a record of his criminal cases?" asked Poole, who had begun to give up hope from this source.

Mr. Purcell rubbed his chin.

"I don't remember to have seen them, inspector. Of course, there's a mass of stuff in the office—old cases, many of them before my time. They might be there. It'd be a long job—"

"Do you want to find Mr. Holkett's murderer, Mr. Purcell?" asked Poole abruptly.

The clerk started.

"Of course, sir, of course."

"Then go through every case you can find first thing tomorrow, and let me know what you find. I'll ring you up at eleven for a first report."

Returning to Scotland Yard, Poole arranged for an advertisement to be put in the Press, and especially the Islington and North London local papers, calling for information from passengers who had travelled with Mr. Holkett the previous evening or from anyone who could throw any light upon the crime. This move brought quick results; Poole had only been at the Yard a few minutes on the following morning when telephone calls came through from two fellow-passengers of Holkett's who had information to give.

One of them, Mr. Raymond Lopez, an author, followed up his message with a personal call at the Yard, possibly with an eye to local colour. He knew Holkett slightly, and on the previous evening had said a few words to him in the train. On alighting at Islington Park he had been separated from him, but had noticed a man in a cloth cap, of not too reputable appearance, accost the barrister, who had stopped to speak to him. Guessing an "old soldier," Lopez had paid no particular attention to him, but thought he might possibly recognise him. He had seen no more.

Mr. Samuel Isaacs meant a call in the City, but it was good value. He also had seen the incident and could go one better than Lopez, because he had noticed that the man in the cloth cap was carrying some sort of raincoat over his arm. This went halfway to tally with Tukes' belated passenger by the next down train; he had worn a raincoat and might well, if quick disguise was wanted, have had a trilby hat in the pocket to substitute for the cap.

On his way back from the City, Poole called at Mr. Holkett's chambers in the Temple and learned that Purcell had not only found the criminal cases, but had had time to extract particulars of some of the more suggestive. Two cases stood out: In 1909 Mr. Holkett had led for the prosecution in a blackmail case at Bedford Assizes, in which the prisoner, James Bight, had been sentenced to twenty years' imprisonment. The judge in the case, Sir Henry Maberley, was dead. In the other case, at Aylesbury in 1905, Holkett had been engaged in the prosecution for murder of Simon Horley, whose sentence of death had been commuted to one of imprisonment for life. There were other cases still unexamined, but Poole, telling Purcell to continue the search, hurried off with what he had got to the record office at the Yard.

Very few minutes were required to discover that Horley had been released in 1925 and was now leading an exemplary life as a chiropodist in the Midlands, whilst Bight, having earned no remission of sentence, had served his full term and been released three weeks previously. He was not, of course, on "ticket," and therefore did not have to report to the police, but he was known to be in the Notting Hill district.

With photographs of both men, together with eight others, Poole revisited Mr. Isaacs and Mr. Lopez and received from the former partial, from the latter definite, identification of Bight as the man in the cloth cap. Tukes, the porter, was as certain as Lopez, in each case it was Bight's peculiar eyes that betrayed him, and further thought he now remembered seeing the man on one of the evening trains on some previous occasions.

"Reconnoitring," thought Poole. It was an attack that would have to be carefully planned, and this was probably only the last stage of twenty years' relentless scheming. Even the knife might have been secretly fashioned in prison, in the astonishing way that old lags had of making bricks without straw. It seemed a fantastic length to which to carry hatred of a man who, after all, had only been the instrument of the law. Still, such cases were by no means unknown.

Feeling that he was now definitely on the right track, Poole, after obtaining a warrant, went to the headquarters of the division in whose area Notting Hill lay. The superintendent in charge soon unearthed an inspector who knew all about Bight, his past career, his recent release, and his probable present whereabouts. Together the two detectives, both in plain clothes, made their way to a gloomy side street in which lay their immediate destination—"The Purple Peter."

Without knocking, Inspector Gorrel pushed open a door and the two found themselves in a small and ill-lit taproom. It was nearly three o'clock, but about a dozen men were seated on the benches round the walls, some with mugs or glasses on the trestle-tables before them, others only smoking. The murmur of voices ceased instantly as the two detectives appeared. After a quick glance round the room, Gorrel strode across to the bar, while Poole remained at the door.

"Afternoon, Hake," said Gorrel to the landlord. "Loppy Bight been here today?"

The landlord, a tall, thin man with a scraggy moustache, looked at him in mild wonder, then turned his eyes to his clients.

"Anyone seen Loppy?" he asked.

There was no reply.

"I've only been at the bar myself a few minutes, inspector," said Hake. "My potman might know; he's gone to his dinner now; you might find him at Casselli's, or if you like to come back in an hour…"

"You know well enough whether Bight's been here or not," said Inspector Gorrel curtly. "He's wanted, and I've got to know where he is. I'll deal with you in a minute."

Turning his back on the bar, Gorrel ran his eye slowly round its patrons. Taking a notebook from his pocket, he began to write in it.

"I know all you fellows," he said, "and I've got your names. I'll see each of you in turn when I've finished with Hake. Bight's wanted for murder, and if anyone knows where he is and doesn't come across, he's down for 'accessory after.' Now, Hake, your parlour."

Signing to Poole to join him, Inspector Gorrel followed Hake into the dingy little room in which, presumably, the landlord entertained his more influential clients.

"They'll not shift," said Gorrel, in reply to his colleague's unspoken question. "They know me and they know that I know them—don't they, Mr. Hake?"

The landlord did not answer, but leant against the mantelpiece and scrutinised his none too clean fingernails. Gorrel's manner changed.

"Now, Hake," he said sharply, "where's Bight?"

The landlord turned his eyes to the detective's face.

"I don't know," he said quietly.

"Oh, yes, you do! He was here this morning and he's been here every day since he came out. Come, now; I'm going to search this place, and if he's on it you'll do ten years. You'd better come across quick."

The landlord shook his head.

"You can search till you're black—it'll not take you long. I don't know where he is."

"You know where I can find him."

A slow smile revealed for the first time a row of yellow and broken teeth.

"I do not, and I doubt if you do, either, Mr. Gorrel."

"Where's he been dossing since he came out?"

"I don't know."

Gorrel struck the table angrily.

"You'd damn well better know something," he snarled.

Poole, whose detective instincts were lacerated by his new colleague's crude methods, thought it time to interpose.

"I don't think we can do any more at the moment," he said. "I suggest I search the house while you go through the others. You've got some men outside by now, haven't you?"

Hake's eyes narrowed: he turned them for the first time on to the Scotland Yard man. Gorrel chuckled.

"Yes," he said. "They were to come up as soon as we'd been settled in ten minutes. Bight'll not get away if he's here—nor will our friend Hake."

The subsequent half-hour, however, proved to be one of the most disappointing in his career. "The Purple Peter" was ransacked from well-filled cellar to filthy garret; not a sign of the wanted man could be found. Nor did Gorrel succeed in wringing one shred of information from the ten sullen innocents whose valuable time had been, they indignantly proclaimed, so wantonly wasted.

"Honour among thieves," chuckled Poole, as the two detectives at last beat their ignominious retreat.

"Honour be blowed. They're too damn frightened of a knife in their liver if they told the truth. But I'll get them. I know one or two places where Bight may be dossing. I— Hold up!"

The two detectives, in their walk back to the station, had turned into a quieter street. As they did so, a woman, approaching them, stumbled and would probably have fallen if Poole had not caught her. As he did so, he felt a piece of paper thrust into his hand. The woman, a pale, slovenly drab, quickly disengaged herself and hurried away. Poole did not so much as raise his hand, and it was not till they reached the police station that he looked at the paper. It was a half sheet of cheap, plain notepaper; on it was written, in a laboured hand:

"He's warned. A peep slipped word of a Yard nosy at the station. You won't find him here now try 7 bells."

"Disguised hand and pretending she's illiterate," said Poole, handing the note to Gorrel. "Where the blazes d'you get this?"

"From the romantic lady who embraced me on the way up. Did you think it was my blue eyes?"

Gorrel stared at him, then intelligence dawned.

"Gosh!" he exclaimed. "That was Mrs. Hake; I thought I'd seen the old pol somewhere. So they're talking, are they?"

"Does this come from Hake?"

"Couldn't say. We've had news from her before. I never could make out whether he knew. It's a good idea—he's, all for 'honour among thieves,' as you said, and she keeps right with us behind his back. No wonder we didn't find the little blighter. What's she mean by '7 bells?'"

"District in Whitechapel. I'll go there straight. You get on to those doss-houses and send word to the Yard. Don't go near Mrs. Hake unless I ask you. A nod's as good as a wink."

Poole was not sorry to get away from the abrupt and rather offensive methods of Inspector Gorrel, though he recognised their effectiveness. Indeed, he reminded himself, the case looked like being a typical example of "real" detective work—as opposed to the subtle, deductive and inductive lines upon which such things were worked in fiction. Here all that he had done was routine—questioning witnesses, looking up records, collecting facts—cold, ruthless facts. These, with the touch of treachery that he had just seen, were the ingredients by which the English police got their results. Relentless machinery and betrayal—coupled with the inevitable mistake that almost every criminal must make.

Having had an experience of the way in which police stations were watched in criminal districts—no doubt there was a "duty roster" for the job—Poole took the precaution to arrive at the Whitechapel Police Station in a West End taxi and to dash quickly up the steps with his coat collar turned up. The driver, previously instructed, turned straight round and drove rapidly away.

"Hallo, young Poole!" exclaimed Superintendent Lammidge, as the detective was shown into his office. "What a' we done wrong now? Delighted to see you, my lad; sit you down."

Poole quickly ran over the facts of the case, ending with Mrs. Hake's cryptic hint.

Lammidge slowly nodded his large head.

"And a very likely place, too," he said. "Seven Bells is 'oney-combed with lie-ups. No doubt your chap's got one that he only uses when he's on his beamers. Wait a minute, though; didn't you say he's only out a fortnight from a twenty-year stretch?"

"Three weeks."

"Then it's any odds it's an old one; those things—last ditches—aren't made in a week or two. It's probably one he had twenty years ago. That may give us a guide—we want it."

He touched a bell.

"Gatling in?" he inquired of the young constable who answered it.

"I'll see, sir."

"Been here a lifetime," whispered the superintendent. "First-class man, but never could keep quite clear of trouble. I wouldn't lose him for worlds. Knows every corner—here he is."

A sturdy constable, with grizzled hair, entered and saluted. The superintendent, introducing him to Poole, explained the problem. Gatling scratched his head.

"Bit of an 'aystack, sir," he said. "These places go on from generation to generation—'anded down like a family business. Bight, you say—don't recollect hearing of it." A pause. "Wait a mo, though. He wasn't copped down here? Then probably he never used that name down here. Any *aliases*, sir?"

Poole took some papers from his pocket.

"Several. Smith, Walker, Murphy, Buckett."

"Buckett? That's got it. Buckett. Now let me think. It was that Sassoon woman we took for harbouring 'Glint' Copeland. She swore Mother Cane had squeaked, so she blew back on her—whole long list of names she gave us of Mother's clients—Buckett was one of the names. We didn't take her up, 'cos we don't if we can help it; like to know who they are and where to find 'em, like spies in the war."

Lammidge whistled.

"Mother Cane, is it? Nice job that'll be—right in the middle of it. She'll be warned before we're within four streets. She's got a boltway, somewhere into Paradise Alley, too, though there's no back-door to her house."

"Then we'll want the flying squad," said Poole; "that'll give them no time."

Quickly Poole made his plans. By telephone he arranged for two cars from the Yard, each with five men, to rendezvous at once, in a quiet street near Liverpool Street Station, where he would meet them and give further orders. A search warrant was to be brought; he already had the warrant for Bight's arrest.

"Now, superintendent, if I might have a taxi. We'll pick you and Gatling up outside the hospital at ten-thirty, sharp."

Poole hurried out to his taxi, called "London Bridge," for the benefit of any listeners, and drove off. Ten minutes later, Superintendent Lammidge, accompanied by P.-C. Gatling, strolled out of the station, as if on a routine tour of inspection, both in uniform. Walking slowly they reached the hospital, a little before ten-thirty, and stopped to talk to the policeman on duty. Hardly had they done so, when two hooded cars glided up; without a word, Gatling slipped into the first, seating himself beside the driver, whilst Lammidge took a similar place in the second.

With a rush that spoke of many cylinders, the two cars got into their stride and, guided by the local men, dashed through narrow and ever narrower streets in their descent upon the wanted man's hiding-place. There was no question of secrecy—passers-by stopped and stared after them; it was purely a question of speed—no system of warning could outpace them. A little short of their destination the second car swung aside, Superintendent Lammidge guiding its occupants to their task of blocking the bolt-hole.

With a screech of brakes too suddenly applied, the police car stopped dead in front of a dirty little house, with blinds drawn over its two windows. Poole sprang from the car, and hammered upon the door—there was neither bell nor knocker. No sound from within. He tried the handle; the door was fast.

"Get ready the ram," he said.

Once more he hammered, accompanying it with a crisp command:

"Open this door; I'm a police officer!"

The top window was slowly raised, and the tousled grey head of an old woman appeared.

"What's all this noise?" she demanded in a shrill voice.

"Open your door. I hold a search warrant!"

The order was greeted by a stream of abuse of almost staggering obscenity. A shout of delight came from the crowd that had collected like vultures, and that was being controlled by uniformed policemen, also apparently sprung from the earth.

"Ram!" said Poole sharply.

The four plain-clothes men who had emerged from the back of the large car with him, were already grasping a thick log of wood, about four feet long, also brought from the car. On his word, they dashed it against the lock of the door. There was a loud crack—but the door did not open.

"Bolts top and bottom. Take the bottom."

As he spoke, two shots rang out from somewhere behind the house. The men hesitated.

"Go on," said Poole. "Superintendent's round there!"

A plain-clothes man from Lammidge's squad pushed his way through the crowd.

"He tried to get over the roofs, out of a skylight at the back!" he panted. "Superintendent put a couple of rounds across his bows, and he dropped back. Don't think he was hit. Still inside."

Poole called to the uniformed sergeant in charge of the local police.

"Clear the street. There may be shooting!"

As he spoke, a hand and arm slipped over the sill of the window, from which Mother Cane had spoken.

"Look out, sir!" cried the constable who had been detailed to watch it, at the same time discharging his pistol at it. As he did so, a stream of bullets squirted from the end of the arm into the cluster of men round the door. Two fell, but the remainder forced their way through the shattered door and, headed by Poole, dashed for the dingy flight of stairs just discernible at the back of the mean hall.

There was a turn halfway up; as he reached it, Poole ducked suddenly and a bullet crashed into the wall behind him. Like a flash, he fired at the figure crouching behind a mattress at the head of the stairs.

It was a lucky shot, and probably saved him his life and the life of several other brave men. As he stepped over the rude barrier, the detective saw at his feet the body of the gunman, surrounded by two Mauser pistols and two revolvers, together with a large pile of cartridges.

He removed a revolver from the limp hand, and as he did so, the man's eyelids lifted, revealing light-grey eyes of appalling malevolence. His lips moved, but the words were drowned in a rush of blood. Mr. Evan Holkett was avenged.

Police-Constable John Bragg in

THESE ARTISTS!

Henry Wade

One of the enduring strengths of Henry Wade's writing was his willing-
ness to experiment, to take chances with his storytelling rather than
producing formulaic work. His interest in describing police work with
a touch of authenticity led him, after years of writing about Inspector
Poole and other senior detectives, to take the unusual step of focus-
ing on a junior officer in action. In 1938, he published not one but two
books featuring a constable called John Bragg. *Released for Death* was
a novel which traced the misfortunes of a cat burglar called Toddy
Shaw, who is framed for a murder by a ruthless criminal associate.
Bragg becomes involved in the later part of the story and the way
Wade describes the impact of his work on his domestic life is interesting and ahead of its time.

This story came from the other book, a collection of Bragg's cases
called *Here Comes the Copper*. In *Queen's Quorum*, a selection of the best
books of short detective stories, Ellery Queen said it was "one of the
very few which trace the vocational advancement of a professional
policeman: in the first story Bragg is an inexperienced patrolman in the
British hinterland and in the final story, supposedly three years later,
he has risen from a humble copper to the exalted position of being a
member of London's CID".

POLICE-CONSTABLE JOHN BRAGG WAS AN AMBITIOUS YOUNG MAN who intended to rise to the highest rank in the Force—Superintendent at least, possibly even Chief Constable. Above that, of course, in the Metropolitan Police Force, there was still this prejudice about bringing in outsiders—soldiers and such like. Bragg knew that to achieve his dearest wish he must not only be a reliable and brave policeman, he must also be an astute detective. At present he was in the uniformed branch (B Division, Chelsea), and competition for the C.I.D. was keen, but a constable who displayed unusual powers of observation was sure to get in. Systematically Bragg set himself to develop those powers; at present they were, he realised, little more than embryonic, but by persistent practice they would develop until his superiors could not fail to notice them.

As he strolled home on completion of a tour of patrol duty on the afternoon of 8th May, 1935, he was following out his principle: Notice and Remember. This was better practice than anything he did on duty, as then he had to take copious notes in case they were wanted as evidence, and Bragg knew that there is no deadlier enemy of memory than a notebook. Off duty, however, he took no notes, he Noticed and Remembered. For instance, outside an artists' colourman's in the King's Road stood a low-lying powerful car, two bucket seats, two minute wind-screens, bonnet strapped down—one of these Brooklands aces, no doubt, though it was odd to find it outside an artists' colourman's. Arda-Rienzi, registration number AWXZ54, licensed for the quarter only... Bragg noticed these facts; for the rest of the evening he would put them out of his mind, but tomorrow morning as he shaved he would recite them, together with the other facts noticed on his way home.

Partly from curiosity he looked into the pigeon-hole in the dashboard and was surprised to see a woman's vanity bag squeezed in together with a small pair of high-heeled shoes. On the driver's side, so presumably belonging to the driver. Not a Brooklands ace after all, then—but there, women were in every game now, more's the pity, thought Bragg.

Turning down a side-street the young constable found plenty to attract and distract him; a chimney in No. 35 was smoking, No. 42 had a Carter Paterson sign in the window, the front door of 60 was being painted. Now he was in the region of big studios; the first to catch his eye was the property, he knew, of Frank Franks, the celebrated sculptor, whose groups and portrait busts fascinated the few and revolted the many, but from whichever cause were always in the public eye. At the moment controversy raged round the commissioning of Franks to do the National memorial to a great soldier. However, that was not Bragg's business; he knew the studio, with its huge north light and towering blank wall broken only by one small window. At the moment that window was clouded with condensed steam; no doubt a bathroom and the artist, contrary to popular belief, having a bath. Or perhaps it was one of those models... Bragg flushed as he thought of artists' models; how any nice girl could stand up there with nothing on in front of a man, artist or no artist... how the artist himself could... better not think about it.

And here, three doors off, was the studio of that painting woman, Delia Featherly—no better than she ought to be, people said. And there was Mrs. Featherly's door opening and a man coming out of it—slinking out of it, Bragg would say. A nasty looking customer, foreigner of sorts, well built and all that, but... another model, no doubt; male model; bah!

The man carried a parcel and his general appearance and behaviour roused the policeman's curiosity as well as resentment. He stopped and waited for the man to come through the little gate.

"You a friend of Mrs. Featherly's?" he asked.

The man showed a row of white teeth in a nervous grin, but did not answer.

"What's in the parcel, eh?"

Bragg gave it a sharp tap with his knuckle. If it was hard and hollow it might be silver or a box of something; on the contrary it was yielding. Again the man grinned and held out his parcel.

"My dancing shoes," he said. "After the sitting the lady like to dance—gramophone. I dance well."

Bragg was conscious of an unpleasant feeling of nausea. These artists! Well, it was his tea time and he was hungry, and unless he was mistaken it would be sheep's brains, a favourite dish. Without a word he turned away and made for home. Perhaps he felt rather disappointed that the incident had not provided a little professional excitement. His self-imposed training was all very well, but the ordinary course of his duty was inclined to be monotonous and even dull.

Superintendent Cleaver, head of B Division, of which Police-Constable Bragg was but a modest pawn, had no such complaint about his duty. Arduous it might be; exasperating it often was, but never dull. He did not particularly care for the locality in which his work lay; Chelsea, with its Bohemian colony, was not the *milieu* best suited for a police-officer who had begun life as a soldier, nor was Cleaver, with rigid Army discipline as a background to his official outlook, the type of man best suited to be the guardian angel of men and women whom he did not in the least understand. However, he was a conscientious officer and tried to deal fairly with facts and circumstances as they presented themselves.

On the morning of 15th May he was, so far from finding life monotonous, inclined to consider it overcrowded with incident. He had just satisfactorily concluded his investigation of a stabbing affair in which ladies had not behaved as ladies should; he was in the depth of an apparently unfathomable problem connected with the disappearance of pictures from a local show; and now Scotland Yard was demanding full and immediate details of the life and habits of that blatant but influential sculptor fellow, Frank Franks.

It appeared that the Belgian police had discovered Mr. Franks' passport, sodden with rain, at the side of a road of no great importance ten miles west of Brussels. Mr. Franks had been expected a week previously in Dinant, where he was to have executed a commission for a portrait bust of the industrial magnate, M. Jules Pollivet, but he had not put in an appearance. The circumstance of the sodden passport was worrying the Belgian police, who had communicated with Scotland Yard, who in turn had passed the job on to Superintendent Cleaver. Well, there was nothing for it but a visit to Franks' studio; an Inspector could do all that was needed equally well, or even a Sergeant, but Franks, for all his Bohemian habits, had influential friends in high places; better, thought Cleaver, to go and do the job oneself.

The great studio sounded hollow and deserted when Cleaver rattled the grotesque knocker on the heavy oak door; there was no bell. Within a minute a window in a modest house next door was thrown up and an untidy female head appeared.

"It's no use you knocking, Sergeant," cried a shrill voice. "'E's aw'y."

Slightly nettled at his loss of rank, Superintendent Cleaver ceased knocking and walked across to the window.

"When did he go? Can you tell me, ma'am?"

"Well, I'm not 'is auntie, and I don't count 'is comin's and goin's, saucy fellow as 'e is, but 'e 'ad a farewell party a week ago yesterday, that's Tuesday, as I do know, m' sister Gertie bein 'ere

and took bad and all that noise goin' on, something crool, constable, and the ladies if you can call 'em such, worse than the men...
these artists!"

"Tuesday evening last week! That would be the 7th. And did he
leave that evening or next day?"

"'Ow should I know? I'm not 'is love bird. You'd better ask the
tridesmen."

That was good advice. Enquiries among the neighbouring tradesmen elicited the fact that no milk or bread had been ordered for the
morning of Wednesday, 8th, neither had any other goods been ordered
or delivered later than the 7th. The matter was clinched by inspection
of the passport, which had now reached London, and which showed
a Belgian stamp, applied on the Flushing boat, dated 8th May. That
settled the time of Franks' leaving England, though there remained
the question, presumably unimportant, as to whether he had slept at
his studio on the night of the 7th, or elsewhere. Here no doubt the
sculptor's friends could help, and Superintendent Cleaver set about the
task of discovering and questioning them.

It was not a difficult task. Franks was a well-known character in
Chelsea; everyone knew him and many knew his friends. Superintendent
Cleaver was soon in possession of a list of those who attended the farewell party on the 7th May, and from this list it was only a matter of
time to select two or three who could give useful information.

Paula Heldwig, Franks' reigning favourite of the moment, knew
all about the sculptor's visit to Dinant; she even knew the price he was
being paid for the commission, a sum which staggered the policeman.
She had not been surprised at hearing nothing from Franks; he never
wrote a letter. But she *was* surprised to hear that he had not fulfilled his
engagement; behind an offhand manner Franks was, Cleaver gathered,
a business man. Paula explained the domestic arrangements of the
studio; Franks did not live there habitually; he had a house, complete

with servants, overlooking Regent's Park; but he did occasionally, if working late, sleep in the studio, and if that happened a woman—Mrs. Jennings, her name was—was summoned to tidy up. Unless Paula happened to sleep in the studio too, and then she generally did the tidying up herself to save paying Mrs. Jennings; Franks did not care to waste his money. The heavy cleaning work in the studio itself was done by Mrs. Jennings' husband, a professional cleaner-up of sculptors' studios, but he also only came when he was sent for.

Superintendent Cleaver interviewed both Jennings and his wife, but neither had been to Franks' studio since 4th May. They had expected to be summoned to clear up the debris of the farewell feast, of which they had heard, but had not been surprised at the omission; nothing an artist did or did not do surprised the Jenningses. Franks was usually good-tempered and pleasant, with occasional fits of rage and a permanent trait of meanness.

No, they had no key to the studio. Mr. Franks was always present himself when any tidying or cleaning was done. He had once experienced wholesale destruction of embryo masterpieces at the hands of a charwoman who suffered, he had said, from spasmodic fits of religious mania; Mrs. Jennings, however, thought the simpler explanation was that Franks had bilked her in the matter of wages.

Of Franks' male friends two, John Durward and Piers Tomblin, seemed to Cleaver most likely to prove useful; Durward because he also was a sculptor and therefore might be expected to know a good deal about Franks' professional life, Tomblin because he was by common consent Franks' greatest friend. As it happened, too, these two men shared a studio, Tomblin being a subject painter; moreover they had been the last to leave after the farewell party. Franks, they were able to say, intended to spend that night in the studio; he had his luggage there, together with the tools of his trade which he would require at Dinant, all ready packed. They had left him, in his usual good spirits, soon after midnight and were under the impression that he intended to travel by the 9.30 a.m. Harwich train from Liverpool Street the next morning.

There could be little doubt that Franks had done that. His large body and auburn beard made him a striking figure; both a ticket collector and a restaurant-car steward on the Harwich train remembered seeing a man answering the description given by the police, though neither knew who he was, nor could say for certain on which day he had travelled. However, the date stamp on the passport settled that point.

As to the fact of his departure, Superintendent Cleaver felt that the evidence was conclusive, but no amount of enquiry provided any explanation of his non-appearance at Dinant, and the curious discovery of his passport. Tomblin did so, so far as to admit that though Franks was always apparently in boisterous spirits he believed that he suffered corresponding periods of depression, when he shut himself up in his studio and, on the pretext of work, refused to see anyone. That might, Cleaver realised, lead to melancholia, and he put it up to Scotland Yard as the only apparent reason for Franks' disappearance, if disappearance there had been. For his own part Cleaver thought it just as likely that Franks had picked up a "friend" somewhere on the journey and was spending a pleasant holiday with her; he suggested that careful enquiries should be made in the neighbourhood where the passport was found, and put the matter from his mind.

Police-Constable Bragg had heard nothing of all this story while Superintendent Cleaver and his divisional detectives were carrying out their investigations. It was not till he got home and found his wife reading the evening paper that he learned what had been going on more or less under his own nose. Not unnaturally piqued that he, the budding C.I.D. star, should have remained so completely in the dark,

Bragg read the meagre story that an enterprising journalist had been able to create from scraps gathered from the tradesmen and artists who had been interrogated; there had been no police statement.

Bragg was not impressed by the story, but one small point did attract his attention: the date of Franks' departure. Something tucked away in his memory caused him to get his wife's confirmation of the fact that sheep's brains were fresh on Wednesdays. He was thoughtful and silent for the rest of the evening and on the following morning repaired to the police station a quarter of an hour earlier than was necessary. Seeking out one of the detective-constables, Bragg learnt from him sufficient further details to justify him in applying for "a word with the Super."

Cleaver was busy with his picture case and not at all anxious to discuss one that he had put out of his mind, but experience had taught him that in police work it was never safe to refuse to listen to a story. He pushed aside a report he had been reading and told Bragg to go ahead and make it snappy.

"I understand it was last Wednesday, the 8th, sir, that Mr. Franks left for the Continent. That would be the morning train?"

"Yes, 9.30 Liverpool Street. As a matter of fact we got word late last night of a milk-roundsman who saw him leave the studio soon after seven; earlier than one would expect, but he travelled by the 9.30 all right; we know that."

"Locked up his studio, sir, didn't he? No one went in after he left?"

"No; so far as we can find, no one did."

"Someone was having a bath there, sir, at 5.45 p.m. that afternoon." Superintendent Cleaver stared.

"How the hell do you know that?" he asked.

"I was passing, sir, and I saw steam condensing on that little window in the north wall. I took it to be a bathroom."

"You're sure it was steam, not dirt?"

"Sure, sir; I saw the moisture trickling down. I thought it was Mr. Franks having an afternoon tub or"—the blush reappeared—"maybe one of those models."

That re-opened the whole question. It could not have been Franks who was having a bath in Chelsea at a time when his boat had just landed him at Flushing, but in view of the Yard's enquiries it was essential to find out just who had been in the studio at a time when all the evidence pointed to its having been empty and locked. Cleaver and his detectives spent the day re-covering the whole ground; the Jenningses, the friends, the tradesmen, the servants at the Regent's Park house—all were questioned again but no one admitted having been in Franks' studio at any time on Wednesday. Superintendent Cleaver himself paid a visit to Scotland Yard, and learning from Chief Constable Thurston that the Belgian police were still without news of Franks and that the Commissioner himself was interested, decided that the time had come to enter the studio.

It would not be an easy matter, without attracting undesirable attention. The door was of solid oak, nobody knew of a duplicate key… Cleaver decided that the small hours of the morning were indicated. As a reward for his contribution, Police-Constable Bragg was allowed to deprive himself of half his night's sleep and join the party which assembled outside the studio at 4.30 a.m. on a cold and misty morning.

"That's the window, sir," he said rather unnecessarily, pointing to the only aperture in the great north wall; it was ten feet up and about two by three in size.

"It's open," said Cleaver, conscious that he had not at his former visit noticed the window at all.

"It wasn't open when I saw it, sir."

Superintendent Cleaver was not pleased with himself.

"Well, that's the way you've got to get in," he said crossly, "and see if you can open the door from the inside"

Helped by a "back" from Detective-Sergeant Ainsworth, Bragg was soon inside and, finding that the lock was of the "slam" type, had no difficulty in admitting his colleagues. His first sight of the great studio had given him a nasty turn; in the centre, towering almost to the thirty-foot ceiling, stood the gigantic figure of a horse, white and somehow frightening in its immobility. On its back, as Bragg now had leisure to observe, sat the rough beginnings of the figure of a man, minus a head and one arm which were represented by mere rods of metal. Even to Bragg's untutored eye, the man's body appeared small and insignificant in comparison with the horse which, whatever horrors of inaccuracy might duly be attributed to it by equine anatomists, did seem to be a fierce and noble animal. By contrast the man, even without his head, appeared puny and *strutting*; Bragg knew just enough about the artist's reputation to realise that this representation of a national hero was probably his idea of a joke.

Superintendent Cleaver and Sergeant Ainsworth made a careful examination of the studio, its screened "bedroom" and the tiny bath-room, without discovering anything of significance. Cleaver studied the sculptured model for a minute of disgusted silence and then turned to a modelling stand on which was some object covered with a cloth. As he removed this Cleaver made a grimace; Bragg imagined this to be caused by the artistic imperfections of the head which was now revealed.

"That'll be the Field-Marshal, sir, no doubt," said Sergeant Ainsworth, pleased with his own perspicacity.

The work, though still in the rough, did show an unmistakable resemblance to the great commander whom his country was delighting to honour. It was not, thought Bragg, nearly so bloody awful as most of the Franks masterpieces which he had seen.

Superintendent Cleaver did not, however, appear to be greatly inter-ested in the question of likeness. He was holding the cloth which had covered the model gingerly to his nose; he now handed it to Sergeant Ainsworth, who obediently did likewise.

"Stinks, sir."

"What of?"

"Dead Hun."

Ainsworth's whole outlook on life reflected the year of horror carved from his impressionable youth.

Bragg started at the words and found his Superintendent staring at him. By common consent all three men drew farther away from the modelling stand. Cleaver was the first to speak.

"Fetch me that brandy out of the cupboard."

He lit a pipe and, having swallowed a stiff peg of brandy, approached the model. Seizing the head in both hands, with a sudden heave he wrenched it from the iron pin on which it was moulded. Instantly a strong stench of putrefaction filled the room. Cleaver put his nose to the pin, then laid the model hurriedly down and made for the bathroom.

The cloth which had covered the head was quite dry, so that the clay (or was it putty? Bragg was uncertain) had become too hard to yield to the fingers, but with the help of a chisel and mallet ten minutes' careful work disclosed what all three men had expected to find—the skull of a human head with scraps of flesh adhering to it.

Another hour revealed the rest of the body, or rather skeleton draped with scraps of flesh, under the clay coating of the roughly sculptured figure which had straddled the horse.

"Where's the right arm?" asked Cleaver.

Search failed to discover it.

"That's why he bolted, then," said the Superintendent. "Killed some poor devil and covered his body with clay—then lost his nerve."

"Man with one arm, sir," suggested Sergeant Ainsworth brightly. "What about the flesh, sir?"

"Burnt it; have a look in the furnace."

A faint smell of burnt flesh seemed to confirm Cleaver's theory. Bragg had remained thoughtful.

"I beg your pardon, sir," he said at last, "but I don't think Mr. Franks did that head."

"Eh?"

"I... I've noticed some of his work, sir, and this isn't like it—too... representational, I think they call it. I think that head is *Franks*."

"My God! But he was seen to leave; seen on the train!"

"Someone like him, sir."

"Then who did this modelling?... the other sculptor—Durward!"

An hour later the party proceeded to the studio shared by Franks' two cronies—the sculptor Durward and the painter, Tomblin. The door was opened by a large, clean-shaven man to whose chin Cleaver at once attached in fancy an auburn beard, and found it satisfactory.

"Good morning, Mr. Tomblin," he said, "sorry to trouble you again. Any news of your friend?"

"Durward? He's out—marketing."

"Early, eh?"

"That's the time to market. You're a bit early yourself, aren't you?"

"Not many people about in this neighbourhood at seven, are there, Mr. Tomblin?"

The artist stared.

"Why do you ask me?"

Superintendent Cleaver strolled across to an easel on which stood an unfinished picture of some Low Country peasants.

"I just thought you might know," he said, peering at the picture as if the brushwork interested him. "You travel abroad yourself, I fancy?"

"Obviously." The big man's tone was hostile, but Bragg thought there was a note of nervousness in it. "You don't think I paint those people from imagination?"

"Can I have a look at your passport, sir?"

Tomblin, who was in the act of lighting a pipe, stood with the match in his fingers till he dropped it with a curse. He seemed uncertain what to do, then walked to a bureau and extracted the passport from a drawer. Superintendent Cleaver idly turned over the pages.

"You've been abroad lately, I see—Belgium."

"Yes, only a flying visit—literally. I had business in Brussels."

"So I see. Here's the date stamp for your return journey—9th May. Curious that there's no stamp for the outward journey, Mr. Tomblin; how do you account for that?"

The big man was white now and his hand trembled as he held it out for the passport, but he forced a careless note into his voice.

"They forgot, I suppose. Done with it?"

Cleaver took no notice of the outstretched hand but slipped the passport quietly into his pocket.

"There will be several questions I shall have to ask you, sir," he said. "I think it will be best if you accompany me to the station."

"It didn't take long to break down *that* story, of course," explained Superintendent Cleaver to the Treasury Solicitor. "And when he heard that his pal had saved the hangman trouble he lost his nerve and confessed. Must have spotted us taking Tomblin away, that Durward, and knew the game was up. Not much in the confession that we hadn't guessed at, sir, but it might have taken some proving. A nice couple of friends, I must say. They stayed on after the rest of the party had gone, knocked Franks on the head and then started to cut him up. Durward, as a sculptor, had studied anatomy, so that wasn't too difficult. The thought they could drain the blood out of the body—there was a lot of talk about that in the Ruxton case—and then burn the flesh in the furnace, but a dead body doesn't bleed much and they were stung over that. Anyway, when they tried to burn it the stink was so bad they were afraid the whole neighbourhood would smell it. So they wrapped the bits up in little parcels and put 'em in Franks' suitcase and Tomblin dropped them out of the porthole of his cabin, one by one."

"Risky job, in daylight."

"They were up against it, sir, and had to take risks. Of course Tomblin was the chap who was seen by the milkman on Wednesday morning. He'd bought a beard, and in Franks' cape and hat he passed muster with anyone who didn't know him well, but that was why he left so early—before other artists were about; there aren't many go marketing before seven. Tomblin went as far as Brussels, dumped the suitcase and cape and hat and beard, and took a plane back. But they had to *prove* that Franks had really crossed on the 8th, so Tomblin dropped Franks' passport out of the plane, trusting to its being found—date stamp and all. The snag was that he hadn't been able to get his own passport stamped on the outward journey; that wouldn't have mattered if we hadn't got curious."

"Surely his absence from home was bound to attract attention?"

"In a normal home, yes, sir. But these artists don't have what you and I would call a home. These two chaps lived together in their studio, did their own catering, an occasional woman in to tidy up, nobody to notice their comings and goings, nobody to ask questions. They were *both* away all Tuesday night, all Wednesday, and most of Wednesday night, when Durward got back, but did anyone notice that? Not a soul."

"Durward stayed in the studio to deal with the bones, eh?"

"That's it, sir, and a hell of a time he must have had fitting 'em round the metal framework and then getting the clay on top and making a decent model all in a day's work. Fortunately for him it was a more than life-size figure or it couldn't have been done. As it was, the head and the right arm beat him. He couldn't get the head to stay firmly on the torso and he didn't dare risk its falling off, so he left it on the stand. The arm was supposed to be up in the air, but that wouldn't stay either."

"Why didn't he change the position, then?"

"Because it had to conform with the small model passed by the Memorial committee. He had to wrap the arm up and take it away with him, tucked inside his coat—nice, it must have felt. Dumped it in the river with a bit of ironwork attached. Crept out in the small hours of Wednesday night, he did."

"Motive?" asked the solicitor.

"Ah, there I think Tomblin's lying. He swears it was Durward who killed Franks in a drunken quarrel about the memorial and that he had to help his pal out of the hole. What about the beard? Had had it a long time—went to a Chelsea Arts Club Ball in it—that happens to be true. But it's my belief that Tomblin was jealous about the woman Paula, just as Durward was jealous about the commission. I'm making enquiries."

"I beg your pardon, sir," interposed Police-Constable Bragg, who was present at the interview in order to give his evidence. "Did you gather why Durward left that window open?"

"Ah, yes, I'd forgotten that window. They used the bath to try and drain the blood away—opened arteries and that sort of thing; got enough out to make a foul mess of the bath, and that's what Durward was doing when you saw the steam—trying to wash away the stains. But he told Tomblin that the smell of blood was so strong even after the marks had gone that he had to open the window in the hopes of its clearing away. Bit of luck your happening to notice that steam, Bragg."

"Luck be damned!" said Police-Constable Bragg. But he said it to himself.

Dr. David Wintringham in

THE CASE OF THE FAULTY DRIER

Josephine Bell

Josephine Bell was, like so many of the names on the contents list of this anthology, a pen-name. Doris Bell Collier (1897–1987) was the author of over sixty novels, most of them mysteries. She was born in Manchester and educated at the Godolphin School in Salisbury (overlapping there with Dorothy L. Sayers) before studying at Newnham College, Cambridge and training in medicine at University College Hospital in London. She married a doctor and for almost a decade the pair of them practised medicine in Greenwich and London. Her knowledge of the area around the River Thames gave particular strength to *The Port of London Murders* (1938), which has been published in the Crime Classics series.

Her first crime novel was rejected, but she and her husband then "realised that we had a very open field for puzzling medical facts relating to death, injury and accident and that our profession offered us a wide range of possible ingenious murders." The result was *Murder in Hospital* (1937), published as by Josephine Bell, because she was professionally debarred from self-promotion; Bell was her second name and her grandmother's maiden name, while Joseph was her father's first name. At first they wrote in alternate chapters before deciding that she should do the writing while he focused on plot development. This book introduced Dr. David Wintringham, who became a series character and features in this story, first published in the *Evening Standard* on 19 December 1949.

"GOOD HEAVENS!" SAID JILL WINTRINGHAM, WITH SURPRISE and feeling in her voice. "What a bit of luck it wasn't me!"

She handed her evening newspaper to her husband, pointing to a paragraph on the front page. David read it aloud.

"'Well-known actress dies in West End beauty parlour... Phoebe Carlton slumped in her chair... The electric lead in the drier had parted causing a short-circuit through the body of the victim.' How could it be you, darling? You aren't a well-known actress."

"Don't be silly, David. Don't you see where it happened?"

He looked again, then lifted his eyes to Jill's head.

"Fingold's, in Knightsbridge. Where you have your own hair done. It looks particularly good too, this evening."

"It was done this afternoon, as you might have noticed before. It was done between twelve-thirty and two, because that was the only time they could fit me in at short notice. If you look at the paper again you will see that the drier packed up about two o'clock."

"So it did."

"It might have been me."

David took this calmly.

"Do they have only one drier?"

She snatched the paper back from him.

"If that's all you care—"

"Half a minute. Let me have it back. Look, it says she was discovered shortly after two. You must have left, or you would have heard the commotion."

"Yes. I went down in the lift at two exactly."

"How do you know that?"

"Because the customers' lift had a notice, 'Not Working', and I looked at the clock above the lifts, and it said two, and at that moment the staff lift came up, so I went down in that."

"I see." David looked at his own watch. "As one who has come back to me from the edge of the grave, will you allow me to take you out to the cinema tonight after dinner?"

"Darling! What shall we see?"

"The Curzon has that rather good new French thing."

"Perfect."

The next evening David came in rather later than usual. Jill met him in the hall.

"I suppose you've seen the latest developments?" she asked.

"In the drier case? Yes, and rather more than that. I've been talking to Steve Mitchell about it."

"Why?"

They had moved into the sitting-room while they were speaking. David lit a pipe with some deliberation before answering.

"Because you were in the building, or had only just left it, at the time it happened. The papers have not got the whole facts of the case yet. Only that there has been a suggestion of foul play, and Scotland Yard has been asked to investigate."

"What did happen exactly?"

"Miss Phoebe Carlton—that was her stage name—the real one was Doreen Brooks. Anyway, the poor girl was discovered by one of the junior assistants, as it was reported last night. But what it omitted to say was that this girl was taking a drier into the cubicle where Miss Carlton was, in order to put it over her hair. In other words, the senior assistant who had set the hair, a man called Henry, had only just finished his job, and gone on to his next client, leaving his junior to fix the drier, fetch the magazines, and clear up after him, generally. Would that be normal?"

"Perfectly normal," Jill answered.

"This girl assistant says she noticed the other drier the moment she entered the cubicle, and was pulling her own machine away again, when she saw Miss Carlton's face."

"How—?" began Jill.

"In the mirror."

"Oh, of course."

"Yes. Of course, to anyone engaged in hairdressing, because I expect they look at the customer more in the mirror than any other way, since they are standing behind them most of the time."

"Yes," said Jill. "I always talk to Henry—"

She stopped dead. They both looked at one another.

"I know," said David. "This Henry went straight to you from Miss Carlton. Your machine had been taken away outside your cubicle by the same girl. She went to fetch a dry towel for Miss Carlton. Your hair was then dry, finished. Henry combed it out or whatever they do; you did your face, put on your hat, and left, paying your bill at the cashier's desk at the end of the hairdressing section of the store. Henry went on to his third client to start her shampoo. He had barely begun when the girl assistant called to him."

"Miss Carlton was not killed by my drier then?" said Jill, who had gone rather white.

"No. It was one that was not used much on account of its weight. It was an older type. Quite efficient, but they only used it if there is a rush on the others. That was the next thing the girl noticed. She says she saw Miss Carlton's face looking awful, swollen and discoloured, with eyes staring and fixed, then she noticed the drier, and thought, 'Something's the matter with that thing. I always hated it.'"

"She thought in those words?"

"So she says."

"Then what?"

"She called to Henry and he went at once, really to curse her for calling out like that, instead of going to him. However, he saw at once something terrible had happened, and sent the girl to tell the management and get a doctor. He then saw that the drier was much lower than it ought to be."

"Lower down over Miss Carlton's head?"

"No. Lower than it would be for anyone sitting normally upright. Otherwise she would have slipped from under it. She was slumped down in the chair, but the drier was still over her head, and the head was lying back against its rim."

"It must have been fixed in that position?"

"Exactly. When Henry reached this conclusion, he began to be suspicious. Up to then he, and the assistant before him, had been thinking in terms of heart attacks or strokes or something of that sort. I am taking a long time to describe it, but all this had occurred in the space of a very few minutes. Henry's thinking took seconds only. The drier was still on: he switched it off. It was lucky he did so or he might have been electrocuted as well as poor Miss Carlton. He next tried to discover if she was still alive, but without moving her, beyond supporting her feet and slipping an extra towel under her neck. A doctor arrived just as he finished that, and found that Miss Carlton was certainly dead. The two men together noted the position of the drier and then moved the body away from it, leaving the machine where it was. When Henry examined the drier he found one of the leads had been cut. At that stage they sent for the police. It was murder, all right."

There was a short silence, then David went on.

"I suppose you did not see any unfamiliar faces while you were at Fingold's. No, I don't mean in the shop. Of course there'd be hundreds, milling around every department. I mean among the assistants in the hairdressing part."

"No. I can't remember any. Why, is there a new one?"

"No. That's just it. No one knows who moved the drier into Miss Carlton's cubicle. Nobody, in the department or outside it, saw an unfamiliar face that afternoon."

"But it must have been a hairdresser, mustn't it? To know about the inside of a drier?"

"Yes. An electrician might understand them. But wouldn't be likely to know how to arrange one over a customer's head. I think the murderer did not intend the crime to be discovered so soon. He or she probably imagined anyone looking into the cubicle would see the back of a customer in a drier and go out again. They forgot the face would show in the mirror."

"That's odd. If the murderer was a hairdresser."

"Very. But on the other hand he or she must have known the time of Miss Carlton's appointment, which of the assistants it was with, and which cubicle she would occupy."

"It ought to be someone who works at the shop or frequents it."

"Exactly. That would account for him or her not being noticed. Even if they were wearing an unusual dress."

"What do you mean?"

"No one would dare tamper with a drier, push it into a cubicle and arrange it over a customer's head, dressed in their own ordinary clothes. The customer for one would notice at once. But in the white coat of the hairdressing department, which is worn by both men and girl assistants, she would not be noticed by busy people, if she kept her head away."

"How could anyone have got hold of an assistant's white coat?"

"Actually one of the men was away that day. His coat was hanging up in the general cloakroom for the staff of the hairdressing floor. It could have been used and replaced. At that time, the normal lunch hour, business was slack. Most of the assistants were in the staff rest room, waiting for their afternoon appointments to start."

"Well then, it could have been done that way by someone outside the department. But who had any possible motive for killing this poor creature?"

"That's the snag. No one. She was not very well-liked in her profession. Rather selfish, her fellow workers at the theatre said, and a bit stand-offish. But nothing extreme. They said she wasn't exciting enough to be hated."

"Poor Miss Carlton!"

"Yes. I think so. Because it appears she was short-sighted, but couldn't wear spectacles in her profession. Probably she didn't always recognise people until they were quite close."

"What about her private life?"

"She had one faithful boy-friend, who has been sharing her flat for four years. No quarrels. No rivals. A very respectable couple, only for some peculiar reason they had never got as far as the registry office. Steve hasn't found a single individual or a single circumstance to provide even the flimsiest of motives."

"Then it must be someone in the shop. Or in her past," added Jill. David looked up quickly.

"In her past. Yes, that's what I said to Steve just before I came away from the Yard. Now, darling, I have just remembered that you said you went down from the hairdressing department in a staff lift. Can you think back and tell me who were in it with you?"

Jill thought for a time.

"Any other customers?" David asked, to encourage her.

"No. Wait a minute. There was the lift man, of course."

"What like?"

"Elderly, ex-service, grey hair, nice old face, straight shoulders, called me 'miss'."

"Good for him. Who else?"

"A cleaner. Down-trodden type in a green overall. Kept in the back corner of the lift. I noticed her because she seemed to belong to the old tradition, not the new, and she smelt of onions."

"Which you resented?"

"Oh, dear me, no. Which I welcomed, because the onions covered up the ghastly scent of the young woman in black. A counter assistant; I think she is on cosmetics. Absolute mask of a face, and eyes as hard as agate; I think that is the usual cliché."

"Nails would do, if they were grey eyes."

"They weren't. Black as sloes, if you can imagine stony sloes."

"Try jet."

"All right. Shall we leave her now? We seem to be going round in circles. The only other member of the lift party was a young man in dark blue dungarees. Engineer type."

"Young mechanic. Hard-faced assistant in cosmetics, which are next door to the hairdressing, aren't they? Cleaner—what age?"

"Oh, quite youngish. Wan-looking, as I said, and depressed."

"Or frightened?"

Jill stared at her husband.

"David! Was it one of those people?"

"Could have been; they were there at the time. So were a lot of other people."

He got up to go.

"I must see Steve again."

"Why?"

"Miss Carlton's past. If it fits in where I think it will, the case is closed."

"But—you don't know who did it?"

"I think I do. But I'll need Steve to prove it."

"Tell me, darling."

"You've got all you need to come to the same conclusion as I have."

"Pig!"

"See you later."

At midnight Jill went to bed, tired of sitting up and of turning the same thoughts over and over in her mind. An hour later David stumbled against her bed and woke her.

"Terribly sorry, darling. I was trying to manage in the dark."

"Did you solve the case?" she asked sleepily.

"Yup. It worked out the way I thought. As a matter of fact, Steve had just got there himself, by a different route."

"How?"

"Digging up the past, as I said we'd have to do. I'll tell you a little story. Once upon a time there were two apprentice hairdressers. They worked together at the same shop and they were friends. They were both rather lazy, and did not try very hard to learn their trade. One of them was Miss Carlton. She had beautiful natural blonde hair, so she was chosen to have it dressed by her boss at a hairdresser's competition for new styles. She was noticed at this competition by a theatrical chap, and soon made her way out of hairdressing into musical comedy choruses. The other apprentice was madly jealous, and broke off their friendship. Eventually this one was found tampering with the till, was dismissed, and went from job to job before finishing up at Fingold's. Miss Carlton came to the shop regularly for her hair-do's and manicure. She was recognised by her former friend, and the old hatred revived, inflamed by the contrast in their present circumstances. I think Miss Carlton's near sight prevented her making the same discovery. So the spite grew, and eventually the murder was planned, and executed, and might have been successful if you had not had your hair washed at short notice between twelve-thirty and two."

"Oh no, David! Then it *was* one of those people in the lift. Which one?"

"It was not."

"Then who?"

"It was the lift girl from the passenger lift. You said yourself it had a 'Not Working' notice on it. She put that on; there was nothing the matter with it. She went to the hairdressers' cloakroom, which she had often done before, since it was the only staff cloakroom on that floor. She nipped into the vacant coat, doctored the drier, killed her victim—who did not see her clearly and had never recognised her as the lift girl who had so often taken her up and down. She slipped back with the coat, and returned to the lift. She made one mistake, perhaps two. She forgot the dead face would be seen in the mirror and the body discovered almost at once. And she overreached herself by putting up that notice. You saw it and took the other lift and remembered the whole incident. If she had just left her lift for a few minutes to go to the cloakroom you would have waited—more or less patiently—and it would have made no impression."

"Someone else might have made a fuss and asked for her."

"Precisely. She knew that. Hence the notice. She had to have time, with no interruptions. She will find it very difficult to explain why—to the jury."

Chief Inspector Moresby in

UNSOUND MIND

Anthony Berkeley

Anthony Berkeley was one of the writing names under which the enigmatic but brilliant Anthony Berkeley Cox (1893–1971) hid his identity from the reading public. Berkeley was born in Watford, the son of a doctor and teacher who owned adjoining properties on Watford High Street. His first two detective novels, both of which featured Roger Sheringham, were published anonymously at first, but subsequently appeared under the Berkeley name. His most famous whodunit, *The Poisoned Chocolates Case* (1929) is set in London, and has been published as a British Library Crime Classic, as have *Murder in the Basement* (1932) and *Jumping Jenny* (1933).

In 1928, Berkeley began to host dinners of leading crime writers at his home in Watford; the success of this venture prompted him to found the Detection Club, which was often known in its early days as the London Detection Club, so high was the proportion of major detective novelists based in the capital. His crime writing was eclectic in both setting and storyline, but *The Piccadilly Murder* (1929) and *Death in the House* (1939)—the title refers to the House of Commons—were both set in London. This story first appeared in *Time and Tide* on 14 and 21 October 1933, and is unusual for featuring Roger Sheringham's regular foil, Chief Inspector Moresby, but not Sheringham himself.

PART I

THE TELEPHONE-BELL AT CHIEF INSPECTOR MORESBY'S ELBOW tinkled. "Hullo, sir? There's a man on the line says he wants to speak to one of the chief officers. Will you take the call, sir?"

"Switch him through," said Moresby.

"Who is that, please?" asked a different and fainter voice.

"Chief Inspector Moresby speaking."

"Chief Inspector, eh? Well, that should do. Listen, Chief Inspector. I'm ringing up to save you bother. I just want to let you know that I'm committing suicide in a minute or two. Prussic acid. The name is Carruthers. I've left a note, of course; this is just to confirm it. Goodbye." The line went dead.

Moresby joggled the receiver-rest. "Trace that call! It's urgent."

The information came through in under two minutes. "Hampstead 15066: Dr. James Carruthers, 42 Hill Walk, Hampstead."

Within a few seconds, Moresby was speaking to the Detective Inspector of the Hampstead Division. "Go round at once to 42 Hill Walk, Dr. James Carruthers. Don't waste a second. He's threatening suicide. Leave word for one of your men to ring up your surgeon, to follow you. I'll meet you there, and bring a doctor too, in case. Hurry, man."

He had been pressing a buzzer on his desk as he spoke.

Three minutes later he was entering a police car in the yard. With him were a doctor, carrying a bag that contained among other things antidotes for prussic acid poisoning, a detective sergeant, and a fingerprint expert. To look at Chief Inspector Moresby, with his burly, bulky frame and his walrus moustache, you would have thought him a deliberate man, slow off the mark. But when the mark is so often that of sudden or threatened death, it is necessary to be able to move off it swiftly. Moresby was no exception to the rule of Scotland Yard.

A constable met them at the door of the house. An open and broken window in the room next to it told a graphic story of unceremonious entrance.

"Inspector Willis inside?" panted Moresby, running up the steps.

"Yes, sir. With the doctor. Carruthers. Our Dr. Peters hasn't got here yet."

Moresby did not waste time asking if Carruthers was still alive. He hurried into the house. "Willis!"

A voice answered from down a passage. Moresby followed the sound, the other two on his heels, and found himself in a surgery. On the floor a man was lying, bent horribly like a bow, his body supported on head and heels. A scream came from the distorted mouth.

"Prussic acid!" muttered the Scotland Yard doctor. "That isn't prussic acid. It's strychnine. Where does he keep his chloroform? Oh, here." He snatched up a jar that was standing open on the surgery counter and sniffed at it.

Moresby drew the divisional detective inspector into the passage. Neither of them could do anything now; the case was in the doctor's hands.

"I got here within nine minutes after you telephoned, sir," murmured Willis.

"I wonder why the deuce he said prussic acid," murmured Moresby.

The body on the floor had relaxed from its dreadful arch and subsided limply. The two detectives watched from the passage as the doctor bent over it.

He rose to his feet, dusting the knees of his trousers. "He's gone," he said briefly. "That was the last convulsion."

Moresby clicked. It could not by any stretch of responsibility be called his fault, and yet he felt as if he had let the man's life slip through his fingers.

"Very rapid," the doctor was muttering. "How long is it since he was speaking to you on the telephone?"

Moresby glanced at his watch. "Twenty-six minutes."

"I'd been here about twelve minutes before you came," confirmed Willis, with a nod.

"H'm!" The doctor rubbed his chin. "Did he speak to you, inspector?"

"Yes," said Willis. "He was pretty bad, but he spoke once between the convulsions. He said: 'Changed my mind. Took strychnine'."

"Ah! He said that."

"Yes; and that's all. I tried to get out of him what the right antidote was, but he wouldn't say. The convulsions were coming on pretty quickly." Willis shuddered. "It's an awful way to die."

"Horrible," muttered Moresby. "Wonder why he changed his mind. Poor devil! I'll bet he was sorry he did. There's no one else in the house?"

"No. We had to break a window to get in. Taking a chance, if it was a spoof call; but we risked it. Lucky we did, too."

Moresby was staring down at the body. "No doubt at all about the cause of death, doctor, I suppose?"

"Good heavens, no; there's no mistaking strychnine poisoning. Except for tetanus, of course; and there's no sign of—hullo, though, what's this?" He picked up one of the dead man's hands. On the ball of the thumb was a piece of sticking-plaster. The doctor peeled it off, and revealed a nasty little wound. "Five or six days old, by the look of it, too."

"Could that have given him tetanus?"

"Certainly it could."

A new voice spoke from the doorway. "Dead, is he? Poor chap, poor chap. Tetanus did set in, then?" It was the divisional surgeon, who had just arrived.

"Why do you say that, doctor?" Moresby asked quickly, before the other surgeon could speak.

The doctor looked slightly surprised. "He's been afraid of it for some days, from that wound on his thumb. He didn't get it cleaned up quickly enough, and thought he might have got something in it."

"You knew Dr. Carruthers, then?"

"Very well indeed. Poor fellow. I should have liked to be with him at the end. It must have been remarkably quick, for tetanus?"

"Yes, far too quick," put in the headquarters surgeon. "Anyhow, we know it wasn't tetanus. It was strychnine." The newcomer was put in possession of the facts.

While the doctors talked, Moresby and the divisional man moved into the consulting-room which adjoined the surgery.

"He'd sent everyone out of the house, you see," remarked the latter.

Moresby nodded absently. "Yes. He's married, I suppose? Your doctor had better take on the job of breaking it to her. What sort of a woman is she?"

"I don't know her, only by sight. Fine-looking lady. It'll be a shock to her. They'd got a reputation round this for being pretty well wrapped up in each other. What he wanted to do it for beats me. He'd got a good practice, and a fine wife. If you'd asked me, I should have named him yesterday as the happiest man in Hampstead."

Moresby shrugged his shoulders. "Why do they do it? But we can't say for certain he did yet, not till after the p.m.; though the doctor didn't seem to have much doubt. Funny that, thought about the tetanus. But he said strychnine to you himself; that's conclusive enough. I supposed this is the note."

Propped against the inkstand on the consulting-room table was an envelope, addressed: "To the coroner."

"It's not sealed," said Moresby, and drew out the sheet of paper inside.

> To the Coroner,
>
> Dear sir: For reasons which concern no one but myself, I am taking my life.
>
> JAMES CARRUTHERS.

"Well, that's to the point, anyhow. I'm not needed here any longer, Willis. You'd better have a look round and see if you can find any of those reasons that concern no one but himself. The coroner will want them, of course. Mrs. Carruthers may be able to help you. I'll be getting along."

"Seems he had another shot at that letter, sir," said Willis from the fireplace. "Look at this."

Lying in the empty hearth was a sheet of charred paper. The ink had turned white in the heat, and by a close scrutiny the words could be made out with fair ease.

> I am sick and tired of this uncertainty, and I can't stand it any longer. What I propose to do may be drastic, but it is better than this wretched existence.
>
> J.C.

"Humph! Toned it down a bit in the second draft. Wait a minute, though! That wasn't meant for the coroner. See the envelope, sir? 'Leila'. That's his wife. Wonder why he burnt it."

"And why did he write on a single sheet of notepaper to her, and a double one to the coroner?" said Moresby. "He seems to have changed his mind a good many times, what with the prussic acid and so on. I don't think I will go just yet after all. I'd like to see the case just tidied up first. We haven't seen the vessel that he took the stuff in yet, have we? I'll put Afford on to that, while you go through his papers."

He went out to the hall, where the sergeant he had brought with him was still waiting, and, having given his instructions, passed on to the surgery.

"Well, there's nothing to keep you, gentlemen. If you could show me his bedroom, doctor, I'll have him moved up there."

"You wouldn't like me to wait and break the news to his wife? It will be a terrible blow to her. They were wrapped up in each other. Poor girl!"

"Thank you, sir, but I don't think there's any need. I'll be staying on a bit myself, and I'll see to it."

"I'll be getting along, then, Chief Inspector," said the headquarters surgeon, and went.

As the two were coming downstairs again, after Moresby had been given a brief idea of the layout of the bedrooms, he turned to the other and said suddenly: "I suppose, doctor, that if he had taken prussic acid, as he said, you wouldn't look during the p.m. for signs of any other poison?"

"Not if the cause of death were obviously prussic acid," returned the other, in some surprise, "and that's quite unmistakable; no, we shouldn't."

"And the analyst would test for prussic acid only?"

"He'd test for prussic acid first, of course; and if he found it I'm quite sure he wouldn't test for anything else. Why?"

"Oh, only something I happened to think of," said Moresby, almost apologetically.

To the constable at the door, when he had seen the doctor out, he said: "Don't let anyone in without reference to me, not either of the maids, nor even Mrs. Carruthers herself."

Then he called Sergeant Afford off his job for a moment to help him get the body upstairs.

Chief Inspector Moresby's actions after that were rather curious. He called the fingerprint man upstairs to him, took him into the Carruthers' joint bedroom (the body had been put in the doctor's dressing-room), and said: "I want you to test the handles of all the drawers in this room, and of the cupboards, for the dead man's own prints. Take a record of them first, and then see if you can find 'em where I said."

He left the man at work, and went down again to the consulting-room.

"Nothing here that I can find," said Inspector Willis, looking up from the desk. "Everything's perfectly in order, hardly any bills; plenty of patients; can't be money trouble."

"I wish that his wife would come back," grumbled Moresby. "She may be able to save us any amount of trouble." He thrust his hands into his pockets and stood staring down at the burnt papers in the hearth. "Wonder who was the last person to see him alive," he muttered.

"It'd save us a whole heap of trouble, too," lamented Willis, "if coroners didn't want to go so deep into their cases. If I was a coroner, that note would be good enough for me; I wouldn't worry about the reasons. Why shouldn't the poor chaps keep 'em secret, if they want to?"

"Coroners always had long noses, and always will," Moresby opined. He walked across to a bookshelf, stood for a moment examining the titles, and then took down Taylor's *Medical Jurisprudence*.

"It says here," he remarked a few minutes later, "that in strychnine poisoning death usually occurs in about two hours after swallowing the stuff. That looks as if he must have taken it pretty well immediately after his lunch. Those maids ought to know something." He put the book back on its shelf and strolled again into the surgery.

On a top shelf stood a jar labelled: Liq. Strych. It was about one-third full.

Moresby was still looking at it when Sergeant Afford came in to report.

"Can't find anything that might have been used as the vessel, sir, except a clean glass in the scullery. Have you been in the dining-room? There's the remains of a meal for one on the table, and a half-full bottle of beer, but no glass. I suggest he took the stuff in beer, and then washed the glass out."

"I wonder why he should do that." Moresby mused.

He looked into the dining-room and then followed Afford to the scullery. On the draining-board stood a single tumbler, globules of water still adhering to its sides. Moresby contemplated it with a puzzled expression. Then he looked searchingly round the room.

The only thing that seemed to hold his attention was an empty beer-bottle, standing on the floor under the sink. While the Sergeant looked on in surprise, Moresby plumped down on his knees and put his nose to the mouth of the bottle, which was unstopped. As he rose he said, in answer to Afford's glance: "That seems to have been washed out, too; at least, there's no smell of beer. Now, why do you think he bothered to do that?"

"Perhaps he didn't, sir, it may have been there for some time. Or perhaps he put the strychnine in the bottle and shook it well up before he poured it out 'Shake well before taking,'" quoted Afford humorously.

Moresby shook his head. "This is the most deliberate suicide I ever struck. Don't touch that bottle and glass."

He marched out of the scullery and lumbered up the stairs into the bedroom.

"How are you getting on, Patterson?"

"Nearly finished, sir. Only this cupboard-knob to do. There's the doctor's prints on three of the dressing-table drawers, but not on any of the cupboards."

"I see," said Moresby; and watched the fingerprint man test the last knob, which proved also to be negative. "There are three articles I want you to try next, Patterson." He described the jar in the surgery, and the bottle and glass in the scullery. "Test all of them for prints of any sort."

The man nodded, and went out of the room.

Moresby waited till he had gone and then sat down at the dressing-table drawers, a grotesquely incongruous figure before the usual array of aids to feminine beauty. The fingerprint man's voice floated up to him from the hall: "What's the Chief want to bother himself with a suicide for? Waste of time, I call it." Moresby smiled his disagreement; some suicides are remarkably interesting.

With experienced fingers he made a swift examination of the contents of each drawer, paying particular attention to the only one on which the doctor's prints had not been found. His large hands rummaged lightly among stockings and handkerchiefs, old bills, powder-puffs, gloves, discarded bags, scribbled notes, the ordinary paraphernalia of a woman's dressing-table drawers. Only to the notes and bills did he pay any attention. When he got up, however, it was with empty hands; everything he had examined had been replaced exactly as he found it.

He turned his back on the dressing-table and looked slowly round the room, his eyes ranging over every piece of furniture with slow deliberation.

When the divisional inspector came upstairs a little later, Moresby had in his hands a small packet of letters tied up with blue ribbon, and was glancing through one of them with complete shamelessness. In reply to the other's questioning look, he said briefly: "Found 'em in a bit of space behind a drawer in her wardrobe; good hiding-place."

"Well, you've found more than I have," grumbled Willis; and then, more eagerly: "Any use to us?"

The chief inspector handed over the letter he had been reading. "Take a look for yourself."

The other glanced through it, a typical love-letter. Phrases here and there caught his eye. "I miss you more than I can find words to write."

"Your sweetness and gentleness…"

"The only woman in the world for me, and always will be."

"… longing to get back and be with you again."

"This is the goods," said Willis coarsely. "Well, we've found the reason all right." Then he turned to the signature, and his expression changed to one of acute disappointment The letter was signed: "Your own adoring Jim."

"Too bad," he said, as he gave the letter back. "I thought you'd get hold of something good. My sakes, I wonder how long they'd been married, for him to write to her like that. Over six years, to my knowledge." A married man himself, Willis managed to look both scornful and envious at the same moment.

"Ah," said Moresby, who was not married.

The constable poked his head in at the door. "Mrs. Carruthers has come, sir," he mouthed. "She's in the hall with the sergeant."

"All right," nodded Moresby; and thrust the packet of letters mechanically into his pocket.

As he ran downstairs he glanced at his watch. The time was twenty minutes to six. He had been in the house for over two hours already.

In the hall a tall woman was standing, her back towards him as he came down the stairs. "But what bad news?" she was saying, in an anxious voice. "I don't understand. Why are you trying to stop me from coming into my own house? Why are the police here at all? If the house has been burgled, why can't you say so?"

Sergeant Afford looked at Moresby with relief.

"It's worse than burglary, I'm afraid, madam," said the chief inspector gently. "You must prepare yourself for very bad news. Won't you come into the drawing-room with me?" He held the door open for her.

"Not—my husband?" Mrs. Carruthers faltered, one gloved hand to her throat. "You don't mean…? He's had an accident? The car…?"

As kindly as he could Moresby told her of the telephone message he had received, and its sequel. Before he had spoken half a dozen words Mrs. Carruthers had swayed, recovered herself, and tottered over to a couch as if her legs could no longer support her. She did not utter a word as Moresby told his story; just sat there and looked at him with her violet eyes painfully wide and an expression in them of almost unbearable horror. Even when he had finished she still sat motionless, as though the very power of movement had left her. Moresby ostensibly turned away to give her time, but kept a wary eye on her in the mirror over the fireplace; he felt extremely uneasy about the possibility of her having a stroke through sheer shock.

At last she managed to force out huskily: "You say… a note? For me?"

"No, madam. It was addressed to the coroner."

"Nothing… for me, at all?"

"I'm afraid not."

She relapsed into her stone-like pose. Moresby fiddled with the ornaments on the mantelpiece. He had thought Mrs. Carruthers a handsome woman when he first saw her; now her face was almost ugly in its strained intensity. From a possible twenty-eight she had changed suddenly to a charitable forty.

"He didn't even—say anything… about me? For you to tell me?" The words seemed forced out of her by a subconscious urge that had taken possession of her impotent consciousness.

"No. He said nothing, except that he had taken strychnine, and not prussic acid. He didn't utter another word."

"Oh." Her unnatural rigidity dissolved. She buried her face in her hands.

Moresby waited patiently.

When her paroxysm was over, he asked her if she felt up to answering a few questions, and proceeded to put them before she could reply, thinking he saw his justification in the quite visible effort with which she pulled herself together and controlled her trembling limbs. He did not ask her at first whether she could throw any light on her husband's action, confining his questions to impersonal matters of fact. Obviously better but still shaken, Mrs. Carruthers answered him in a voice that slowly became steadier, though every now and then a look of utter bewilderment appeared in her fine eyes, as if the realisation of what had happened had struck her once more with ever-fresh incredulity.

The story Moresby obtained from her was simple enough. Her husband had been alone in the house at lunch-time. The two servants, who were sisters, had been promised a day's holiday to attend their parents' silver-wedding festivities, and had left the house soon after eleven o'clock, after setting the table with cold food for the doctor's lunch. She herself had been lunching at the flat of a friend in Kensington, whose name and address she gave; after lunch she and her friend had gone to the West End to do some shopping and had had tea at one of the big stores, whence she had come straight home. When had she left the house in the morning? At about a quarter past twelve, and her husband was still out on his rounds; he rarely got in to lunch before half-past one.

Moresby approached the delicate subject of Dr. Carruthers' reasons for his action, but Mrs. Carruthers could offer no help at all; she simply could not understand it. They had been so happy together. Nor could she understand how her husband could have done such a thing without leaving any word for herself at all, and pressed Moresby again and again on the point; she seemed to think that he must have found something and be concealing it from her. At last Moresby told her of the charred paper in the hearth; could she suggest what the "uncertainty" might be to which he referred?

"Oh!" Mrs. Carruthers cried. "Oh, I see now. Oh, why didn't you tell me before? Poor, poor James."

"What do you see, madam?" Moresby asked patiently.

"He was so terribly afraid of getting tetanus from a bad place he had on his thumb. It—it was really a morbid fear. He was convinced that he would get it and die. I tried to joke him out of it, but for the last week he has been getting more and more depressed. Oh, how terrible—how terrible! He might never have had it at all. Inspector, haven't you learned everything you want now? I can't answer any more questions. I simply can't. Oh, please leave me alone now."

As, in fact, he had now learned everything he wanted, Moresby did leave her, with a few clumsy words of sympathy.

In the hall he collected his men and glanced enquiringly at Patterson, who told him in a low voice that he had found the doctor's fingerprints on all three articles. Afford and Patterson were then packed into the police-car and sent back to Scotland Yard, and Moresby offered to stroll back to the district station with Willis, "to help get out of the report."

"Phew!" said Willis, as they got underway. "Nasty business that. Made me miss my tea, too. What do you say to a glass of beer before we go to the station, Mr. Moresby? This is a very good house we're just coming to."

"Yes," said Moresby.

They turned into the private bar, empty but for themselves. "Surprised to see you taking so much trouble over a suicide, sir," remarked Willis, when the barman had served them and gone. The room was cut off from the other bars, and their voices could not be overheard.

Moresby looked at him quizzically. "So you think the doctor committed suicide, Willis, do you?"

"Don't you, Mr. Moresby?" asked Willis, in astonishment.

"I do not," Moresby replied with energy. "I know he was murdered; but I'm bothered if I know how to prove it."

PART 2

"How do you make out that it was murder, sir?" asked Willis.

"I'll tell you," said Moresby. "There were a number of curious little facts, you remember, that you wouldn't expect in a suicide case. The doctor ringing up, the washed glass, still more the washed bottle, the burnt note to his wife, the open chloroform jar on the surgery counter as if he'd been trying to give himself the proper antidote to his own poison; the whole place reeked of chloroform. But what put me on to the idea that things mightn't be so simple as they looked was his changing his mind from prussic acid to strychnine. Why on earth should he change his mind from a quick, not too painful poison to the most painful of the whole lot? The only reason I could see was that he had the strychnine in him already, knew his case was hopeless, and intended to finish himself off less painfully; but the strychnine convulsions caught him and stopped him getting at the prussic acid at all."

"Coo!" said Detective-Inspector Willis unprofessionally.

"Somebody wanted Dr. Carruthers out of the way, Willis—someone who knew that there was quite a possibility of him getting tetanus, and knew, too, that the symptoms of strychnine poisoning are pretty well the same as those of tetanus. I haven't the least doubt that the doctor's death was intended to be put down to tetanus; and with his own fears so widely expressed, it wasn't anticipated that there'd be any trouble about the death certificate. But just to make things certain, that letter addressed to his wife was left somewhere handy, to be found if it was wanted and not if it wasn't."

"But—wasn't it a genuine letter?"

"Genuine so far as the doctor had written it but not genuine so far as its meaning went. It was the back page torn off a longer letter, if I'm right and it referred to something quite different and I shouldn't be at all surprised if it wasn't the possession of that letter, and the realisation of what those words could be made to imply, that was responsible for the doctor's death."

"But the letter to the coroner, sir, and him ringing you up. Oh, I see. You mean it wasn't him on the telephone at all?"

"Oh, yes it was. I'll tell you what happened. The doctor came in, had his lunch, poured himself out a glass of beer, and drank it off. It wasn't till he'd got it down that he realised how bitter it was. 'That's funny,' he thinks. 'Tastes almost as if there's something in it. And yet it's a new bottle. Well, well.' And he takes something to get rid of the bitter taste—a bit of cheese, perhaps. Then he thinks: 'Now's my chance. Servants out. Leila's out. I'll have a scout round.' Upstairs he runs, and starts going through his wife's dressing-table drawers."

"Why ever did he do that, sir?"

"Because he was her husband, and desperately in love with her, and therefore jealous; and therefore suspicious; and he's got a pretty good idea, and perhaps more than an idea, that she isn't as true to him as he'd like. Well, he goes through two drawers, and in the third he finds that bit torn off his letter, in an envelope on which he himself had once written 'Leila.' And at about the same time, I should imagine, the first convulsion comes along. He knows all right then; he's been poisoned, with strychnine. He runs down to the surgery as soon as he can move, and sees there's a good deal less in the strychnine jar than there should be; that makes him certain. He gets down the chloroform jar, and starts trying to dope himself. He daren't call another doctor in, because that would give away the fact that he's been poisoned; and his one idea now is to shield the person who poisoned him, even at the risk of his own life. Perhaps he doesn't care much for life now in any case, knowing what he knows at last.

"So between the spasms, instead of going on doping himself, he carries that beer-bottle out to the scullery, empties it and rinses it out, and the glass, too, and writes that note to the coroner. By that time he knew it was hopeless; he couldn't save himself now even if he wanted to, and the convulsions are coming on quicker and quicker; he can hardly drag himself about between them. So he rings us up at Scotland Yard, and then crawls back to the surgery to get the prussic acid. But he's left it too late. He can't even stand up. He has to stick it out. That's all."

"You mean… Mrs. Carruthers?"

"His wife put the strychnine in the beer-bottle before she left home. She murdered him all right, Willis. But we'll never get her. He's covered her traces too well. My goodness, he must have loved her."

"But—why did she, sir? Where's the motive?"

"In my pocket, man. Those letters. You made a bad mistake there, Willis. Jimmy isn't such an uncommon name, you know. Besides, she called him 'James.' Those letters weren't in the same handwriting as the note to the coroner."

"Oh! But you've got them, Mr. Moresby. Surely…?"

"No, we can't do a thing, that I can see. It'll give her a nasty jar when she finds they're gone; but the evidence of suicide is too strong for us. And, of course, I may be wrong from beginning to end; there's always that possibility. But, mark my words: if, not too long ahead, Mrs. Carruthers marries a man whose Christian name is James, that will prove me right."

Eleven months later Detective-Inspector Willis received a cutting from *The Morning Post*. There was no letter with it, but the paper in which it was folded bore the address of Scotland Yard.

The cutting ran as follows:

"Grey—Carruthers. On November 19, at St. Agatha's, N.W., James Roland Grey, second son of Robert Grey, of Wellington, Dorset, to Leila Joan Carruthers, only daughter of Mr. and Mrs. Herbert Thomas, of The Mount, Bishop's Stratford; very quietly, owing to mourning in bride's family."

Detective Inspector Field in

MAN IN BOND STREET

Anthony Gilbert

Anthony Gilbert was the principal pen-name of Lucy Malleson (1899–1973). She was born in London and spent most of her life in and around the capital, although in her self-deprecating memoir *Three-a-Penny* (1940), published under another pseudonym, Anne Meredith, she described her origins as "Yorkshire with a dash of Scotch". While working as a secretary, she went to see *The Cat and the Canary*, a popular mystery play then running at the King's Theatre, and decided she could write something as good, thus launching a prolific career in the crime genre.

She used a variety of backgrounds, but many of her stories were set in London, and she described the city evocatively in *Three-a-Penny*, in which she discusses "an enchanting game" she indulged in one August, asking herself: "What does London look like to a stranger? Does it seem vast? Beautiful? Mysterious? Strange?" These thoughts led her to write a novel: "I had anticipated that this book would sweep London. Actually it was hardly noticed by anyone and did not sell more than three or four hundred copies." Such, unfortunately, is so often the author's lot. Her best-known series character was a London solicitor, Arthur Crook, but this story, first published in the *Daily Express* on 15 April 1935, features the less-renowned Inspector Field.

"THERE ARE SOME MEN," REMARKED DETECTIVE INSPECTOR Field, taking up his second pint, "whose misfortunes are in a sense their advantages. There was a man in the Bible like that, if you remember, which I don't.

"And look at deaf men when it comes to after-dinner speeches and sermons and the next-door people's wireless of an evening. I knew a blind man once whose wife got a skin complaint in the face so it was a shock just to see her. But it didn't worry him; he couldn't, and he lived to be ninety.

"Which reminds me of a man I used to see a good bit of the year before the war in Bond-street. One of these hopeless cripples he was, with one leg two inches shorter than the other, and he wore a great boot on the bad foot and had to go on sticks.

"I remember the first time I saw him, because it was the time of the big Bond-street ramp. You'll remember it, I expect. I hadn't been in the force long, and I thought of it as my first big chance. The whole country was talking of some jewel gang that was robbing people right and left.

"Things were getting pretty bad. The police were being laughed at everywhere.

"I was as ambitious as Lucifer, and this seemed to me my great chance for promotion. But though I kept my eyes skinned I didn't make any startling discoveries and no arrests at all.

"It was just about this time that I first saw the Lame Man. I'd been watching a girl who seemed to me to be acting rather suspiciously, when I heard a yell behind me and I flashed round to see the fellow hoisting himself on to the pavement on his two sticks and a big red car drawing up alongside. It was easy to see what had happened. He'd been crossing the road, and being slow he'd been almost run down.

"The car stopped—you didn't nearly run down a cripple and clap your foot on the accelerator in those days, and Bond-street had a cachet the present generation wouldn't recognise—and the window was let down with a run. A big man with a blond moustache put his head out and said, 'Not hurt, are you? By Jove! that was a narrow shave. Did the car touch you?'

"Now a real beggar would have seen his chance there. He'd have got ten bob easy out of the man and probably more just by threatening to make a scene, specially with a policeman next door. But my man said, ''Sall right, guv'nor. My fault. Fact is, I can't get used to them cars.'

"The gentleman laughed. 'London's no place for you,' he said. 'You should live quietly in the country somewhere away from all this racket.'

"The cripple looked a bit indignant. 'I daresay,' he said, 'and be chased and gored to death by cows and fair deafened by nightingales. Thank you, I've 'ad some. Besides, I like a bit of life.'

"The man in the car laughed again and put his hand in his pocket. The cripple said, 'Thank you very much, sir, and good luck,' and the car went on.

"'Found a new way of getting a living?' I asked the fellow as he shuffled towards me.

"He was sharp, like these London chaps generally are. 'Dessay half-a-crown 'ud be a good price for your life,' he said. 'I look a bit 'igher my*self*. Still, thank you for the 'int. There's not many ways of getting on for a man like me.'

"Mind you," continued Field, earnestly, "I don't for a moment believe I put the idea into his head. I wouldn't be surprised to know he'd been getting four or five pound a week for years for not letting people kill him. But I suppose Bond-street was a bit richer than the other places, because after that I saw a good deal of him.

"He wasn't always just not getting run over; you don't want to do these things too often. There's always nosey people watching and thinking, not having anything else to do. But he had plenty of side-lines: he'd whip open the doors of cars and taxis, and though the people inside might wish he'd mind his own business they'd give him something for his trouble.

"Of course if I'd ever seen him beg that would be a different matter; but he was too sharp for that. He'd just stand by. That might have gone on for months but for a little accident that happened to him one afternoon. Either he slipped or else someone jostled him—anyway, one of the sticks he carried fell down and rolled almost to my feet. I bent down to pick it up and I saw on the bottom a little thing like a clip. I daresay it wouldn't have meant much to most people, but I recognised it at once.

"It's quite an old dodge of thieves. The little clip unfastens a man's shoelace and then the crook taps him on the arm and points out that with a bit of luck in another minute he'll break his neck or his nose. Then while he's stooping down and tying the lace the crook goes through his pockets.

"As soon as I saw that—though I didn't give any sign that I knew anything—I began to think a lot. The first thing was—this chap was a crook. And if he was a crook he was probably an impostor, too.

"Think for a minute. Where did this chap loiter? Outside jewellers, and so far as I could see nowhere else.

"I'd always taken it for granted that what was slipped into his hand was a bit of silver, but I didn't know. And what simpler or safer disguise could he have worn? It was all Scotland-yard to a soda-cake no one would ever drop on him. But suppose it was true—suppose those women passed him stolen gems or rings as they came out?

"I had to work carefully. I didn't want to let on that I knew the game by taking the fellow up and finding he'd really only got a shilling; because some of his bluff would be genuine: the fellow was no fool. Then came the theft of the Burlington ruby. It belonged to the Dowager Lady Burlington who had a house in Mayfair; it's been pulled down now; there's flats there these days.

"The ruby was one of those things connoisseurs almost break their hearts over, and you'll probably know that a ruby's much more valuable than a diamond often. Anyway, this one was insured for £50,000, and no company's going to stand for a job like that without some fight. The place was lousy with police—that's how the Dowager's butler put it—and suspicion fell on young Aubrey Dyke, who'd just got engaged to the dowager's youngest daughter.

"It was known he hadn't much money, as they counted it, but even so it seemed a bit thick to tell him to his face, as the Dowager did, that every one knew he'd only proposed to Kathleen Burlington to get a chance at snooping the ruby. It was a pretty rotten time for him. All the papers announced the smash of the engagement, and he offered to clear out at once.

"'Thank you, Mr. Dyke,' said the old lady, 'but I should prefer your interview with the police to take place before you go.'

"They didn't bring it home to him, of course, and the old lady was clever enough to realise that he wouldn't bring a libel action, because that would mean dragging the girl into it. But there was a lot of unpleasantness.

"I'd got it firmly into my head that my cripple was involved in all this, and that sooner or later the ruby would come into his possession. My carking fear was that he wouldn't be in Bond-street when it was passed him, but I had to take that chance. I might have warned my superiors, but the odds were that he wasn't a lame man in other districts, he was something quite unrecognisable. About four days after the ruby disappeared I saw him wandering about round a new fashionable café in Bond-street; it was run by a Hungarian, with a full Hungarian staff and the most magnificent band in Europe.

"People were going in and out, and I kept my eyes glued to my man; any one of the people might be the thief or his accomplice, and I wasn't going to look in another direction, not even if a car mounted the pavement and charged me to distract my attention. Presently Mr. Dyke's car rolled up and the chauffeur jumped down and opened the door. Mr. Dyke was a handsome young man with a very happy sort of manner, but he looked pretty jumpy today. And no wonder. He said something to the commissionaire as he went in, and no sooner had he disappeared than I saw my lame friend come shuffling round to talk to the shover.

"So that's it, I thought. The shover's in the gang. You'll often find in these big put-up affairs that ladies' maids and valets and footmen are involved; either they're bought over or they're in the gang before they get the job. A gang doesn't mind waiting a precious long time to get a big haul. I was watching to see what happened when some one spoke to me. A shabby little old woman wanting to know the way some street I'd never heard of. That's an old dodge, too. It makes you turn your back for a minute or half a minute, and that's long enough for half the crimes in the calendar.

"I said, 'Sorry, mum. I don't think you've got the name right.'

"She said. 'Do you call yourself a policeman?' To me, that was seeing myself an inspector in no time at all.

"I lost patience with her. I said, 'Second on the right and first on the right again.'

"I don't think she believed me: I could feel her standing there, and for a minute I thought she might knife me. You could feel her trembling with rage. But she went on at last, and I saw the commissionaire of the café come down to the cripple, who was hanging about round the doorway and tell him to clear off.

"'What's the matter with you?' said the cripple. 'You don't own the pavement, do you?'

"The commissionaire got angry and there were heated words, and suddenly the chauffeur shot out his fist and laid the other man out. That gave me my chance.

"'What's all this?' I said. I couldn't have asked for anything better. Now I could take the pair of them into custody, and I was willing to wager my stripes that they wouldn't get away before we knew a lot more about the Burlington ruby than we did at the moment.

"'You can't go knocking people down here,' I said to the chauffeur. 'You'll have to come along with me. This isn't your private house: you can't behave how you like here.'

"'I don't mind coming with you,' said the chauffeur fiercely. 'But you take him as well.' He pointed to the commissionaire. 'He began it.'

"The commissionaire had slowly got up. 'I did nothing,' he protested angrily. 'I told this beggar he must not beg here.'

"'I'm not a beggar. And I'll ask you to show when I've ever asked a penny off of any one,' said the cripple, just as furious. 'And I'd have knocked you down myself, only me being the man I am it couldn't be done.'

"There was a big crowd collected by now, too big, because for all I knew half the gang was there, so I was glad to see Mr. Dyke coming out of the café.

"'What's all this?' he asked. 'What on earth have you been doing, Plater?' That was to the chauffeur.

"We all told him what Plater had been doing and I said I was sorry, but they'd all have to come along with me to the station.

"The commissionaire said he couldn't come, but Plater chipped in that if the commissionaire wasn't going to make a charge we couldn't take him along either. I meant to get Plater and the other fellow at the station, and the long and short of it was that the whole lot of us went off together in Dyke's car, with me driving. I was half mad with excitement. I didn't know whether we had the ruby but I was dead sure we were on its track. The commissionaire made his charge and the sergeant took down a statement, and presently Dyke went off to say a word for Plater, I suppose.

"I hung about by myself, wondering how much longer this suspense was going to last and suddenly the door opened, and Fletcher came in. A hard man, Fletcher, but just: he'd see to it a man got his share of the swag in any haul.

"'Oh, Field,' he said to me, 'a complaint's just come in about you.'

"That was so different from what I'd expected that I could only just stare.

"'Yes,' Fletcher went on. 'You've heard of Lady Hendrie?'

"All London knew about Lady Hendrie, her brilliant past and her mysterious present, how she always slept in her coffin and kept the light burning all night and had a skull on her bureau to remind her what lay ahead.

"'She reports that she asked the constable on duty in Bond-street less than an hour ago the way to Mulgrave-square, and he treated her with levity and disrespect. You remember the lady?'

"'Was that who she was?' I exclaimed. 'I thought she was all part of the frame-up, and I meant to get the ruby.'

"I didn't know, you see, how much of the story he'd heard.

"'Oh, you brought that in all right,' said Fletcher in his cool way. 'I bet you enjoyed yourself, too. It's fun being a constable, Field, isn't it?'

"I began to go a bit shivery. 'Beg pardon, sir. I don't quite understand.'

I saw him wandering about round a bit more enthusiasm, as any man would.

"'Yes, Field,' he went on in a dreamy sort of voice, as if he hadn't heard me, 'it must be fun arresting your superior officer for being the leading light of a gang of jewel thieves. I must say I didn't expect things to turn out quite this way. I let you into the secret, by rolling my stick to your feet, just to show you something was going on. I thought you'd be useful as a stand-by. I didn't know,' he began to shake with laughter, 'you'd mistake me for the criminal.

"'Still,' he was suddenly quiet again, 'all's well that ends well. We've got Dyke—oh yes, he took it; the old dowager was right every time, and, anyway we've been after that lad for years—and we've got Slim Archie, the commissionaire, you know. You hadn't recognised him? Ah, you hadn't studied his profile. His ears, Field. Always remember that nothing can disguise an ear.

"'Dyke had just slipped him the ruby as he went into the café. That's why our plain-clothes man had to knock him down. Oh, it was a great scheme, but the police aren't such a back number as some people think. And you can't say they're not persevering; we were two years working Wilson into that job as Dyke's chauffeur.'

"I was dumb. I didn't know where to look. But I knew who came out last on the list. Not Dyke and not Slim Archie, but me, me that had practically got the chair at Scotland-yard a half-hour before.

"'It's all right,' Fletcher encouraged me. 'Your picture'll be in all the papers. We're seeing to that. And you're going to have all the kudos. I don't suppose the people that matter—the people at headquarters, say—will ever forget your share of the Burlington ruby case.'

"And they never have," concluded Field grimly. "It got so bad I couldn't hear a ruby mentioned without jumping. One thing, it put me out of love with publicity once and for all. It's a mug's game and when you think there's men and women that'll pay an agent hundreds of good pounds every year to get their names and faces in the Press, well, it just shows it's gospel truth what they say, that there's a mug born every minute."

Superintendent Aldgate in

DEATH ON NELSON'S COLUMN

Eric Bennett

Eric Oswald Bennett (1909–1985) is, by a considerable distance, the most obscure author whose work appears in this collection, so he deserves the longest introduction. I'm indebted to Jamie Sturgeon for directing me to this story and for supplying what information I have about him. He was born in London and educated at Christ's Hospital and Worcester College, Oxford. He seems to have written only one novel, *Murder in the Admiralty* (1941), which has a curious claim to fame. It was published in 1945 as a "green Penguin" title (number 497 in the main series) at a time when paper rationing meant that the quality of production was poor, with the result that most copies were so brittle that they disintegrated. As a result, it is now a rare and collectible title, which featured as the eighth most valuable "green Penguin" in a YouTube video by the bibliophile Jules Burt, who (in 2022) estimated the value of this little-known paperback at £350. At the time of writing, however, I was unable to locate any copies for sale on the internet, anywhere in the world.

Murder in the Admiralty was serialised in the *Evening Standard* prior to its original publication. Bennett, who lived in Thaxted, Essex, was a journalist who wrote for the *Daily Express*, *Sunday Chronicle*, and *Sunday Express*, as well as the magazine *John Bull*. His work for newspapers and magazines included a series of four tales of sporting murder which were published in 1948 in a volume costing a shilling. *Sports Crimes*, a quartet of extracts from Superintendent Aldgate's casebook, concerned sudden death at an assortment of major sporting occasions: a Test Match, the Derby, the F. A. Cup Final, and Wimbledon. Each case involved an intriguing method of murder: a poisoned cricket ball, a revolver controlled by sound waves, a hypodermic needle in the stud of a football boot, and a needle in a tennis ball. Aldgate also investigated in "Murder on the Beach", a four-part story from the *Evening Standard* in August 1939 and a five-part radio thriller, "Watt Was the Murderer's Name", broadcast on the Forces Network in February and March 1941. The following story appeared in the *Evening Standard* as a "five-part thriller" in the week commencing 5 June 1939.

ALTHOUGH IT WAS JUNE AND THE SUN WAS UP AND A CLEAR blue sky stretched above a London that was yawning and rumbling into life, there was a nip in the air. The metal of Landseer's dour-faced lions was cold to the touch, and Henry Cockspur, the steeplejack, cursed them amiably as he hauled his ladders up to the base of Nelson's Column.

"That's the worst of these special jobs," he grumbled, jabbing his first ladder upright against the stonework of the column. "Give me those irons, boy. They shove 'em at you in a hurry, and you have to get up at dawn to do 'em."

Cockspur looked across Trafalgar Square. From one corner the red type of a row of the previous night's *Evening Standard* bills stared back at him:

WORLD CONFERENCE FOR LONDON	ROOSEVELT SAILS	HITLER ACCEPTS

Cockspur read the last one out to himself and spat dispassionately at the tail of the nearest lion.

"Fancy polishing up old Nelson and hanging the flags out for him," he murmured and began to climb.

It was a long job fastening his ladders one on top of the other and clamping them securely to the stone, but Henry Cockspur rose slowly with the sun.

He looked down on the cleaners in the Square. They were clearing away the debris of a political meeting which had been held at the column the night before, and he saw the tattered remnant of a paper banner shouting WE DON'T WANT...

As he climbed higher he saw the first buses gliding below him like brightly-painted beetles, and the air around began to hum with the noise of London life. And presently, as he glanced round after testing a ladder he saw that another fresher row of red type was commanding a corner of the Square with:

ASCOT:	ASCOT:	ASCOT:
CARD AND	AJAX	FALCON'S
FORM	SUMS UP	FINALS

But the steeplejack was aloof, godlike. He was climbing to the skies and hauling his ladders up behind him. Only the pigeons, wheeling and crying, were living in his world.

He reached at last the head of the column and braced himself for his most difficult task. Above him the broad platform on which the Nelson statue stands shut out his view of the sky. His last ladder had to reach the edge of this platform by leaning away from the column, so that when he climbed round the overhang his body would perch perilously at an angle of 45deg., back to the ground, but 145ft. above it.

Standing on the top half of the last ladder Cockspur flung out a kind of grappling hook to the platform above. After some struggling he secured a line safe enough to climb up to the platform, his assistant waited just below him with the last ladder.

"All right," said Cockspur, and swung himself out into space.

His knuckles gripped the grimy stone edge of the platform; his feet, dangling, appeared to stamp the square fountains out of sight.

Cockspur tensed his muscles and heaved his head and shoulders over the edge of the platform... heaved his head straight into the face of another man.

For the first time in forty years the steeplejack lost his nerve. His scream was lost in the harsh cries of the pigeons. Only his terrified assistant saw his body roll half-balanced on the edge, his legs kick wildly in the air.

Sudden realisation of his own danger brought the man back to normal. His muscles acted automatically; he became a steeplejack once more through habit.

He pulled himself over the platform edge and sank down on his knees to stare at the face which had been waiting for him at the top of Nelson's Column.

Then he became a frightened man again. That was a dead face. He put out a hand to touch it and quickly drew it back.

The dead man was lying full length on the platform staring with wide, empty eyes, across the roofs of London to where the Thames was sparkling in the morning sun. The colossal stone Nelson towered above and stared blindly with him.

On that little island of stone, high above the roar of London, there was silence.

The steeplejack felt the sweat running on the palms of his hands. Then he looked down again and saw a dark pool oozing from beneath the dead man.

Blood. The red-black of blood. For some crazy reason he thought of the red ink of the newspaper bills. But this...

A shout from below roused him. He looked over the edge of the platform.

"All right," he snapped at his assistant. "Let's have that ladder."

The mechanical business of fastening the top of the ladder helped to clear his mind. When it was ready he ordered the assistant to go down at once. He took one more look at the body, and then went down the column so fast that he was on the base before his assistant had finished dusting his hands.

When a dishevelled and excited man, clasping the arm of a young policeman, marched into Cannon-row police station and declared that there was a dead man on top of Nelson's Column, the station sergeant was undecided whether to ring for the ambulance or give the joker a taste of the cells.

But when at last Cockspur established his identity, the excitement of the police was equal to his own. Even Superintendent Aldgate, of the Yard, who was getting liverish and bored with crime, became interested, and it was he who led the party of officials who followed Cockspur back to Trafalgar-square.

The Super's enthusiasm abated when he stared up at the column.

"I've done some things for the Force in my time, but I'll give every murderer in the country a free pass for the World's Fair before I climb up that thing," he said.

He looked round at his subordinates and picked out the photographer.

"You will have to go up. Get all you can. I want detail plates of every square yard of that platform and the pedestal of the statue and that dollop of old rope. After that, I think we'll leave things to you, Mr. Cockspur. You and your assistant could no doubt get a bit of rope round the body and lower it better than we could. Hopkinson, get a cordon put round this base."

The photographer, followed by the sympathetic Cockspur, made the long climb. Aldgate and the police waited impatiently for him to finish.

Then, at last, after much signalling and shouting to the satisfaction of the crowd that was rapidly filling the Square and staring up at the strange performance on the column, the body was swung clear of the platform and lowered gently to the ground.

They rested it carefully upon a police cape in the shadow of a brazen lion. Aldgate leaned over.

"Good God," he shouted. "Marriner!"

"Marriner?" echoed Inspector Jeans. "Not…"

"Yes, of course. Robert Marriner, the Foreign Secretary."

Superintendent Aldgate eased himself into his office chair and picked up the pile of damp prints that lay on his desk. The photographer had done his work well.

There, as clear as the dawn which had lit the steeplejack's work, lay Robert Marriner, the Foreign Secretary, stone dead at the foot of the stone Nelson. There was the little pool of blood. There was the rigid stare on Marriner's face as he looked out across London. In one print was a glimpse of the Square below, dotted with ant-like figures. That one made Aldgate snort and close his eyes… height had more horror for him than murder.

He opened his eyes again to answer the house telephone. Would he go and see the Commissioner at once? Yes, he would.

The Commissioner was obviously worried.

"Look here, Aldgate," he began. "The Foreign Secretary…"

"I know, sir. I've found him. On top of Nelson's Column."

"What the devil are you talking about?"

Aldgate explained three times before the Commissioner was convinced that the Superintendent hadn't cracked up under the strain of a long career of police work.

"I've never heard anything so fantastic in my life," he groaned at the end of it.

Aldgate shifted his weight from one foot to the other.

"What were you going to tell me, sir?" he asked.

"Only that Mrs. Marriner had 'phoned. He hadn't been home all night. I sent for Phipps, his bodyguard. Phipps says that he was working late at the F.O. last night, and left hurriedly about eight o'clock... apparently after receiving a telephone call. He told Phipps that he was off on private business and expressly warned him not to follow. Phipps thought it was a woman. So did I... until you came in."

"Car? Taxicab?" suggested the Superintendent.

"No. Phipps said that he walked up Whitehall."

"Hm. He couldn't very well walk up Nelson's Column," murmured the Super. "Do you mind if I telephone, sir? The medical report should be ready by now."

It was, and Aldgate summarised it for his chief.

"Been dead about twelve hours when we found him. Stabbed through the heart with a thin sharp instrument... dagger, stiletto, or even lancet. Very little bleeding. He had also been hit over the head with a blunt instrument, but that blow probably did nothing more than stun him. That's all, sir."

The two men stared at each other in silence. Then at last the Commissioner asked:

"What do you know, Aldgate?"

"Only this, sir. He was killed up there... on the column."

"But that makes it more fantastic than ever. Why do you think that?"

"There was no blood splashes on the column and none on the base. If someone had hauled the dead man up there, it is almost certain there would have been slight traces of blood. There isn't a drop."

"But how on earth could anyone get a man like Marriner to climb up Nelson's Column? And how could he get up there? You say that this steeplejack only fixed his ladders this morning?"

"He started at dawn, sir. And didn't leave the job until he had got to the top. And he was working in daylight the whole time, with an assistant watching him."

"Then Marriner somehow got to the top of the column... in the middle of London... between eight o'clock last night and dawn. And his murderer. It's certain murder, I suppose?"

"Certain. The weapon has gone. And the photographs of the body leave no doubt."

Suddenly the Commissioner brought his fist down on the desk.

"I've got it. A fire escape. You remember there was a big display last night... recruiting for the Auxiliary Fire Services. Now a man with an escape..."

Aldgate was shaking his head.

"I had thought of that, sir. But the longest escape in the brigade is only 100ft. And Nelson's Column is 145, to say nothing of the odd six inches."

The Commissioner was dashed, and there was another silence. At last he said:

"Why Nelson's Column?"

"I was thinking of that very thing," answered Aldgate. "And I think I know the answer. Supposing you wanted to get a man of Marriner's importance out of the way and make it appear that he had disappeared... bolted of his own accord.

"You could kidnap him, but you wouldn't be able to hold him very long in this country. Or you could kill him, but then you have the body to hide. Now bodies hidden in rivers, marshes, quarries, mines, and all the obvious places have a nasty habit of being accidentally discovered... and also they have to be carried for miles across country. A clever murderer knows he could hardly hope to keep Marriner's body hidden like that.

"But here, close at hand, is the obvious hiding place. The one place right in the middle of London that nobody can see. Nelson's Column wasn't due to be cleaned for years. By the time the missing Foreign Secretary would normally have been discovered, there would have been just a skeleton.

"But Hitler threw a spanner into the scheme. It was only last night that the Office of Works decided that his acceptance of an international conference in London was worthy of a clean-up of monuments and an elaborate decoration of the West End. Hence the providential appearance of Mr. Cockspur."

The Commissioner nodded thoughtfully. "Yes," he agreed. "That seems sound. But it postulates a reason for Marriner's disappearance. After all…"

He broke off to answer the telephone.

When he put the receiver down he looked at Aldgate with new respect.

"I think you are absolutely right," he said quietly. "And the missing reason appears to be at hand. That was Hargor, of the City Police. You had better go along and see him.

"It appears that they are on the edge of the biggest financial scandal they've had for years. And the people involved are the old-established firm of solicitors, Marriner, Williams and Marriner… apparently there were other pigeons, besides those in Trafalgar-square, attracted by our late lamented Foreign Secretary."

The City police were plumb worried. It appeared that they only knew the first things about the coming scandal, but those things were bad enough.

The legal firm of which the dead Minister was a partner had been fiddling with the trust funds which they superintended. The amount would run into hundreds of thousands… but worse than that was the scandal. Big names would be involved.

Even if Robert Marriner had taken little active part in the affairs of the firm since he had embraced a political career, he was still the senior partner. And they weren't quite sure how much he knew.

That's why Hargor was anxiously waiting for a lead from the Yard.

Superintendent Aldgate said nothing about the death of the Foreign Secretary until he had heard every known detail of the smash. He didn't want to excite his colleague unduly and he wanted to gauge his reaction when he said quietly:

"And now Robert Marriner has disappeared."

"Good Lord," said Hargor. "Then he was in it."

"So somebody was anxious for the world to think," agreed Aldgate, and told the rest of the story.

"You mean," said Hargor, when he had assimilated the facts of the murder on Nelson's Column, "that someone killed him, but wished it to be assumed that Marriner had disappeared of his own accord because of this scandal."

"Exactly. Exit Mr. Marriner. Completely discredited. And no hunt for a murderer, because no one would have suspected murder."

"Well, now," said Hargor. "The obvious murderer then would have been Marriner's active partner, a man named Ericson. Particularly as he seems to be the one who profited most out of the swindles. In fact, I'm pretty sure that Marriner had no idea of what was going on."

"Why 'would have been'?"

"Because Mister Ericson made his getaway last night. He hired a private airplane from Heston. He had to when he heard that the auditors were at work. Unfortunately for us, and for him, he never arrived at Le Bourget. The pilot's theory is that Ericson stepped overboard into the Channel."

"Like Loewenstein?"

"Like Loewenstein. I suppose," added Hargor tentatively, "Marriner couldn't have been in the same plane. I mean, suppose that he was killed in the air and pitched out, there's just a chance that he would land on Nelson's Column."

"A million to one chance," laughed Aldgate. "And in any case he would have been a mangled mass of pulp, whereas the Marriner murder was quite a neat job. By the way, how sudden was this smash?"

Hargor shrugged.

"Anyone with particularly good sources of information might have picked up rumours in the last two or three days, but it wasn't until yesterday that we heard anything definite. Why?"

"Someone might have learned enough to frighten Marriner?"

"Not as high as Nelson's Column."

"No, you oaf. But enough to lure him away with a telephone call. Enough to frighten him into making a secret appointment with a stranger who evidently had information which could ruin him?"

"Oh, I get you. Yes. I think that was possible"

"Thank you. Let me know if you get anything else."

Aldgate went back to the Yard. There was no news, but Inspector Jeans was obviously excited about something.

"I've found out," he began before Aldgate could settle his bulk comfortably in his chair, "that Marriner had a bitter feud with Sir Martin Bleate, the Permanent Under-secretary at the F.O. And yesterday they had one hell of a row, which ended with Marriner humiliating Bleate in public. Now Bleate, as you know sir, is a quick-tempered man…"

Aldgate held up his hand wearily.

"Forget all you've read about motive," he told the Inspector. "Just tell me *how* the murderer got Marriner to the top of that column, and I'll soon tell you *who* he is."

"I was coming to that," answered Jeans. "I also discovered that when Sir Martin Bleate was a young man, he was famous or notorious for his college climbing feats at Oxford."

Aldgate sat up.

"Sounds all right," he said at last. "But it doesn't get us very far, or does it?"

"It's a line," suggested Jeans. "I'm having Bleate watched."

"All right," said Aldgate. "I'm all for enthusiasm."

Jeans winced. He had been at Oxford himself and was Hendon

trained, and there were times when Aldgate was uncompromisingly old school, which is not the same thing as old school tie.

On his way home down Whitehall that night Aldgate scowled up at Nelson's Column. Nelson, high and aloof, stared coldly back, the dumb witness of the murder.

The steeplejack's ladders were still clamped against the column, but Aldgate had forbidden Cockspur to work there, and a constable was on duty at the foot of the ladders.

The Superintendent had an uneasy feeling that he ought to go up the column. The blood ran to his head at the thought of it and he nearly turned his car over the kerb. A constable on point duty walked over to reprimand him, recognised the Super, and turned his head quickly the other way.

Supper and soft slippers could not ease Aldgate's mind. He was on the case all the time.

He ignored his own advice to the Inspector and sat back to think of motives. Who would gain by making Marriner disappear?

There was certainly Ericson. There was Bleate. And both of those could have had the required information about the state of his firm's finances. Was there anyone else?

Wait a minute. What would be the public effect of Marriner's death? It might wreck the international conference. Who stood to gain by that? Armaments manufacturers. Who stood to lose by the conference, if Hitler really did come to a Western agreement with the European powers and America? Only Japan.

Well, that was an uninspiring list; Ericson, who was now dead, but could have killed Marriner before he died; Bleate; an unknown armament maker; Japan.

Better go to bed. He was switching the light off when the telephone rang. It was the operator from the Yard.

"Long distance call for you, sir. He says it's urgent. A Mr. Ericson."

Mr. Ericson's remarks were to the point. His voice over the telephone was smooth.

"Listen," he said. "I'm just ringing up to save your time and my trouble. You can trace this call if you like, but my airplane's ready and I shall be safely in a country that has never heard of extradition before you can say 'Operator.'

"I've just read the evening papers, and I see that Marriner's been murdered. Well, don't get it into your head that I did it. I've got a complete alibi, and if you ever catch me, which is unlikely, I'll prove it. I may have swindled poor old Marriner, but I didn't kill him. I just took the trouble to ring up, because even Scotland Yard would have seen through that airplane disappearance of mine sooner or later. Goodbye."

"Thank'ee," murmured Aldgate, and rang up the Yard. As he went up the stairs to bed he said to himself, "That was a smart move on Ericson's part—but does it let him out or put him in?"

Sleep brought no answer to the problem. Nor did the results of the Yard's routine inquiries.

The Foreign Secretary had not been seen from the time he left his office at 8 p.m. until the morning when he was found dead. There were no family troubles. Mrs. Marriner was distracted. Aldgate was up against a blank wall… and Nelson's Column.

It took him an hour of prayer and sweating to make up his mind to do it. Then he sent for Cockspur.

"Do you think I could climb that perishing thing?" he asked the expert.

Cockspur looked at the Superintendent's bulk and grinned.

"Lor, yes. It's easy. Just keep your head up and your eyes to the front and don't look down."

"I shan't. And what's more, you're going up first and we are going to be roped together," answered Aldgate, firmly.

The steeplejack was quite willing. Nothing was likely to upset his nerve—unless somebody had left another corpse on top of the column.

It was a slow climb, and it fascinated the crowd which gathered daily in the Square. Since the discovery of Marriner's body the crowds had been dense; hundreds of people stood for hours staring up at Nelson as if they expected him to rain corpses upon the earth.

They gave a cheer when Aldgate reached the platform and was hauled on to it by Henry Cockspur. Aldgate was puffing, and he had to lean against the statue for some minutes, struggling with a desire to vomit.

"Take it easy, sir," said Cockspur, sympathetically. "Don't look down. Look across at Big Ben, that'll take your mind off it."

Aldgate recovered at last and stared about him. There was the bloodstain, small and dark, against the grime. There was the disturbance in the caked soot where the body had lain. He looked round for other marks, and called out suddenly to the steeplejack.

"What do you make of that?" he said, pointing to a mark on the base of the statue.

"Something's been rubbed against there," said the steeplejack.

"A rope. You can see it was passed right round the statue base. There's a distinct mark on the grime this side, where it tightened. But where…?"

He leaned against the statue and stared into the sky. Around him the pigeons wheeled and swooped. Some of them were carrying the titbits they had snatched from the crowd in the Square below. They whirled around, now lighting on the statue, now cutting fantastic flights, now crooning at the two men who had invaded their eyrie.

Aldgate watched them idly as they spun dizzily around him. Suddenly he stiffened.

"I want to go down," he said.

"All right, sir," answered Cockspur, who thought that nausea had overcome the Superintendent again. "Let me lower you over this edge first, and I'll follow. Don't go too fast, and keep your eyes on my heels."

As soon as they reached the base of the column, Aldgate was off at a trot across the Square. He was interrupted by Inspector Jeans with a note.

"Urgent memo from the Commissioner, sir."

"To hell with memos, come with me," snapped the Superintendent.

Nevertheless, as he continued his jog trot across the Square and over the Strand crossing, he managed to tear open the note and read the Commissioner's remarks:

> F.O. believe political motive for Marriner murder. International conference entirely due his influence, and may now be wrecked. Marriner considered only British statesman capable reconciling Hitler, Daladier, Roosevelt. F.O. expect Hitler jilt conference any minute now.

Aldgate jerked his companion to a stop and suddenly pointed upwards to the top story of one of the huge office buildings that surround Trafalgar-square.

"See that window? We want to get in that office," and with that he was off again, into the building and impatiently holding open the lift gates for the bewildered Jeans.

The lift rocketed them up to the top floor. And there was a pause while Aldgate and Jeans calculated their exact position with regard to the Square and Nelson's Column.

Then Aldgate flung open the door of a room. It was a small office and completely empty. There was neither carpet nor furniture, and it did not seem to have been occupied for some time. But although the window was tight shut the office did not smell musty.

Aldgate without a word walked to the window and stood by the corner of it, so that he could see out without being seen. Jeans, from the back of the room, saw that the view was dominated by the top half of Nelson's Column.

The two men waited in silence, staring out over the Square.

Presently one of the pigeons that had been wheeling round the column flew straight across to the window-sill outside their room. Before Aldgate could fling the window up the pigeon was off again across the Square.

"Open the window," snapped the Super, and Jeans flung up the sash.

A minute later the pigeon flew back, straight into the room.

"Shut it," roared Aldgate, at the same time flinging himself on the bird.

Jeans stared open-mouthed as his superior officer rose from the floor, spitting dust and feathers but triumphantly clasping the pigeon.

"Get me a bird cage," shouted Aldgate. "I've got my first witness."

Jeans shrugged. The old man had gone daft at last.

"Hurry up," snapped the Superintendent. "I don't want to stand here all day like a ruddy bird fancier. Don't you know," he said more calmly, as the pigeon tried desperately to flutter to freedom, "that these wings I'm holding were the killer's wings?"

After the excitement of his pigeon-catching, Superintendent Aldgate sat back in his office and waited for the results of routine work.

His minions questioned the lessors of the offices in the building where the bird had been caught. They chased from address to address, and, like pigeons themselves, brought tiny scraps to his nest.

Meanwhile the Special Branch were also at work, and many curious pieces of information from foreign parts were conveyed to the Superintendent. And finally after a long telephone conversation with the Chief Constable of Bedlington in the Midlands, he sent for Inspector Jeans.

"Oh. Jeans," he said in the soft voice that told the Inspector that the boss was pleased with himself. "I've got a couple of tickets for the Bedlington Empire tonight. Would you like to come?"

"Certainly, sir," answered the Inspector, determined not to show surprise.

"We can catch the 7.10 and have dinner on the train, because I only want to see the last act," said Aldgate.

On the train Jeans could not restrain his curiosity.

"What are we going for?" he asked.

"To arrest the murderer of Marriner," answered Aldgate as casually as he asked for the salt.

"But… what's the pigeon got to do with it?"

"I observed, from my excellent viewpoint on top of Nelson's Column—you really should go up there some time: bracing air, fine scenery—that whereas most of the pigeons were flying aimlessly hither and thither, one bird was flying straight across the Square, round the statue and back. Does that convey anything to you?"

"No," confessed Jeans.

But Aldgate wouldn't say another word.

They were met at the station by the Chief Constable of Bedlington and escorted in state to the stage door of the Empire.

"They're on now," whispered a constable, who was standing in the wings.

"Who's on?" asked Jeans testily.

"The Flying Fakasakis," answered the constable in surprise, and light began to dawn on Jeans.

He followed the Super to the edge of the stage. The Flying Fakasakis, a Japanese troupe of acrobats, were at the climax of their turn.

A tight wire had been stretched from the stage to the gallery. Spotlights picked out its taut steel as it climbed steeply to the back of the house.

And to the rolling of drums, to the gasps of the audience as he passed above their heads and craning necks, a Japanese acrobat was walking up the tight wire with another member of the troop upon his back.

Suddenly Jeans realised that he was watching a twice nightly performance—of the Nelson's Column mystery.

Suddenly the drums ceased to roll. The wire walker had reached the gallery. Then, crash. A reverberating echo from the big drum and he slid backwards down the wire, balancing perfectly with his human burden and flourishing a gay little paper umbrella.

They reached the stage. The girl acrobat jumped off the wire walker's back. They bowed to the cheering audience. And then the man half turned, caught sight of Aldgate ambling towards him.

In a flash he was walking up the wire again. Aldgate ran on to the stage, but he was powerless to follow the little Japanese along the wire.

The man turned his head to grin at Aldgate's discomfiture. Then he called out to the crowd below in a sing-song voice:

"Get out of your seats quickly, please."

Jeans saw him put the little bottle to his lips, sway unsteadily on the wire, and then crash headlong into the stalls.

"It was a political job all right," explained Aldgate as they travelled back to London. "That wire walker has been a leading political agent for years, and he had instructions to wreck the conference and discredit the Foreign Secretary by any means he could. And, of course, the efforts of Mr. Ericson, of which he must have learned through his own secret service channels, gave him the opportunity. Just as I explained in the first place…"

"I know," interrupted the exasperated Jeans. "You were quite right about the motive for using Nelson's Column all along. But how did he do the murder?"

"Well, you saw his act. It was nothing to him to walk along a tight rope or wire carrying a body, whether a live partner or an unconscious Foreign Secretary. Heights and distances wouldn't worry him. I remember the Flying Fakasakis once walked a tight wire between the two towers of the Crystal Palace.

"I have had a talk with his little girl partner, who's in the Bedlington cells now as an accessory, and everything happened as I thought.

"Fakasaki had found out enough about Ericson's game to persuade Marriner on the telephone to come and see him, at once and in private. And when Marriner turns up at the Trafalgar-square office, Fakasaki slugs him over the head, humps him on his back, walks the wire in the dark—whoever would think of looking straight up in the air at about two in the morning in Trafalgar-square on a pitch black, moonless night?— dumps the body, stabs him, walks back and then hauls the wire in."

"But how did he get the wire out?" shouted the exasperated Jeans.

Aldgate grinned maliciously.

"That's where the bird comes in," he answered. "Fakasaki could walk the wire in the dark, but he couldn't fix it in the dark.

"What he could do was to train a homing pigeon to fly out from that window, round the Nelson statue and fly back to him. It took him a day or two, but he had the time to spare.

"When he was ready to receive Marriner he sent the pigeon out on the return flight round the Nelson statue with a waxed cord attached to his leg, so that when the pigeon returned there was a continuous thread running from the window, round the base of the statue, and back to the window.

"Now then. All he had to do was to release the pigeon, fasten both ends of the cord in his room and leave it. Who could possibly notice a thin piece of waxed cord stretching across Trafalgar-square from a top-storey window to the column?

"But when it was dark, and he had Marriner senseless in his office, he could complete his job.

"To one end of the cord he attached a length of thin wire. Then catching hold of the other end—the one the pigeon had brought back—he began to haul gently.

"It is an old trick. Prison-breakers used to do it regularly. Pulling gently and carefully, so that there was no danger of the thread breaking, he went on hauling until he had drawn the wire round the statue base.

"To the end of the wire was attached a thicker wire, and to the end of that was attached a still thicker and heavier wire, and so he went on until he had run a length of Mr. Fakasaki's own tested stage cable round the statue. So long as the weight was increased gradually there was never any fear of one of the wires snapping, and Mr. Fakasaki, remember, was a wire expert. He knew how to keep drawing in his end of the wire without putting too much tension on the section which was running round his "pulley"—the statue base.

"After that everything was straightforward. Mr. Fakasaki only made one mistake. That was when he let the pigeon go. He had taught the bird one trick it couldn't forget.

"It's a good thing I did go up that perishing column after all. By the way, Jeans, remind me to get some bird seed or whatever it is pigeons eat. I'm going to keep that bird."

"I thought you didn't like pets," murmured Jeans.

"Pet be damned. I owe that bird a living. He saved my reason!"

Colonel March in

THE CRIME IN NOBODY'S ROOM

Carter Dickson

Carter Dickson was the transparent alias employed by John Dickson Carr (1906–77) for his series of novels and stories featuring Sir Henry Merrivale, together with a handful of other stories. John was born in Pennsylvania, but he married an Englishwoman and became an ardent Anglophile, living in England for many years and setting the majority of his mysteries there. In early 1933, the Carrs took a flat in Guilford Street, London and John enjoyed traipsing around the city, which supplied the setting for his second book to feature Dr. Gideon Fell; *The Mad Hatter Mystery* (1933) boasts a particularly evocative description of the Tower of London. Carr's interest in true crime led him to write a book about a real life killing on Primrose Hill, *The Murder of Sir Edmund Godfrey* (1936).

From 1936, Carr became a pillar of the Detection Club, which had rooms in Gerrard Street, Soho; the first foreigner to be elected to the Club's membership, he was soon asked to become Secretary. In his biography by Douglas G. Greene, he is described as the Club's unofficial photographer. He also joined the short-lived Black Maria Club, which focused on true crime and was based at the London home of F. Tennyson Jesse before war intervened. He used the Carter Dickson name for a series of short stories about Colonel March of Scotland Yard, whose physical bulk was inspired by that of Carr's friend and fellow Detection Club member John Rhode. The Colonel never appeared in a novel, but was played on TV by Boris Karloff. This story was first published in the *Strand Magazine* in June 1938 and was later collected in *The Department of Queer Complaints* (1940).

B ANDS WERE PLAYING AND SEVEN SUNS WERE SHINING; BUT this took place entirely in the head and heart of Mr. Ronald Denham. He beamed on the carpark attendant at the Regency Club, who assisted him into the taxi. He beamed on the taxi-driver. He beamed on the night porter who helped him out at his flat in Sloane Street, and he felt an irresistible urge to hand banknotes to everyone in sight.

Now, Ronald Denham would have denied that he had taken too many drinks. It was true that he had attended an excellent bachelor party, to celebrate Jimmy Bellchester's wedding. But Denham would have maintained that he was upheld by spiritual things; and he had proved his exalted temperance by leaving the party at a time when many of the guests were still present.

As he had pointed out in a speech, it was only a month before his own wedding to Miss Anita Bruce. Anita, in fact, lived in the same block of flats and on the same floor as himself. This fact gave him great pleasure on the way home. Like most of us, Denham in this mood felt a strong urge to wake people up in the middle of the night and talk to them. He wondered whether he ought to wake up Anita. But in his reformed state he decided against it, and felt like a saint. He would not even wake up Tom Evans, who shared the flat with him—though that stern young business man usually worked so late at the office that Denham got in before he did.

At a few minutes short of midnight, then, Denham steered his way into the foyer of Medici Court. Pearson, the night porter, followed him to the automatic lift.

"Everything all right, sir?" inquired Pearson in a stage whisper. Denham assured him that it was, and that he was an excellent fellow.

"You—er—don't feel like singing, do you, sir?" asked Pearson with some anxiety.

"As a matter of fact," said Denham, who had not previously considered this, "I do. You are full of excellent ideas, Pearson. But let us sing nothing improper, Pearson. Let it be something of noble sentiment, like—"

"Honestly, sir," urged Pearson, "if it was me, I wouldn't do it. *He's* upstairs, you know. We thought he was going to Manchester this afternoon, to stay a week, but he changed his mind. He's upstairs now."

This terrible hint referred to the autocrat of Medici Court, Cellini Court, Bourbon Court, and half a dozen other great hives. Sir Rufus Armingdale, high khan of builders, not only filled London with furnished flats which really were the last word in luxury at a low price; he showed his pride in his own merchandise by living in them.

"No special quarters for me," he was quoted as saying, with fist upraised for emphasis. "No castle in Surrey or barracks in Park Lane. Just an ordinary flat; and not the most expensive of 'em either. That's where I'm most comfortable, and that's where you'll find me."

Considering all the good things provided in Armingdale's Furnished Flats, even his autocratic laws were not much resented. Nor could anyone resent the fact that all the flats in a given building were furnished exactly alike, and that the furniture must be kept in the position Rufus Armingdale gave it. Medici Court was "Renaissance," as Bourbon Court was "Louis XV": a tower of rooms like luxurious cells, and only to be distinguished from each other by an ornament on a table or a picture on a wall.

But Sir Rufus's leases even discouraged pictures. Considering that he was something of an art-collector himself, and had often been photographed in his own flat with his favourite Greuze or Corot, some annoyance was felt at this. Sir Rufus Armingdale did not care. You either leased one of his flats or you didn't. He was that sort of man.

Otherwise, of course, Ronald Denham's adventure could not have happened. He returned from the bachelor party; he took Pearson's advice about the singing; he went up in the automatic lift to the second floor; and he walked into what the champagne told him was his own flat.

That he went to the second floor is certain. Pearson saw him put his finger on the proper button in the lift. But nothing else is certain, since the hall upstairs was dark. Pushing open a door—either his key fitted it or the door was open—Denham congratulated himself on getting home.

Also, he was a little giddy. He found himself in the small foyer, where lights were on. After a short interval he must have moved into the sitting-room, for he found himself sitting back in an armchair and contemplating familiar surroundings through a haze. Lights were turned on here as well: yellow-shaded lamps, one with a pattern like a dragon on the shade.

Something began to trouble him. There was something odd, he thought, about those lampshades. After some study, it occurred to him that he and Tom Evans hadn't any lampshades like that. They did not own any bronze book ends either. As for the curtains...

Then a picture on the wall swam out of oblivion, and he stared at it. It was a small dull-coloured picture over the sideboard. And it penetrated into his mind at last that he had got into the wrong flat.

Everything now showed itself to him as wrong: it was as though a blur had come into focus.

"Here, I'm sorry!" he said aloud, and got up.

There was no reply. The heinousness of his offence partly steadied him. Where in the name of sanity was he? There were only three other flats on the second floor. One of these was Anita Bruce's. Of the others, one was occupied by a brisk young newspaper man named Conyers, and the other by the formidable Sir Rufus Armingdale.

Complete panic caught him. He felt that at any moment a wrathful occupant might descend on him, to call him a thief at worst or a snooper at best. Turning round to scramble for the door, he almost ran into another visitor in the wrong flat.

This visitor sat quietly in a tall chair near the door. He was a thin, oldish, well-dressed man, wearing thick-lensed spectacles, and his head was bent forward as though in meditation. He wore a soft hat and a thin oilskin waterproof coloured green: a jaunty and bilious-looking coat for such a quiet figure. The quiet light made it gleam.

"Please excuse—" Denham began in a rush, and talked for some seconds before he realised that the man had not moved.

Denham stretched out his hand. The coat was one of those smooth, almost seamless American waterproofs, yellowish outside and green inside; and for some reason the man was now wearing it inside out. Denham was in the act of telling him this when the head lolled, the smooth oilskin gleamed again, and he saw that the man was dead.

Tom Evans, stepping out of the lift at a quarter past one, found the hall of the second floor in complete darkness. When he had turned on the lights from a switch beside the lift, he stopped short and swore.

Evans, lean and swarthy, with darkish eyebrows merging into a single line across his forehead, looked a little like a Norman baron in a romance. Some might have said a robber baron, for he carried a briefcase and was a stern man of business despite his youth. But what he saw now made him momentarily forget his evening's work. The hall showed four doors, with their microscopic black numbers, set some distance apart. Near the door leading to Anita Bruce's flat, Ronald Denham sat hunched on an oak settle. There was a lump at the base of his skull and he was breathing in a way Evans did not like.

It was five minutes more before Denham had been whacked and pounded into semi-consciousness; and to such a blinding headache that its pain helped to revive him. First he became aware of Tom's lean, hook-nosed face bending over him, and Tom's usual fluency at preaching.

"I don't mind you getting drunk," the voice came to him dimly. "In fact, I expected it. But at least you ought to be able to carry your liquor decently. What the devil have you been up to, anyway? Hoy!"

"He had his raincoat on inside out," was the first thing Denham said. Then memory came back to him like a new headache or a new explosion, and he began to pour out the story.

"—and I tell you there's a dead man in one of those flats! I think he's been murdered. Tom, I'm not drunk; I swear I'm not. Somebody sneaked up behind and bashed me over the back of the head just after I found him."

"Then how did you get out here?"

"Oh, God, how should I know? Don't argue; help me up. I suppose I must have been dragged out here. If you don't believe me, feel the back of my head. Just feel it."

Evans hesitated. He was always practical, and there could be no denying the bruise. He looked uncertainly up and down the hall.

"But who is this dead man?" he demanded. "And whose flat is he in?"

"I don't know. It was an oldish man with thick glasses and a green raincoat. I never saw him before. Looked a bit like an American, somehow."

"Nonsense! Nobody wears a green raincoat."

"I'm telling you, he was wearing it inside out. If you ask me why, I'm going to bat my head against the wall and go to sleep again." He wished he could do this, for he could not see straight and his head felt like a printing-press in full blast. "We ought to be able to identify the flat easily enough. I can give a complete description of it—"

He paused, for two doors had opened simultaneously in the hall. Anita Bruce and Sir Rufus Armingdale came out, in different stages of anger or curiosity at the noise.

If Evans had been more of a psychologist, he might have anticipated the effect this would have on them. As it was, he stood looking from one to the other, thinking whatever thoughts you care to attribute to him. For he was an employee of Sir Rufus, as manager of the Sloane Square office of Armingdale Flats, and he could risk no trouble.

Anita seemed to take in the situation at a glance. She was small, dark, plump, and fluffy-haired. She was wearing a négligée and smoking a cigarette. Seeing the expressions of the other three, she removed the cigarette from her mouth in order to smile. Sir Rufus Armingdale did not look so much formidable as fretful. He had one of those powerful faces whose features seem to have run together like a bull-pup's. But the old dressing-gown, fastened up at the throat as though he were cold, took away the suggestion of an autocrat and made him only a householder.

He breathed through his nose, rather helplessly, until he saw an employee. His confidence returned.

"Good morning, Evans," he said. "What's the meaning of this?"

Evans risked it. "I'm afraid it's trouble, sir. Mr. Denham—well, he's found a dead man in one of the flats."

"Ron!" cried Anita.

"A dead man," reported Armingdale, without surprise. "Where?"

"In one of the flats. He doesn't know which."

"Oh? Why doesn't he know which?"

"He's got a frightful bump on the back of his head," said Anita, exploring. She looked back over her shoulder and spoke swiftly. "It's quite all right, Tom. Don't get excited. He's d-r-u-n-k."

"I am not drunk," said Denham, with tense and sinister calmness. "May I also point out that I am able to read and write, and that I have not had words spelled out in front of me since I was four years old? Heaven give me s-t-r-e-n-g-t-h! I tell you, I can describe the place."

He did so. Afterwards there was a silence. Anita, her eyes shining curiously, dropped her cigarette on the autocrat's hardwood floor and ground it out. The autocrat seemed too abstracted to notice.

"Ron, old dear," Anita said, going over and sitting down beside him, "I'll believe you if you're as serious as all that, but you ought to know it isn't *my* flat."

"And I can tell you it isn't mine," grunted Armingdale. "There certainly isn't a dead man in it. I've just come from there, and I know."

If they had not known Armingdale's reputation so well, they might have suspected him of trying to make a joke. But his expression belied it as well. It was heavy and lowering, with more than a suggestion of the bull-pup.

"This picture you say you saw," he began. "The one over the side-board. Could you describe it?"

"Yes, I think so," said Denham desperately. "It was a rather small portrait of a little girl looking sideways over some roses, or flowers of some kind. Done in that greyish-brown stuff; I think they call it sepia."

Armingdale stared at him.

"Then I know it isn't mine," he said. "I never owned a sepia drawing in my life. If this young man is telling the truth, there's only one flat left. I think I shall just take the responsibility of knocking, and—"

His worried gaze moved down towards the door of the flat occupied by Mr. Hubert Conyers, of the *Daily Record*. But it was unnecessary to knock at the door. It opened with such celerity that Denham wondered whether anyone had been looking at them through the slot of the letter-box; and Hubert Conyers stepped out briskly. He was an unobtrusive, sandy-haired little man, very different from Denham's idea of a journalist. His only extravagance was a taste for blended shadings in his clothes, from suit to shirt to necktie; though he usually contrived to look rumpled. He was always obliging, and as busy as a parlour clock. But his manner had a subdued persuasiveness which could worm him through narrower places than you might have imagined.

He came forward drawing on his coat, and with a deft gesture he got into the middle of the group.

"Sorry, sorry, sorry," he began, seeming to propitiate everyone at once. "I couldn't help overhearing, you know. Good evening, Sir Rufus. The fact is, it's not my flat either. Just now, the only ornaments in my sitting-room are a lot of well-filled ashtrays and a bottle of milk. Come and see, if you like."

There was a silence, while Conyers looked anxious.

"But it's got to be somebody's flat!" snapped Sir Rufus Armingdale, with a no-nonsense air. "Stands to reason. A whole confounded sitting-room can't vanish like smoke. Unless—stop a bit—unless Mr. Denham got off at some other floor?"

"I don't know. I may have."

"And I don't mind admitting—" said Armingdale, hesitating as everyone looked at him curiously. The autocrat seemed worried. "Very well. The fact is, *I've* got a picture in my flat something like the one Mr. Denham described. It's Greuze's 'Young Girl with Primroses.' But mine's an oil painting, of course. Mr. Denham is talking about a sepia drawing. That is, if he really saw anything. Does this dead man exist at all?"

Denham's protestations were cut short by the hum of an ascending lift. But it was not the ordinary lift in front of them; it was the service lift at the end of the hall. The door was opened, and the cage grating pulled back, to show the frightened face of the night porter.

"Sir," said Pearson, addressing Armingdale as though he were beginning an oration. "I'm glad to see *you*, sir. You always tell us that if something serious happens we're to come straight to you instead of the manager. Well, I'm afraid this is serious. I—the fact is, I found something in this lift."

Denham felt that they were being haunted by that phrase, "the fact is." Everybody seemed to use it. He recalled a play in which it was maintained that anyone who began a sentence like this was usually telling a lie. But he had not time to think about this, for they had found the elusive dead man.

The unknown lay on his face in one corner of the lift. A light in the roof of the steel cage shone down on his grey felt hat, on an edge of his thick spectacles, and on his oilskin waterproof. But the coat was no longer green, for he was now wearing it right-side-out in the ordinary way.

Anita, who had come quietly round beside Denham, seized his arm. The night porter restrained Tom Evans as the latter bent forward.

"I shouldn't touch him, sir, if I was you. There's blood."

"Where?"

Pearson indicated a stain on the grey-rubber floor. "And if I'm any judge, sir, he died of a stab through the heart. I—I lifted him up a bit. But I don't see any kind of knife that could have done it."

"Is this the man you saw?" Armingdale asked Denham quietly.

Denham nodded. Something tangible, something to weigh and handle, seemed to have brought the force back to Armingdale's personality.

"Except," Denham added, "that he's now wearing his raincoat right-side-out. Why? Will somebody tell me that? Why?"

"Never mind the raincoat," Anita said close to his ear. "Ron, you don't know him, do you? You'll swear you don't know him?"

He was startled. She had spoken without apparent urgency, and so low that the others might not have heard her. But Denham, who knew her so well, knew that there was urgency behind the unwinking seriousness of her eyes. Unconsciously she was shaking his arm.

His wits had begun to clear, despite the pain in his skull; and he wondered.

"No, of course I don't know him. Why should I?"

"Nothing! Nothing at all. Ss-t!"

"Well, I know him," said Hubert Conyers.

Conyers had been squatting down at the edge of the lift, and craning his neck to get a close view of the body without touching it. Now he straightened up. He seemed so excited that he could barely control himself, and his mild eye looked wicked.

"I interviewed him a couple of days ago," said Conyers. "Surely you know him, Sir Rufus?"

"'Surely' is a large word, young man. No, I do not know him. Why?"

"That's Dan Randolph, the American real-estate king," said Conyers, keeping a watchful eye on Armingdale. "All of you will have heard of him: he's the fellow who always deals in spot cash, even if it's a million. I'd know those spectacles anywhere. He's as near-sighted as an owl. Er—am I correctly informed, Sir Rufus, that he was in England to do some business with you?"

Armingdale smiled bleakly. "You have no information, young man," he said. "And so far as I'm concerned you're not getting any. So that's Dan Randolph! I knew he was in England; but he's certainly not made any business proposition to me."

"Maybe he was coming to do it."

"Maybe he was," said Armingdale, with the same air of a parent to a child. He turned to Pearson. "You say you found him in that lift. When did you find him? And how did you come to find him?"

Pearson was voluble. "The lift was on the ground floor, sir. I just happened to glance through the little glass panel, and I see him lying there. So I thought I'd better run the lift up here and get you. As for putting him there—" He pointed to the *recall* button on the wall outside the lift. "Somebody on any floor, sir, could have shoved him in here, and pressed this button, and sent him downstairs. He certainly wasn't put in on the ground floor. Besides, I saw him come into the building tonight."

"Oh?" put in Conyers softly. "When was this?"

"Might have been eleven o'clock, sir."

"Who was he coming to see?"

Pearson shook his head helplessly and with a certain impatience. "These ain't service flats, sir, where you telephone up about every visitor. You ought to know we're not to ask visitors anything unless they seem to need help, or unless it's somebody who has no business here. *I* don't know. He went up in the main lift, that's all I can tell you."

"Well, what floor did he go to?"

"I dunno." Pearson ran a finger under a tight collar. "But excuse me, sir, may I ask a question, if you please? What's wrong exactly?"

"We've lost a room," said Ronald Denham, with inspiration. "Maybe you can help. Look here, Pearson: you've been here in these flats a long time. You've been inside most of them—in the sitting-rooms, for instance?"

"I think I can say I've been in all of 'em, sir."

"Good. Then we're looking for a room decorated like this," said Denham. For the third time he described what he had seen, and Pearson's expression grew to one of acute anguish. At the end of it he shook his head.

"It's nobody's room, sir," the porter answered simply. "There's not a sitting-room like that in the whole building."

At three o'clock in the morning, a sombre group of people sat in Sir Rufus Armingdale's flat, and did not even look at each other. The police work was nearly done. A brisk divisional detective-inspector, accompanied by a sergeant, a photographer, and a large amiable man in a top-hat, had taken a statement from each of those concerned. But the statements revealed nothing.

Denham, in fact, had received only one more mental jolt. Entering Armingdale's flat, he thought for a second that he had found the missing room. The usual chairs of stamped Spanish leather, the refectory table, the carved gewgaws, greeted him like a familiar nightmare. And over the sideboard hung a familiar picture—that of a small girl looking sideways over an armful of roses.

"That's not it!" said Anita quickly.

"It's the same subject, but it's not the same picture. That's in oils. What sort of game do you suppose is going on in this place?"

Anita glanced over her shoulder. She had dressed before the arrival of the police; and also, he thought, she had put on more makeup than was necessary.

"Quick, Ron; before the others get here. Were you telling the truth?"

"Certainly. You don't think—?"

"Oh, I don't know and I don't care; I just want you to tell me. Ron, you didn't kill him yourself?"

He had not even time to answer before she stopped him. Sir Rufus Armingdale, Conyers, and Evans came through from the foyer; and with them was the large amiable man who had accompanied Divisional-Inspector Davidson. His name, it appeared, was Colonel March.

"You see," he explained, with a broad gesture, "I'm not here officially. I happened to be at the theatre, and I dropped in on Inspector Davidson for a talk, and he asked me to come along. So if you don't like any of my questions, just tell me to shut my head. But I do happen to be attached to the Yard—"

"I know you, Colonel," said Conyers, with a crooked grin. "You're the head of the Ragbag Department, D-3. Some call it the Crazy House."

Colonel March nodded seriously. He wore a dark overcoat, and had a top-hat pushed back on his large head; this, with his florid complexion, sandy moustache, and bland blue eye, gave him something of the look of a stout colonel in a comic paper. He was smoking a large-bowled pipe with the effect of seeming to sniff smoke from the bowl rather than draw it through the stem. He appeared to be enjoying himself.

"It's a compliment," he assured them. "After all, somebody has got to sift all the queer complaints. If somebody comes in and reports (say) that the Borough of Stepney is being terrorised by a blue pig, I've got to decide whether it's a piece of lunacy, or a mistake, or a hoax, or a serious crime. Otherwise good men would only waste their time. You'd be surprised how many such complaints there are. But I was thinking, and so was Inspector Davidson, that you had a very similar situation here. If you wouldn't mind a few extra questions—"

"As many as you like," said Sir Rufus Armingdale. "Provided somebody's got a hope of solving this damned—"

"As a matter of fact," said Colonel March, frowning, "Inspector Davidson has reason to believe that it is already solved. A good man, Davidson."

There was a silence. Something unintentionally sinister seemed to have gathered in Colonel March's affable tone. For a moment nobody dared to ask him what he meant.

"Already solved?" repeated Hubert Conyers.

"Suppose we begin with you, Sir Rufus," said March with great courtesy. "You have told the inspector that you did not know Daniel Randolph personally. But it seems to be common knowledge that he was in England to see you."

Armingdale hesitated. "I don't know his reasons. He may have been here to see me, among other things. Probably was. He wrote to me about it from America. But he hasn't approached me yet, and I didn't approach him first. It's bad business."

"What was the nature of this business, Sir Rufus?"

"He wanted to buy an option I held on some property in—never mind where. I'll tell you in private, if you insist."

"Was a large sum involved?"

Armingdale seemed to struggle with himself. "Four thousand, more or less."

"So it wasn't a major business deal. Were you going to sell?"

"Probably."

Colonel March's abstracted eye wandered to the picture over the sideboard. "Now, Sir Rufus, that Greuze, 'Young Girl with Primroses.' I think it was recently reproduced, in its natural size, as a full-page illustration in the *Metropolitan Illustrated News*?"

"Yes, it was," said Armingdale. He added: "In—sepia."

Something about this afterthought made them all move forward to look at him. It was like the puzzle of a half-truth: nobody knew what it meant.

"Exactly. Just two more questions. I believe that each of these flats communicates with a fire-escape leading down into the mews behind?"

"Yes. What of it?"

"Will the same key open the front door of each of the flats?"

"No, certainly not. All the lock-patterns are different."

"Thank you. Now, Mr. Conyers—a question for you. Are you married?"

Hitherto Conyers had been regarding him with a look of watchful expectancy, like an urchin about to smash a window and run. Now he scowled.

"Married? No."

"And you don't keep a valet?"

"The answer to that, Colonel, is loud and prolonged laughter. Honestly, I don't like your 'social' manner. Beston, our crime news man, knows you. And it's always, 'Blast you, Beston, if you print one hint about the Thing-gummy case I'll have your hide.' What difference does it make whether I'm married or not, or whether I have a valet or not?"

"A great deal," said March seriously. "Now, Miss Bruce. What is your occupation, Miss Bruce?"

"I'm an interior decorator," answered Anita. She began to laugh. It may have been with a tinge of hysteria; but she sat back in a tall chair and laughed until there were tears in her eyes.

"I'm terribly sorry," she went on, holding out her hand as though to stop them, "but don't you see? The murder was done by an interior decorator. That's the whole secret."

Colonel March cut short Armingdale's shocked protest.

"Go on," he said sharply.

"I thought of it first off. Of course there's no 'vanishing room.' Some sitting-room has just been redecorated. All the actual furnishings, tables and chairs and sideboards, are just the same in every room. The only way you can tell them apart is by small movable things—pictures, lampshades, bookends—which could be changed in a few minutes.

"Ron accidentally walked into the murderer's flat just after the murderer had killed the old man. That put the murderer in a pretty awful position. Unless he killed Ron too, he was caught with the body and Ron could identify his flat. But he thought of a better way. He sent that man's body down in the lift and dragged Ron out into the hall. Then he simply altered the decorations of his flat. Afterwards he could sit down and dare anyone to identify it as the place where the body had been."

Anita's face was flushed with either defiance or fear.

"Warm," said Colonel March. "Unquestionably warm. That is why I was wondering whether you couldn't tell us what really happened."

"I don't understand you."

"Well, there are objections to the redecoration. You've got to suppose that nobody had ever been in the flat before and seen the way it was originally decorated. You've also got to suppose that the murderer could find a new set of lampshades, pictures, and book-ends in the middle of the night—Haven't you got it the wrong way round?"

"The wrong way round?"

"Somebody," said March, dropping his courtesy, "prepared a dummy room to begin with. He put in the new lampshades, the bookends, the copy of a well-known picture, even a set of new curtains. He entertained Randolph there. Afterwards, of course, he simply removed the knick-knacks and set the place right again. But it was the dummy room into which Ronald Denham walked. That, Mr. Denham, was why you did not recognise—"

"Recognise what?" roared Denham. "Where was I?"

"In the sitting-room of your own flat," said Colonel March gravely. "If you had been sober you might have made a mistake; but you were so full of champagne that your instinct brought you home after all."

There were two doors in the room, and the blue uniform of a policeman appeared in each. At March's signal, Inspector Davidson stepped forward. He said:

"Thomas Evans, I arrest you for the murder of Daniel Randolph. I have to warn you that anything you say will be taken down in writing and may be used in evidence at your trial."

"Oh, look here," protested Colonel March, when they met in Armingdale's flat next day, "the thing was simple enough. We had twice as much trouble over that kid in Bayswater who pinched all the oranges. And you had all the facts.

"Evans, as one of Sir Rufus's most highly placed and trusted employees, was naturally in a position to know all about the projected business deal with Randolph. And so he planned an ingenious swindle. A swindle, I am certain, was all he intended.

"Now you, Sir Rufus, had intended to go to Manchester yesterday afternoon, and remain there for a week. (Mr. Denham heard that from the night-porter, when he was advised against singing.) That would leave your flat empty. Evans telephoned to Randolph, posing as you. He asked Randolph to come round to your flat at eleven o'clock at night, and settle the deal. He added that you *might* be called away to Manchester; but, in that event, his secretary would have the necessary papers ready and signed.

"It would have been easy. Evans would get into your empty flat by way of the fire-escape and the window. He would pose as your secretary. Randolph—who, remember, always paid spot cash even if it involved a million—would hand over a packet of banknotes for a forged document.

"Why should Randolph be suspicious of anything? He knew, as half the newspaper-reading world knows, that Sir Rufus lived on the second floor of Medici Court. He had seen photographs of Sir Rufus with his favourite Greuze over the sideboard. Even if he asked the hall porter for directions, he would be sent to the right flat. Even if the hall-porter said Sir Rufus was in Manchester, the ground had been prepared and Randolph would ask for Sir Rufus's secretary.

"Unfortunately, a hitch occurred. Sir Rufus decided not to go to Manchester. He decided it yesterday afternoon, after all Evans's plans had been made and Randolph was due to arrive. But Evans needed that money; as we have discovered today, he needed it desperately. He wanted that four thousand pounds.

"So he hit on another plan. Sir Rufus would he at home and his flat could not be used. But, with all the rooms exactly alike except for decorations, why not an *imitation* of Sir Rufus's flat? The same plan would hold good, except that Randolph would be taken to the wrong place. He would come up in the lift at eleven. Evans would be waiting with the door of the flat open, and would take him to a place superficially resembling Sir Rufus's. The numbers on the doors are very small; and Randolph, as we know, was so near-sighted as to be almost blind. If Evans adopted some disguise, however clumsy, he could never afterwards be identified as the man who swindled Randolph. And he ran no risk in using the flat he shared with Denham."

Anita interposed. "Of course!" she said. "Ron was at a bachelor party, and ordinarily it would have kept him there whooping until two or three o'clock in the morning. But he reformed, and came home early."

Denham groaned. "But I still can't believe it," he insisted. "Tom Evans? A murderer?"

"He intended no murder," said Colonel March. "But, you see, Randolph suspected something. Randolph showed that he suspected. And Evans, as a practical man, had to kill him. You can guess why Randolph suspected?"

"Well?"

"Because Evans is colour-blind," said Colonel March.

"It's too bad," Colonel March went on sadly, "but the crime was from the first the work of a colour-blind man. Now, none of the rest of you could qualify for that deficiency. As for Sir Rufus, I can think of nothing more improbable than a colour-blind art-collector—unless it is a colour-blind interior decorator. Mr. Conyers here shows by the blended hues of brown or blue in his suits, shirts, and ties that he has a fine eye for colour effect; and he possesses no wife or valet to choose them for him.

"But Evans? He is not only partially but wholly colour-blind. You gave us a spirited account of it. Randolph's body was sent up in the lift by Pearson. When Evans stepped forward, Pearson warned him not to touch the body, saying that there was blood. Evans said: 'Where?'— though he was staring straight down in a small, brightly lighted lift at a red bloodstain on a grey-rubber floor. Red on any surface except green or yellow is absolutely invisible to colour-blind men.

"That was also the reason why Randolph's waterproof was put on inside out. Randolph had removed his hat and coat when he first came into the flat. After Evans had stabbed him with a clasp-knife, Evans put the hat and coat back on the body previous to disposing of it. But he could not distinguish between the yellow outside and the green inside of that seamless oilskin.

"You, Mr. Denham, let yourself into the flat with your own key: which in itself told us the location of the 'vanished' room, for no two keys are alike. I also think that Miss Bruce could have told us all along where the 'vanished' room was. I am inclined to suspect she saw Randolph going into your flat, and was afraid that you might be concerned in the murder."

"Oh, well," said Anita philosophically.

"Anyway, you spoke to a corpse about his coat being inside out; and Evans rectified the error before he put the body in the lift. He had to knock you out, of course. But he genuinely didn't want to hurt you. He left the building by way of the fire-escape into the mews. He disposed of his stage-properties, though he was foolish enough to keep the money and the clasp-knife on his person, where they were found when we searched him. When he came back here, he used the main lift in the ordinary way as though he were returning from his office. And he was genuinely concerned when he found you still unconscious on the bench in the hall."

There was a silence, broken by Armingdale's snort.

"But colour-blindness! What's that got to do with the solution? How did you come to think the murderer must have been colour-blind to begin with?"

Colonel March turned to stare at him. Then he shook his head, with a slow and dismal smile.

"Don't you see it even yet?" he asked. "That was the starting-point. We suspected it for the same reason Randolph suspected an imposture. Poor old Randolph wasn't an art-critic. Any sort of coloured daub, in the ordinary way, he would have swallowed as the original 'Young Girl with Primroses' he expected to see. But Evans didn't allow for the one thing even a near-sighted man does know: colour. In his effort to imitate the decorations of Sir Rufus's flat, the fool hung up as an oil-painting nothing more than a sepia reproduction out of an illustrated weekly."

Dr. Gideon Fell in

THE LOCKED ROOM

John Dickson Carr

John Dickson Carr based the appearance of his principal detective, Dr. Gideon Fell, on that of his literary idol G. K. Chesterton. Fell's long career began with *Hag's Nook* in 1933 and continued until *Dark of the Moon*, thirty-four years later. His status as the most gifted solver of locked room mysteries was underlined by his famous (and fascinating) "Locked Room Lecture", which occupies a chapter in Carr's *The Hollow Man* aka *The Three Coffins*, regarded by many as the finest impossible crime story ever written. But his expertise isn't confined to crime; at one dinner he discusses "the origins of the Christmas cracker, Sir Richard Steele, merry-go-rounds—on which he particularly enjoyed riding—Beowulf, Buddhism, Thomas Henry Huxley, and Miss Greta Garbo."

Over the years he appeared in several radio plays and five short stories, published between 1936 and 1957. This story was first published in the *Strand Magazine* in July 1940. As Carr's biographer Douglas Greene has pointed out, when the Second World War was declared, Carr—who was travelling from Britain to his native United States—returned back to England, immediately, a kind of gallantry not matched by Francis Seton in this story.

YOU MAY HAVE READ THE FACTS. FRANCIS SETON WAS FOUND lying on the floor behind his desk, near death from a fractured skull. He had been struck three times across the back of the head with a piece of lead-loaded broom-handle. His safe had been robbed. His body was found by his secretary typist, Iris Lane, and his librarian, Harold Mills, who were, in the polite newspaper phrase, "being questioned."

So far, it seems commonplace. Nothing in that account shows why Superintendent Hadley of the C.I.D. nearly went mad, or why ten o'clock of a fine June morning found him punching at the doorbell of Dr. Gideon Fell's house in Chelsea.

Summer touched the old houses with grace. There was a smoky sparkle on the river, and on the flower-veined green of the Embankment gardens. Upstairs, in the library, with its long windows, Superintendent Hadley found the learned doctor smoking a cigar and reading a magazine.

Dr. Fell's bulk overflowed from a chair nearly large enough to accommodate him. A chuckle animated his several chins, and ran down over the ridges of his waistcoat. He peered up at Hadley over his eyeglasses; his cheeks shone, pinkly transparent, with warmth of welcome. But at Hadley's first words a disconsolate expression drew down the corners of his moustache.

"Seton's conscious," said Hadley. "I've just been talking to him."

Dr. Fell grunted. Reluctantly he put aside the magazine.

"Ah," he said. "And Seton denies the story told by the secretary and the librarian?"

"No. He confirms it."

"In every detail?"

"In every detail."

Dr. Fell puffed out his cheeks. He also took several violent puffs at the cigar, staring at it in a somewhat cross-eyed fashion. His big voice was subdued.

"Do you know, Hadley," he muttered, "I rather expected that."

"I didn't," snapped Hadley. "I didn't; and I don't. But that's why I'm here. You must have some theory about this impossible burglar who nearly bashed a man's head off and then disappeared like smoke. My forthright theory is that Iris Lane and Harold Mills are lying. If... hullo!"

Standing by the window, he broke off and glanced down into the street. His gesture was so urgent that Dr. Fell, with much labour, hoisted himself up wheezily from the chair and lumbered over to the window.

Clear in the strong sunshine, a girl in a white frock was standing on the opposite pavement, by the railings, and peering up at the window. As Dr. Fell threw back the curtains she looked straight into their eyes.

She was what is called an outdoor girl, with a sturdy and well-shaped body, and a square but very attractive face. Her dark-brown hair hung in a long bob. She had light-hazel eyes in a tanned, earnest face. Her mouth might have been too broad, but she showed fine teeth when she laughed. If she was not exactly pretty, health and vigour gave her a strong attractiveness which was better than that.

"Iris Lane," said Hadley ventriloquially.

Dr. Fell, in an absent-minded way, was startled. He would have expected Francis Seton's typist to be either prim or mousy.

When she saw the two men at the window, Iris Lane's expressive face showed many things. Disappointment, surprise, even fear. Her knee moved as though she were about to stamp angrily on the pavement. For a second they thought she would turn and hurry. Then she seemed to come to a decision. She almost ran across the street toward the house.

"Now what do you suppose—?" Hadley was speculating when the doctor cut him short.

"She wants to see me, confound you," he roared. "Or she did want to see me, until you nearly scared her off."

And the girl herself confirmed it a moment later. She was making an attempt to be calm and even jaunty, but her eyes always moved back to Hadley.

"It seems," she said, after a quick look round the room, "that I'm always trailing the Superintendent. Or he's always trailing me. I don't know which."

Hadley nodded. He was noncommittal.

"It does seem like that, Miss Lane. Anything in particular on your mind now?"

"Yes. I—I wanted to talk to Dr. Fell. Alone."

"Oh? Why?"

"Because it's my last hope," answered the girl, raising her head. "Because they say nobody, not even a stray dog, is ever turned away from here."

"Nonsense!" said Dr. Fell, hugely delighted nevertheless. He covered this with deprecating noises which shook the chandelier, and an offer of refreshment. Hadley saw that the old man was half hooked already, and Hadley despaired.

Yet it seemed impossible to doubt this girl's sincerity. She sat bolt upright in the chair, opening and shutting the catch of a white handbag.

"It's quite simple," she explained, and hunched her shoulders. "Harold Mills and I were alone in the house with Mr. Seton. There was nearly three thousand pounds in the safe in his study."

Dr. Fell frowned.

"So? As much money as that?"

"Mr. Seton was leaving," said Iris Lane, with an effort. "He was going abroad, to spend a year in California. He always made his decisions suddenly—just like that." She snapped her fingers. "We didn't know anything about it, Harold and I, until he broke the news that morning. The man from the bank brought the money round; Mr. Seton put it into the safe, and told us why he had sent for it. That meant we were out of our jobs."

And she began to tell the story.

Of course (Iris admitted to herself), her nerves had been on edge that night. It was caused partly by losing a good job at a moment's notice, partly by the thick and thundery weather round the old house in Kensington, and partly by the personality of Francis Seton himself.

Francis Seton was a book-collector. When Iris had first answered his advertisement for a secretary-typist, she had expected to find someone thin and ancient, with double-lensed spectacles. Instead she found a thickset bull of a man, with sandy hair and a blue guileless eye. His energy was prodigious. He animated the old house like a humming-top. He had the genuine collector's passion; he was generous, and considerate when it did not inconvenience him.

But he whirled off at a new tangent that morning, a hot overcast day, when he called Iris Lane and Harold Mills into his study. They had been working in the long library on the first floor. The study, which opened out of it, was a large room with two windows overlooking a tangled back garden.

Seton stood by the big flat-topped desk in the middle of the study. Out of a canvas bag he was emptying thick packets of banknotes, one of which fell into the waste-paper basket.

"Look here," he said, with the confiding candour of a child. "I'm off to America. For a year at least."

(He seemed pleased at the way his hearers jumped.)

"But, sir—" began Harold Mills.

"Crisis!" said Seton, pointing to a newspaper. "Crisis!" he added, pointing to another. "I'm sick of crises. California's the place for me. Orange groves and sea breezes: at least, that's what the booklets say. Besides, I want to make old Isaacson sick with my 1593 *Venus and Adonis* and the 1623 folio."

His forehead grew lowering and embarrassed.

"I've got to let you both go," he growled. "I'd like to take you both with me. Can't afford it. Sorry; but there it is. I'll give you a month's salary in place of notice. Damn it, I'll give you *two* month's salary in place of notice. How's that?"

Beaming with relief now that this was off his chest, he dismissed the subject briskly. He gathered up the packets of banknotes, fishing the dropped one out of the waste-paper basket. It made his face crimson to bend over, since Dr. Woodhall had warned him about high blood pressure; but he was all energy again.

A little iron safe stood against one wall. Seton opened it with his key, poured the money into a tin box, closed the safe, and locked it. In a vague way Iris noted the denominations on the paper bands round the packets of notes. A little treasure-trove. Almost a little fortune.

Perhaps because of the heat of the day, there was perspiration on Harold Mills's forehead.

"And when do you want to leave, sir?" he asked.

"Leave? Oh, ah." Seton considered. Day after tomorrow, he decided.

"Day after tomorrow!"

"Saturday," Seton explained. "Always a good ship leaving. Yes, make it Saturday."

"But your passport—" protested Iris.

"That's completely in order," said Seton cooly.

The word which flashed through Iris Lane's mind just then was "robbed". She could not help it. There are times with everyone when the sight of so much money, all in a lump, makes the fingers itch and brings fantastic dreams of what might be.

She didn't mean it—as she was later to explain to the police. But there was a tantalising quality in what had happened. Only yesterday she had been safe. Only a week ago she had returned from a holiday in Cornwall, where there had been little to do except lie on lemon-coloured sands in a lemon-coloured bathing-suit; or feel the contrast between sun on baking shoulders and salt water foaming and slipping past her body, in the cold invigoration of the sea. The future would take care of itself.

And more. There was a pleasant-looking man, just on the right side of middle age, who came to do sketches at the beach. They were such intolerably bad sketches that Iris was relieved to discover he was a doctor from London.

By coincidence, a breeze blew one of the sketches past her, and she retrieved it. So they fell into conversation. By coincidence, it developed that the man's name was Charles Woodhall; and that he was Francis Seton's doctor. It astounded Iris, who saw in this a good omen of summer magic. She liked Dr. Woodhall. He was as good a talker as Seton himself, without Seton's untiring bounce. And he knew when to be comfortably silent.

Dr. Woodhall would sit on a camp-stool, attired in ancient flannels, tennis shoes, and shirt, and draw endless sketches of Iris. A cigarette would hang from the corner of his mouth. He would blink as smoke got into one eye, and amusement wrinkles deepened from the corners of his eyes almost back to temples that were slightly grey. Meantime, he talked, he talked happily of all things in earth and sky and sea. He also offered a profound apology for the bad sketches. But Iris, though she secretly agreed with him, kept them all; and so passed the fortnight.

They would meet again in London.

And she had a good job to go back to there.

All the future looked pleasant—until Francis Seton exploded every-thing that morning.

The thunderstorm, which had been imminent all day, broke late in the afternoon.

It brought little relief to Iris. She and Harold Mills went on with their work and were still working long after dinner, in the library under the shaded lamps and the rows of books behind their wire cages. It was a rich room, deep-carpeted like every other room in the house; but it was tainted with damp. Iris's head ached. She had sent off two dozen letters, and arranged every detail of Seton's trip: all he had to do now was pack his bag. Seton himself was in the study, with the door closed between, cleaning out the litter in his desk.

Harold Mills put down his pen.

"Iris," he said softly.

"Yes?"

Mills glanced toward the closed door of the study, and spoke still more softly.

"I want to ask you something."

"Of course."

She was surprised at his tone. He was sitting at his own writing-table, some distance away from her, with a table lamp burning at his left. The light of the lamp shone on his flat fair hair, brushed with great precision round his head, on his waxy-coloured face, and on his pince-nez. Since he was very young, it was only this pince-nez which gave him the sedate and donnish appearance; this, or the occasional slight fidgeting of his hands.

He almost blurted out the next words.

"What I mean is: are you all right? Financially, I mean?"

"Oh, yes."

She didn't know. She was not even thinking of this now. Dr. Woodhall had promised to drop in that evening, to see Seton. It was nearly eleven now. Seton, who always swore that his immense vitality was due to the regularity of his habits, was as regular as that clock over the mantelpiece. At eleven o'clock he would smoke the last of the ten cigarettes allowed him a day, drink his one whisky and soda, and be in bed by eleven-thirty sharp. If Dr. Woodhall didn't hurry…

Iris's head ached still more. Mills kept on talking, but she did not hear him. She awoke to this with a start.

"I'm sorry. I'm afraid I didn't catch—?"

"I said," repeated the other, somewhat jerkily, "that I'm sorry for more reasons than one that we're leaving."

"So am I, Harold."

"You don't understand. Mine is rather a specialised job. I'll not get another in a hurry." Colour came up under his pince-nez. "No, no, that isn't what I mean. I'm not complaining. It's very decent of Seton to provide two months' salary. But I'd hoped that this job would be more or less permanent. If it turned out to be that, there was something I wanted to do."

"What was that?"

"I wanted to ask you to marry me," said Mills.

There was a silence.

She stared back at him. She had never thought of him as awkward or tongue-tied, or anything like the man who now sat and cracked the joints of his knuckles as though he could not sit still. In fact, she had hardly ever thought of him at all. And his face showed that he knew it.

"Please don't say anything." He got to his feet. "I don't want you to feel you've got to say anything." He began to pace the room with little short steps. "I haven't been exactly—attentive."

"You never even…"

He gestured.

"Yes, I know. I'm not like that. I can't be. I wish I could." He stopped his pacing. "This fellow Woodhall, now."

"What about Dr. Woodhall?"

He never got the opportunity to say. This was the point at which they heard, very distinctly, the noise from the next room.

When they tried to describe it afterward, neither could be sure whether it was a yell, or a groan, or the beginning of incoherent words. It might have been a combination of all three. Then there were several soft little thuds, like the sound of a butcher's cleaver across meat on the chopping block. Then silence, except for the distant whisper of the rain.

That was the story which Iris Lane began to tell at Dr. Fell's flat. Both Dr. Fell and Superintendent Hadley listened with the closest attention, though they had heard it several times before.

"We didn't know what had happened," said Iris, moving her shoulders. "We called out to Mr. Seton, but he didn't answer. We tried the door, but it wouldn't open."

"Was it locked?"

"No; it was warped. The damp from the rain had swollen and warped the wood. Harold tried to get it open, but it wouldn't work until he finally took a run and jumped at it."

"There was nobody in the study except Mr. Seton," she went on. "I know, because I was afraid we should see someone. The place was brilliantly lighted. There's a big bronze chandelier, with electric candles, hanging over the flat-topped desk in the middle. And there was even a light burning in the cloakroom—it's hardly more than a cupboard for a washbasin, really—which opens out of the study. You could see everything at a glance. And there wasn't anybody hiding in the room."

She paused, visualising the scene.

Francis Seton lay on the far side of the desk, between the desk and the windows. He was unconscious, with blood coming out of his nostrils.

His cigarette, put down on the edge of the desk, was now scorching the mahogany with an acrid smell. The desk chair and a little table had been overturned. There was a stain on the thick grey carpet where his glass had been upset, together with a stoppered decanter which had not spilt, and a siphon enclosed in metal crossbands. Seton was moaning. When they turned him over on his side, they found the weapon.

"It was that hollow wooden thing with lead inside," said Iris. She saw it as vividly as though it lay on the carpet now.

"Only six or seven inches long, but it weighed nearly a pound. Harold, who'd started to study medicine once, put his fingers down and felt round the back of Mr. Seton's head. Then he said I'd better hurry and phone for a proper doctor.

"I had backed away against the windows—I remember that. The curtains weren't quite drawn. I could hear the rain hitting the windows behind me. I looked round, because I was afraid there might be somebody hiding in the curtains. We pulled the curtains back on both windows. Then we saw the edge of the ladder. It had been propped up against the right-hand window, from the garden below. And I noticed something else that I'll swear to, and swear to, and go on swearing to until you believe me. But never mind what it was, for a minute.

"I ran out to phone for Dr. Woodhall, but it wasn't necessary. I met him coming up the stairs in the front hall."

There were several things she did not tell here.

She did not say how heartening it was to see Dr. Woodhall's shrewd, humorous face looking at her from under the brim of a sodden hat. He wore a dripping mackintosh with the collar turned up, and carried his medicine case.

"I don't know how he got in," Iris went on. "Mr. Seton had dismissed the servants after dinner. The front door must have been unlocked. Anyway, he said, 'Hullo; is anything wrong?' I think I said, 'Come up quickly; something terrible has happened.' He didn't make any comment. But when he had examined Mr. Seton he said it was concussion of the brain all right, from several powerful blows. I asked whether I should phone for an ambulance. He said Mr. Seton wasn't in shape to be moved, and that we should have to get him to bed in the house.

"When we were carrying him to his bedroom, things started to fall out of his pockets. The key to the safe wasn't there: it had been torn loose from the other end of his watch-chain. And he kept on moaning.

"You know the rest. The safe had been robbed, not only of the money, but of two valuable folios. Apparently it was all plain sailing. There was the ladder propped against the window-sill outside. There were scuffed footprints in a flower bed below. It was a burglar. It must have been a burglar. Only—" She paused, clearing her throat. "Only," she went on. *"both those windows were locked on the inside."*

Dr. Fell grunted.

Something in this recital had interested him very much. He drew in several of his chins, and exchanged a glance with Superintendent Hadley.

"Both the windows," he rumbled, "were locked on the inside. You're quite sure of that? Hey?"

"I'm absolutely positive."

"You couldn't have been mistaken?"

"I only wish I could have," said Iris helplessly. "And you know what they think, don't you? They think Harold and I caught him and beat his head in.

"It's so awfully easy to think that. Harold and I were alone in the house. We were sitting outside the only door to the study. There was no intruder anywhere. Both the study windows were locked on the inside. It—well, it just couldn't have been anybody else but us. Only it wasn't. That's all I can tell you."

Dr. Fell opened his eyes.

"But, my dear young lady," he protested, blowing sparks from his cigar like the Spirit of the Volcano, "whatever else they think about you, I presume they don't think you are raving made? Suppose you had faked this burglary? Suppose you had planted the ladder against the window? Would you and Mills then go about swearing the windows were locked in order to prove that your story couldn't be true?"

"Just a moment," said Superintendent Hadley sharply.

Hadley was beaten, and he knew it. But he was fair.

"I'll be frank with you, Miss Lane," he went on. "Before you came in, I was telling Dr. Fell that Mr. Seton is conscious. He's talked to me. And—"

"And?"

"Mr. Seton," said Hadley, "confirms your story in every detail. He clears you and Mills of any complicity in the crime."

Iris said nothing. All the same, they saw her face grow white under its tan.

"He says," pursued Hadley, in the midst of a vast silence, "that he was sitting at his desk, facing the door to the library. He swears he could hear you and Mills talking in the library. His back, of course, was toward the windows. He agrees that the windows were locked, since he had just locked them himself. At a few minutes past eleven, he heard a footstep behind him. A 'shuffling' footstep. Just as he started to get up, something smashed him across the head, and that's all he remembers. So it seems you were telling the truth."

"H'mf," said Dr. Fell.

Iris stared at Hadley. "Then I'm not—you're not going to arrest me?"

"Frankly," snapped the Superintendent, "no. I'm sorry to say I don't see how we can arrest anybody. The windows were locked. The door was watched. There was nobody hidden in the room. Yet someone, by the victim's own testimony, did get in and cosh Seton. We've got a blooming miracle, that's what we've got; and, if you don't believe me, come along and talk to Seton for yourself."

Francis Seton lived, and nearly died, in the grand manner. His bedroom was furnished in the heavy, dark and florid style of the Second French Empire, with a four-poster bed. He lay propped up with his neck above the pillows, glowering out of a helmet of bandages.

"Time's nearly up," warned Dr. Charles Woodhall, who stood at one side of the bed. His fingers were on Seton's wrist, but Seton snatched the wrist away.

Superintendent Hadley was patient.

"What I'm trying to get at, Mr. Seton, is this. When did you lock those two windows?"

"Told you that already," said Seton. "About ten minutes before that fellow sneaked up and hit me."

"But you didn't catch a glimpse of the person who hit you?"

"No, worse luck. Or I'd have—"

"Yes. But *why* did you lock the windows?"

"Because I'd noticed the ladder outside. Couldn't have burglars getting in, could I?"

"You didn't try to find out who put the ladder there?"

"No. I couldn't be bothered."

"At the same time, you were a little nervous?"

For some time Iris Lane had the impression that Seton, if it were not for his injury, would have rolled over on his side, buried his face in the pillows, and groaned with impatience. But the last question stung him to wrath.

"Who says I was nervous? Nervous! I'm the last man in the world to be nervous. I haven't got a nerve in my body." He appealed to Dr. Woodhall and to Harold Mills. "Have I?"

"You've got an exceptionally strong constitution," replied Dr. Woodhall blandly.

Seton appeared to scent evasion here. His bloodshot eyes rolled, without a turn of his neck, from Woodhall to Mills; but they came back to Hadley.

"Well? Anything else you want to know?"

"Just one more question, Mr. Seton. Are you sure there was nobody hidden in the study or the cloakroom before you were attacked?"

"Dead certain."

Hadley shut up his notebook.

"Then that's all, sir. Nobody hidden, before or after. Windows locked, before and after. I don't believe in ghosts, and so the thing's impossible." He spoke quietly. "Excuse me, Mr. Seton, but are you sure you were attacked after all?"

"And excuse *me*," interrupted a new voice, thunderous but apologetic.

Dr. Fell, whose presence was somewhat less conspicuous than a captive balloon, had not removed his disreputable slouch hat: a breach of good manners which ordinarily he would have deplored. But his manner had a vast eagerness, like Old King Cole in a hurry. Iris Lane could not remember having seen him for some minutes. He lumbered in at the doorway, with one hand holding an object wrapped in newspaper and the other supporting himself on his crutch-handled stick.

"Sir," he intoned, addressing Seton, "I should regret it very much if my friend Hadley gave you an apoplectic stroke. It is therefore only fair to tell you that you were attacked, and very thoroughly battered about the head, by one of the persons in this room. I am also glad the police have kept your study locked up since then."

There was a silence as sudden as that which follows a loud noise.

From the newspaper Dr. Fell took out a soda-water siphon, and put it down with a thump on the centre table. It was a large siphon, bound round with metal bands in a diamond design.

And Dr. Fell reared up.

"Dash it, Hadley," he complained, "why couldn't you have told me about the siphon? Ten days in a spiritual abyss; and all because you couldn't tell me about the siphon! It took the young lady to do that."

"But I did tell you about a siphon," said Hadley. "I've told you about it a dozen times!"

"No, no, no," insisted Dr. Fell dismally. "You said 'a' siphon. Presumably an ordinary siphon, the unending white bulwark of the English pub. You didn't say it was this particular kind of siphon."

"But what the devil has the siphon got to do with it anyway?" demanded Hadley. "Mr. Seton wasn't knocked out with a siphon."

"Oh, yes, he was,"

It was so quiet that they could hear a fly buzzing against one half-open window.

"You see," continued Dr. Fell, fiery with earnestness, "the ordinary siphon is of plain glass. It doesn't have these criss-cross metal bands, or that nickelled cap at the other side of the nozzle. In short, this is a 'Fountain-fill' siphon; the sort which you fill yourself with plain water, and turn into soda water by means of compressed-air capsules."

Enlightenment came to Superintendent Hadley.

"Ah!" chortled Dr. Fell. "Got it, have you? The police, as a matter of ordinary routine, would closely examine the dregs of a whisky glass or any decanter found at the scene of a crime. But they would never think twice about a siphon, because the ordinary soda-water siphon can't possibly be tampered with. And yet, by thunder, *this* one could be tampered with!"

Dr. Fell sniffed. He lumbered over to the bedside table, and picked up a tumbler. Returning with it to the centre table, he squirted some of the soda into the glass. He touched his tongue to it.

"I think, Mr. Harold Mills," he said, "you had better give yourself up for theft and attempted murder."

★

Dr. Fell chuckled as he sat again in his own library at Chelsea.

"And you still don't see it?" he demanded.

"Yes," said Dr. Woodhall.

"No," cried Iris Lane.

"The whole trick," their host went on, "turns on the fact that the 'Mickey Finn' variety of knockout drops produces on the victim exactly the same sensation as being struck over the head: the sudden bursting explosion of pain, the roaring in the ears, and almost instant unconsciousness.

"Mills had a dozen opportunities that day to load the 'Fountain-fill' siphon with the drug. He knew, as you all knew, exactly when Francis Seton would drink his one whisky and soda of the day. Mills had already removed what he wanted from the safe. Finally, he had propped up a ladder outside the study window to make the crime seem the work of a burglar. All he had to do then was to wait for eleven o'clock.

"At eleven o'clock Seton drank the hocused mixture, cried out and fell, knocking over a number of objects on the carpet. Since the whole effect of this drug depends on a violent cerebral rush of blood, a man already suffering from high blood pressure would be likely and even certain to bleed from the nostrils. It provided the last realistic touch."

Dr. Fell growled to himself, no longer seeming quite so cherubic. Then he looked at Iris.

"Mills," he went on, "deliberately fiddled with the door, pretending it was stuck: which it was not. He wanted to allow time for the imaginary burglar to loot the safe. Then he ran in with you. When he turned Seton over, he took that piece of lead-filled broom-handle out of his sleeve, slipped it under the body, and dramatically called your attention to it.

"Next, you remember, he felt at the base of Seton's skull in pretended horror, and told you to go out and phone for a doctor. As a result of this, you also recall, he was for several minutes completely alone in the study."

Iris was looking at the past, examining each move she herself had made.

"You mean," she muttered, "that was when he—?" She brought up her arm in the gesture of one using a life-preserver.

"Yes," said Dr. Fell. "That was when he deliberately struck several blows on the head of an unconscious man to complete his plan.

"He removed the key to the safe from Seton's watch-chain. In case the police should be suspicious of any drinks found at the scene of a crime, he rinsed out the spilled whisky glass in that convenient cloakroom, and poured into the glass a few drops of harmless whisky from the decanter. He had no time to refill and recharge the siphon before you and Dr. Woodhall returned to the study; so he left it alone. A handkerchief round his hand prevented any fingerprints. Unfortunately, mischance tripped him up with a resounding wallop."

Dr. Woodhall nodded.

"You mean," he said, "that Seton noticed the ladder, and locked the windows?"

"Yes. And the unfortunate Mr. Mills never discovered the locked windows until it was too late. Miss Lane, as you have probably discovered, is a very positive young lady. She looked at the windows. She knew they were locked. She was prepared to swear it in any court. So Mills, floundering and drifting and never very determined except where it came to appropriating someone else's property, had to keep quiet. He could not even get at that betraying siphon afterward, because the police kept the room locked up.

"He had one bit of luck, though. Francis Seton, of course, never heard any footsteps behind just before the attack. Anybody who takes one look at the thick carpet of the study cannot fail to be convinced of that. I wondered whether the good Mr. Seton might be deliberately lying. But a little talk with Seton will show you the real reason. The man's boasted vitality is killing him: it has got him into such a state of nerves that he really does need a year in California. Once he saw that ladder outside the window, once he began to think of burglars, he was ready to imagine anything."

Iris was glancing sideways at Dr. Woodhall. Woodhall, a cigarette in the corner of his mouth, was glancing sideways at her.

"I—er—I don't like to bring it up," said Iris. "But—"

"Mills's proposal?" inquired Dr. Fell affably.

"Well, yes."

"My dear young lady," intoned Dr. Fell, with all the gallantry of a load of bricks falling through a skylight, "there you mention the one point at which Mills really showed good taste. Discernment. *Raffinement*. It also probably occurred to him that a criminal who propose marriage places the lady in a blind-eyed and sympathetic mood if the criminal should happen to make a slip in his game afterward. But can you honestly say you are sorry it was Mills they took away in the Black Maria?"

Iris and Dr. Woodhall were not even listening.

Sergeant Dobbin in

SERGEANT DOBBIN WORKS IT OUT

J. Jefferson Farjeon

Joseph Jefferson Farjeon (1883–1955) is an author who had disappeared into obscurity long before his lively thrillers were brought to the attention of a contemporary readership as a result of the British Library's decision to republish a number of them in the Crime Classics series. At the age of fourteen, Joe Farjeon started working as a secretary for his father, Benjamin Farjeon, an author and prominent figure on the London literary scene; unfortunately, the pair had a troubled relationship, perhaps as a result of Joe feeling the pressure of unrealistic paternal expectations. Joe soon found he could earn extra money through journalism, and became increasingly successful in his own right.

His breakthrough came with a play, *No. 17*, which premiered at New Brighton (then in Cheshire) before enjoying a good run in London's West End. He turned the story—which was also filmed by Alfred Hitchcock—into a novel, and settled into a career that was just as prolific as his father's had been. He spent much of his life in London, and for many years lived on Finchley Road. This story, written in his later years, first appeared in the *Evening Standard* on 26 September 1950.

A T 6.49 A.M. ON A CRISP SEPTEMBER MORNING THE TELEPHONE rang at Little Warbridge police station, and Sergeant Dobbin only just saved himself from gashing his chin with his razor. Not much happened at Little Warbridge, and when it did Sergeant Dobbin always had to deal with a secret emotion. It had to be secret, because policemen are not supposed to express any, but the sergeant had plenty beneath his official uniform, and whenever the telephone rang at an unusual time—a rare occurrence—he always experienced a somewhat ingenuous hope that this might herald his Big Chance. After all, you never knew, did you?

Half dressed, he hurried down to the room from which the bell was jangling and lifted the receiver.

"Little Warbridge police station," he said, in a firm voice intended to convey that he had been up for hours. Then his eyes popped, and he fought a most unworthy sense of pleasure. "What's that? Dead? On the floor?… Yes… Yes… Would you speak a little more slowly, I can't quite…" The agitated voice at the other end became slightly more controlled. "Yes… Yes… I've got it. Uphill, you say? Yes, I know the house. Please don't touch or move anything, sir… That's the idea. Thank you, sir; I'll be right along."

Replacing the receiver, he waited for a few seconds, then lifted it again.

"Warbridge 57." To his surprise he was answered almost immediately. "Dr. West? Sergeant Dobbin speaking from the station. Could you go at once to Uphill, Bell Lane, and meet me there? The Wethertons' place. Yes, sir, very urgent indeed." The sergeant's voice grew in importance. "It sounds like a murder case, but of course... Thank you, that's fine. Sorry to get you out of bed, sir, so early in the... Oh, were you? Well, come to that, sir, so was I."

Two minutes later he was on his motor-bike, speeding towards Uphill.

On the way he reviewed what he knew of the house and its occupants. This was not very much. The house stood by itself at the top of a hill, and its occupants were two brothers, Tom and Konrad Wetherton. Of Konrad, who had telephoned to him, he knew very little. He had only met him once and had found him a rather nervy man in the middle twenties, but he had seen Tom more often, generally going into the local pub. "But he won't be going there again," the sergeant reflected grimly, for it was Tom's body that lay at this moment on the floor awaiting his inspection. Well, that was all the back history he could think of, and it didn't amount to a row of pins. The present history was that Konrad had just returned from Manchester on a night train and had found his brother lying dead on his bedroom carpet.

The motor-bike chugged up the hill and stopped at the house on the top. Konrad Wetherton, hatless but still wearing a light overcoat, stood in the porch, the front door wide open behind him, and he came forward unsteadily as the sergeant dismounted.

"This—this is ghastly!" he gasped.

"It sounds pretty bad, sir," answered the sergeant.

"I haven't touched anything," went on Wetherton. "As soon as we rang off I came down here and waited; I thought that best. Of course, if one could have done anything—I mean, if my brother had only been—but, as it was, I thought—"

"You're quite certain he's dead?" the sergeant interposed.

"Oh yes. You'll see that at once. Otherwise I'd have telephoned for a doctor. Perhaps we ought—"

"One's coming, sir. Will you show me up?"

Konrad Wetherton turned, and the sergeant followed him into the house and up to a bedroom on the first floor. The door was ajar, and the sergeant, waving his agitated host away, stood regarding it for a few moments, and then gave it a gentle shove. As it swung slowly inwards, Tom Wetherton's prone body came into view. There was no doubt about it. He looked dead. And a closer survey soon proved that he was.

"Seems to have been hit on the head," said the sergeant. He glanced quickly around for some implement, but saw none. "And you found him just like this, you say?"

"Just as you see him, Sergeant," replied Wetherton.

"Is there anybody else in the house?"

"No. Only the two of us."

"And you've been away, you tell me?"

"I'm only just back from Manchester."

"What time did you arrive back, if I may ask?"

"Just before I phoned to you, that's all. Say, three or four minutes. The moment I saw what had happened—"

He gave a little despairing shrug.

"You telephoned to me?"

"Yes."

"Then you'd have got in here at about a quarter to seven, we might put it."

"About then, yes. It would be."

"Did you have any conveyance from the station?" came the next question after a slight pause.

"Eh? No, I walked. I only had a suitcase."

"I saw one in the hall downstairs."

"Yes. I put it there after letting myself in."

"I see," said Sergeant Dobbin, and began moving round the room. He asked casually, "Instead of taking it up to your room?"

Konrad Wetherton blinked, then nodded without offering any explanation. Was one necessary? But the sergeant did not pursue the point. Instead he asked, "And what did you do then, sir?"

"When?" jerked Wetherton.

The sergeant gave him a quick covert glance. Something seemed to have happened to him. Something new had entered his expression.

"After you had put your suitcase down?"

"Oh yes. Of course. I—I came upstairs."

"To go to your room?"

"Well, yes."

"What took you into this one?"

"What do you mean? The door was open." Wetherton spoke emotionally. "Wasn't that enough? I—I don't understand—"

His words trailed off. "It's something on this table," thought the sergeant. "Something's upset him, and he's trying not to let me know." It was a small table by the bed. The bedclothes were disarranged, as though someone had hastily left it. Probably someone had. But the table was the point of interest at the moment. What was on it? Glass of water. Cigarette case. Ashtray. Smoked in bed, eh? No ashes. Instead, the tray contained a slender tube of Veganin tablets. Did that imply anything? Silver frame, with photo of attractive female. Very attractive female. He turned to Wetherton, whose eyes were glassy.

"Would this be your brother's wife, sir?" he enquired.

"*No!*" The word came with venomous emphasis. Then was repeated more quietly: "No."

"I beg your pardon. I see—just a friend—"

"What do you mean?"

"Nothing, sir." Sergeant Dobbin's interest began to tighten. "Might I ask, sir, whether you were expected back this morning?"

Wetherton's hesitation was too obvious to be concealed, and before he had decided on his reply a sharp rapping sounded on the front door below. The sergeant swore softly at this ill-timed interruption, though his fast-working mind quickly turned it to account.

"That'll be the doctor, sir," he said. "Would you kindly go down and let him in?"

As though glad to escape, Konrad Wetherton left the room; and freed of his presence, the sergeant continued his search, his mind working swiftly as he did so.

"No, not *Tom's* wife, but *Konrad's*! Was he wild to see that photograph by his brother's bed, or was he! Not only wild, but frightened, too, because, of course, he should have got rid of that before phoning me up! *They* never knew he was coming back like he did! Probably he only went away so as to come back and catch 'em. It was a try-out. He leaves his bag in the hall and comes up quietly and catches 'em together. Let's take a whiff at the pillow." Sergeant Dobbin's nose descended to the pillow and he sniffed. "Evening in Paris? That's no man's scent, anyway. Good enough! And after he's packed her off, we have the row, and Konrad crashes Tom's head with—what?"

His eyes roamed to the fireplace. Tongs, hearth-brush, but no poker. Now, if there'd been a poker... Hey! What was he thinking about? No poker! *There wasn't any poker!*

He had just found it under the bed when Konrad returned, accompanied by Dr. West. The poker was still in his hand, gingerly held.

"'Morning, Sergeant," said Dr. West crisply, and added on his way to the lifeless figure on the floor, "Is that what did it?"

"You can help me to decide," answered Dobbin, and turned to Konrad. "Do you know where I found this, sir?"

Konrad stared at the poker with fascinated eyes and shook his head.

"Behind the window curtain," lied Dobbin rashly.

"Did you?" murmured Konrad.

H'm. Pity, that! He showed no sign of having detected the lie and the sergeant wondered ruefully whether he were trying to be too clever. Perhaps Konrad Wetherton was not such a fool as the sergeant had begun to suspect? But, after all, a clever rascal would surely have feigned some grief over the death of his brother—Konrad had shown none; merely horror—and if he had intended to blind the police by phoning them up he should have fixed a few false clues to assist in the operation.

A minute or two of silence went by while the doctor made his examination. When the preliminaries were over, the doctor said:

"Yes, you'll have to look for fingerprints on your poker, Sergeant. There is little doubt it finished him off."

"Finished him off?" repeated the sergeant.

"He was in a bad state of health, anyway. I attended him. Did you know that, Mr. Wetherton."

"I knew he was a sick man—largely through his own fault," replied Konrad. "We needn't mince matters. But I am often away, and I didn't know he had consulted you."

"When you say we needn't mince matter—" began Dr. West.

"He was drinking himself to death," said Konrad. "Nor was that his only weakness."

"But the immediate cause of death was that crack on his head," insisted Dobbin.

"Oh, certainly—occurring on a weakened constitution," nodded the doctor.

"How long would you say he has been dead?"

"I'd put it at from three to four hours."

"Oh! As long as that?"

"And nearer four than three. I haven't had many details. Didn't anybody in the house hear anything?"

Konrad Wetherton exclaimed eagerly: "There wasn't anybody else in the house—that is, besides whoever did it. I was away. On my way back from Manchester. There are no servants living in. A maid comes at nine and leaves at six. So, you see, there wasn't anybody here to hear anything. Someone must have broken in and—"

"Yes, I think I'll have a look round the front door and lower windows," interposed the sergeant. "I'll be with you again in a minute."

Sergeant Dobbin had a second purpose in leaving the room. His theory was going to pieces. If Tom Wetherton had been dead for at least three hours, and if Konrad had killed him, how had he filled the long interim? Had he waited all those hours deliberately? His overcoat was the only thing that suggested a recent arrival… Trains… Time-table… What train *would* he have arrived on, if not a recent one.

In the hall fortune was kind, though only to prove cruel. He found a time-table beside the telephone directory, and, being good at time-tables, he had soon worked out the only night connections from Manchester to Warbridge. The first, an early one, got in at 10.29 p.m. The last, a late one, got in at 6.15 a.m. There was no train in between.

"So where do we go from here?" pondered Dobbin, as he began examining windows and doors. "Half an hour from the station means he walked in round about eleven o'clock last night or six-forty-five this morning. The latter fits his story; the former doesn't fit anywhere! All right. Wipe him out. Find someone else. No sign of forced entry yet. There needn't have been any forced entry if the murderer was already in the house. Nobody was supposed to be in the house bar Tom Wetherton himself. But if he slept with someone—and if that lady was Mrs. Konrad Wetherton—yes, there may have been a row between them? P'r'aps Tom wanted a bit more than she was willing to give him, eh? Ah, what about that now? Out of bed she jumps. Fool ever to have got in. Out he jumps after her. She flies for poker. Bangs him a whopper, and down he goes, and out he konks, being already weakened by his bad habits! Now, if that happened between three and four, say, the timing would be right. Plenty of time for her getaway, after flinging the poker under the bed—or did it just roll there?—before Konrad comes back and makes his discovery."

Warming to this new theory, Sergeant Dobbin moved towards the front door for a final examination of it, and as he did so a letter shot through the slit and landed in his stomach to the sound of the postman's salvo.

He caught the envelope before it slipped to the ground, and he was holding it in his hand, vaguely regarding its American stamp, when footsteps behind him made him turn. Dr. West and Konrad Wetherton were coming down the stairs.

"Well, I've done all I can for the moment, Sergeant," said the doctor. "I don't suppose you'll want the body moved till the inspector's seen it?"

"Naturally not," answered the sergeant rather gruffly. Was the doctor trying to teach him his own business? This was just the preliminary investigation in response to Konrad Wetherton's SOS, and, of course, higher authorities would have to be brought along; but if possible he wanted to greet the higher authorities with the mystery solved, to help him on the way to become a higher authority himself, and a minute or two more or less would make no difference to the cause of justice. "I'm phoning the inspector in a moment, sir. You can wait for him?"

Dr. West glanced at his watch. "Yes, if you get him here before too long."

"What's that? A letter for me?" exclaimed Wetherton suddenly.

"Yes, sir. Just come."

Wetherton snatched the letter from the sergeant's hand. He was in a bit of a hurry for it, wasn't he? The doctor lit a cigarette, while the sergeant watched Wetherton fiddle with the envelope.

"Find anything down here?" asked the doctor a little impatiently. "My own belief is that a burglar's been in the place."

"Oh? What makes you think that?"

"Well, doesn't everything point to it? And then—of course, there may be nothing in this—but when Tom Wetherton came to see me he boasted that ten years ago, when his wind was sounder, he won a gold cup. 'If you visit me next time instead of my visiting you,' he said, 'you'll see it in my bedroom.' I didn't notice it."

Hallo! This was a new idea! Mrs. Konrad Wetherton would hardly go to bed with her brother-in-law in order to steal a gold cup! Sergeant Dobbin glanced at Konrad, but Konrad seemed to have forgotten them. He was standing apart, absorbed in his letter.

Quietly the sergeant turned and ran up to the bedroom. A quick glance round the room revealed an unoccupied space on an otherwise rather overstocked mantelpiece. The surface of the mantelpiece was dusty, but a circle in the middle of the empty space was dustless.

The sergeant descended, perplexed. The doctor looked at him enquiringly. Konrad Wetherton was still reading his letter. "It must be an absorbing letter," thought the sergeant, "to occupy his mind at a moment like this."

"Excuse me, Mr. Wetherton," said the sergeant, "but do you happen to know where your brother's gold cup is?"

Konrad raised his eyes from his letter and blinked.

"Gold cup? Isn't it on the mantelpiece?"

"No, sir, it isn't. Looks as if someone might have gone off with it, and maybe a few other things we'll find missing, though I haven't found any signs yet of forced entry."

"Could it have been a visitor?" suggested the doctor.

"Ah! Could it?" said Sergeant Dobbin, and after a moment's hesitation took a chance, without any idea where it might lead. "That lady whose photograph—"

"What the hell!" cried Konrad, suddenly waking up. "That lady is in America! I'm just reading a letter from her! Would you like to read it yourself?"

"No, of course not, sir. I just thought—"

"Well, you just thought wrong! I don't know what you're driving at," he went on excitedly, "but if it interests you this is a letter accepting my offer of marriage! Oh yes, and now you'll want to know what her photograph was doing in my brother's room. It had no right to be there! It ought to have been in my room, but I expect he took it while I was away because he was fond of her, too, though she'd already turned him down! Do you want any more? All right, you shall have it. One reason she turned him down was because he was too fond of women. I've no doubt my brother *did* have a visitor last night. He'd got in with a tough crowd and was getting too chummy with the woman who bossed it!"

"Pity you didn't mention that before, sir," grunted Dobbin. "Was that why you returned so unexpectedly?"

"What? No! Why should it have been? I returned because I got through my business a day earlier than I'd planned, and I was in a hurry to know whether this letter had turned up for me—as it has!" He paused, while the sergeant and the doctor exchanged glances. "Good heavens! You don't mean that—that woman—?"

"That's what I do mean," said the sergeant, on his way to the phone, "and if he picked her up at the Pig and Whistle that'll be a good start for tracing her. Love and larceny, that's my name for it, but if the feller wakes up too soon with thieving tarts of that kind, then there's trouble!"

And then Sergeant Dobbin phoned up the inspector.

It was, of course, just bad luck that the gold cup had been pawned that day to pay for a carouse, that Tom Wetherton had arrived home bibulous, that a few minutes after he had tumbled into bed he had tumbled out again in a drunken nightmare, that he had seized a poker (as his own fingerprints eventually proved) to fight an imaginary foe, that he had tripped and cracked his skull, and that Sergeant Dobbin's insensitive nose could not detect the difference between Evening in Paris and eau-de-Cologne.

Sergeant Dobbin did not get promotion. But he remains hopeful.

Albert Campion and Divisional Detective
Chief Inspector Charles Luke in

MUM KNOWS BEST

Margery Allingham

Margery Allingham (1904–66) was born in Ealing to a family of writers, although shortly after her birth the Allinghams moved to Essex.
Margery returned to London in 1920, studying drama and speech
training at Regent Street Polytechnic. She was precociously talented
and while there, she wrote a verse play, *Dido and Aeneas*, which was per-
formed at St. George's Hall and the Cripplegate Theatre (with scenery
designed by her future husband, Pip Youngman Carter). She and Pip
married and moved to Tolleshunt D'Arcy in Essex, but London settings
featured in many of her finest novels, and her series detective, Albert
Campion, lived in a flat above a police station in Bottle Street, Piccadilly.
The twice-yearly journal published by the Margery Allingham Society
is known as the *Bottle Street Gazette*.

Death of a Ghost (1934) is memorably set in and around "the Lafcadio
House and Studios in Little Venice, Bayswater, London"; the first edition
had delightful endpapers with a map of the crime scene. Many good judges,
including J. K. Rowling, regard *The Tiger in the Smoke* (1952) as Allingham's
masterpiece; the titular "Smoke" was a well-merited nickname for London,
especially prior to the enactment of clean air legislation of the mid-50s.
This story, anthologised in the posthumously published short story collection *The Allingham Case-book* (1969) as "Mum Knows Best", first appeared
as "Mother Knows Best" in the *London Evening News* on 12 May 1954.

M RS. CHUBB'S "LITTLE ROOM", WHICH HUNG LIKE A SIGNAL-BOX over the great circular bar of the Platelayers' Arms, was unusually deserted for the time of day, which was six o'clock on a fine warm evening. Only two or three of the habitués were present, but Charley Luke, the D.D.C.I. of the district, was there, and so was his old friend Albert Campion, startled at the moment into mild astonishment.

Luke was speaking. "Mum? Of course I've got a mum." He was aggrieved and his diamond-shaped eyes opened as wide as his prominent cheek-bones would permit. "What do you think? That I sprang in full uniform from the head of an Assistant Commissioner?" As was his custom, he gave a brief pantomimic display to illustrate his words and managed to look for a second like a piece of early Greek statuary, boldly costumed by a spiv tailor. "Not on your life," he went on, settling down again on the table where he had been sitting. "I've got a mum, all right. Two jam pots high and boss of all she surveys. Perceptive, that's what mum is."

He hunched himself suddenly and, by peering at us from under his lids and pulling his lips down over his teeth, gave us a sudden startling glimpse of a new and doughty personality.

"What she knows, she knows she knows," he said. "She's got a twenty-two carat heart, was born within sight—much less sound—of Bow Bells, and takes a poor view of policemen."

Luke grinned at Campion. "Her dad was killed in the Melbourne Street Raid when he was a Sergeant C.I.D.; she married a Superintendent and then there's me coming along. She's had a packet to put up with."

"What exactly has she got against the profession?" inquired Mr. Campion with interest. "Always assuming, of course, that the question is without personal offence."

"Not at all, chum." Luke's magnificent teeth showed for an instant above the pewter rim of his tankard. "She thinks we're a weak-minded, unsuspicious lot, too slow to catch a pussycat. And so we are, by her standards. If she wore a helmet, none of you would go out without your rear lights, and she can smell breath over the telephone. I caught her out once though. Whenever she comes the acid, I promise to buy her a diamond necklace. That sends her back to the gas stove."

He presented his back to us, hunched and sulky, so that we caught an image of an angry, elderly person minding her own business grudgingly.

"It was before I got my step up," he said, referring to his Chief Inspectorship. "I'd just taken over this manor and I was going steady, playing myself in. As you know, this isn't a posh district exactly, but it's been posh and there are, so to speak, remnants of poshness scattered about." He waved a hand to the open doorway where the flight of stairs led down into the stucco wilderness of the area north of the park.

"I'd got my office nice and clean, decided which peg to hang my hat on, and started reading up the 'pending' file, when in came my first bit of homework, a nice respectable old housekeeper, all gloves and embarrassment, and would I please come and see her Dear Old Master who'd been made a fool of and wanted to speak to someone BIG. I hinted the D.O.M. might demean himself and come down to see the D.D.I., but that wouldn't do. The Dear Old Master was too old, too ill, too silly, too upset. It sounded as though he was dropping to bits, so I took my hat off the peg and went down the road with her to inspect the ruin." He paused and his diamond-shaped eyes became reflective.

"I expected a nice clean house, you know," he went on. "But wacky! Luxury! Enormous great rooms full of gorgeous junk!" His long hands, which were never quite still when he was talking, drew some remarkably vivid shapes in the air. One received an impression of vast quantities of baroque furniture, statuettes, pictures and floating drapery. At the end of the swift performance he rubbed an imaginary piece of material between thumb and forefinger. "Velvet," he said. "Carpets, too. I was over my ankles in lush! Well, I saw the old boy and I thought he was one of his own idols until he spoke. He was sitting by the fire in a high-backed chair and he looked as if the last hundred years hadn't meant much to him. But he was very nice, you know. Very charming and even 'wide' in his own way. I took a shine to him. The story he had to tell was familiar enough—old-fashioned and not even out of the ordinary; but he told it very well and very politely, if you see what I mean—didn't expect ME to be a mug. He could laugh at himself, too. I've been hearing versions of the story all my life. The old chap had been out in his car with a chauffeur driving and they had crossed the park in a rainstorm. Presently, what should they see but a young woman, not too well dressed but quite respectable, caught by her high heel in a grating in the road. The old boy stopped the car and told his man to help her get free. After that they had to give her a lift home because the heel had come off. She gave a very decent address in this neighbourhood and they drove her to it, but didn't wait to see her go in."

He sighed and we shook our heads over the duplicity of young women.

"Meanwhile, of course," Luke continued, "on the drive he had heard The Tale. It was a good one. She was very young and she said she was a student at a dramatic school, that she lived with her mother who was a widow, and that she was determined to go on the stage. He asked her to tea one day in the following week and the old house-keeper, glad to see him amused, baked a special cake. So it went, all through the season until he'd grown quite fond of the poppet. As far as I could hear he never gave her anything but cake and the visits were restricted to formal tea parties. He was that sort of old boy. But the time came, naturally, when she did her stuff—'came to her bat', as we say in the trade." Luke pushed his hat on to the back of his head and blinked at us innocently.

"It's wonderful to me," he announced, "how certain stories just happen to work. Everybody's heard 'em, women are born knowing how to tell 'em, yet they never fail. Tell the truth—say, you've counted your money and you haven't as much as you thought—and no one will believe you. But come out with one of these old Cinderella yarns and Bob's your Uncle! You've got a happy and contented audience digging in its hip pocket. This girl told the one about the ball—I believe she really did call it a ball—where she was to meet The Impresario. She'd got a dress but—ahem—no jewellery." Luke favoured us with a leer of quite horrific archness, fluttering his lashes and widening his mouth like a cat's. "He fell for it," Charley went on, "went through all the motions except one. He did not ring for the chauffeur and drive her down to Cartier's for something suitable. Not at all. He trotted off to his study, unlocked the secret safe, and came back with something which must have startled her out of her wits. It was a single string diamond necklace. Family stuff, worth the Lord knows what. I had a full description of it, complete with weights of the individual stones and all the rest. He lent it to her for the evening. He told me that without a tremor, but I could see he knew he'd asked for it. He said she was so young and so guileless and had come to the house so often—that's where she was so clever—that he trusted her."

Luke wrinkled up his long nose with weary resignation. "After that it was just the usual," he went on, flicking away the details with a bony hand. "No girl, tea party deserted, no girl next day. Housekeeper consulted, talk, chauffeur sent round to the house where they had taken her on the first occasion. Finds out she's not known there… All the ordinary palaver. And there is my poor old pal without his sparklers and without his little ray of sunshine who, no doubt, is shining somewhere else all lit up like a perishing Christmas tree. That was where I came in." Luke shook his head. "The public believes in us if mum doesn't," he said. "Think of it. What an assignment!"

"So you didn't get the necklace back?" someone said.

Luke lifted up his hand.

"Don't hurry me," he protested. "Let me have my pleasure. I tried. We worked on it for months. The only description of the girl which we sifted—from the report of the three of them—housekeeper, chauffeur, and old boy—was that she was five foot one, two or three inches high; that she was pretty, innocent looking, 'like a flower', that her eyes and hair were 'blue and brown', 'hazel and black', 'brown and dark'. The diamonds were easier, but not much. It was a single string, you see. The value lay in the size and purity of the stones. The jewellers helped more than anybody. They all agreed that the necklace couldn't be disposed of over here without making a bit of a stir in the trade and that if it were broken up it would lose so much in value that they rather thought an effort would be made to get it to the Continent intact. We warned the Customs and shook up all the likely fences. I put the thing in the hands of a really good boy by name of Gooley, who was a sergeant of mine, and I got on with my other work."

Luke paused and accepted the cigarette Campion offered him. "It was one Sunday afternoon in August," Charley continued. "Hot? I thought I was being rendered down! I was sitting in mum's backyard reading the paper and trying to make a noise like someone weeding a path, when Gooley came through on the blower. He was in a terrific state. He thought he'd got her, he said, or he thought he knew where she was. In the last report I'd had from him he'd mentioned some rumours he'd picked up of a diamond necklace owned by a member of the chorus at the New Neapolitan. He'd followed these up like a sensible lad, but the show had closed, making the job more difficult.

Now he had got wind of the string of ice again and had pinned it down to a troupe of seventeen dancers who were just going off to Holland. In fact, they were actually at Liverpool Street Station, waiting for the boat train which was mercifully late. He was ringing up from the platform and they were all in the tea-room, chattering like a parrot house and laughing as if they'd got something on their minds." Luke grinned at the recollection.

"Poor Gooley," he went on. "He reported that they were *all* covered with diamonds! He said he'd never seen such a blaze. And he guessed that all the cheap jewellery counters of Western London must have been cleared. He was certain that the real necklace must have been amongst them, but for the life of him he didn't know where. He asked if he could pull them all in." The D.D.C.I. spread out his hands. "I wasn't quite as senior as I am now," he remarked, "so before answering I asked for the name of the management. When I heard it I thought twice. The Customs angle was difficult too. They'd help, of course, but if the train was late and the boat was waiting they wouldn't thank me if I sent 'em on a wild-goose chase. Gooley was by no means certain, and being alone he couldn't watch seventeen girls at once. 'We'll have to pick her out,' he said to me. 'Can't you bring an expert? He could look the necklaces over and pick the right one at once.'"

Luke rubbed his hand over his forehead and we remembered the heat of the day. "Expert!" he said bitterly. "Anyone who had brains enough to be an expert was out of London that afternoon. I only had half an hour. The old boy and his servants were away in Scotland and it looked as if I'd have to turn it up and let Gooley down. There wasn't a soul I could produce on the spur of the moment. Then I had a brainwave. 'Hold it,' I said to him. 'I'm coming and I'll bring someone who knows most things.'" He beamed at us. "I took mum," he said.

"It was quite ticklish work getting her there in time, but she arrived at last—little black hat crammed over her eyes, best coat buttoned up to hide her house dress, second best umbrella for defence. We found Gooley as arranged, by the bookstall. He was sweating with heat and anxiety, and his jaw dropped when he saw who I'd got with me. 'Is that…?' he began. 'Greatest living expert,' I said hastily. 'Where are they?' He pointed to the upstairs tea-room. 'They're getting ready to make a move,' he said, 'train's due in ten minutes.'"

Luke rubbed his hands with remembered excitement.

"We put mum in," he said. "Just like putting a ferret down a hole. She went through the glass doors and we stood one on either side. The idea was for her to take sights, spot the real diamonds, and then nip out and tell us. But there was nothing like that. Within a matter of minutes there was the Ma and Pa of a row inside. We hadn't time to get in. As we moved, a girl came flying out into our arms, making a bolt for it. Seconds later, mum followed, very dignified except that there was a cup of tea all over her where the kid had chucked it the moment she had asked her to take off her necklace." Luke wagged his head. "Poor mum! She was very pleased with herself until we all four got back to the station, roused the jeweller from Crumb Street, and got him to take a squint through his spy-glass at the kid's necklace. Net value Five Guineas and he didn't know how they did it at the price, he announced. 'Cheer up, mum,' I said to her. 'How could you tell diamonds, duck? You never had any except the little black 'un you call your eyes. Besides, it wasn't as if it mattered. By that time the girl had broken down and come across with the whole story, and I'd got through to Harwich where they'd picked up the real necklace."

As he ceased to speak, Mr. Campion took off his horn-rim spectacles. "Oh, I *see*. Mrs. Luke picked the *girl*."

The D.D.C.I. nodded. "Seventeen lovelies, five others on the staff, and four schoolmistresses who had nothing to do with it," he announced. "Mum took one look round and picked the only wrong 'un in the room. She'd seen her picture in the sensational Sunday rag she takes. Couldn't think what the story had been, but she knew it must be a police case because that's the only news she reads. It was eighteen months before—but she remembered!" Luke chuckled. "All the girls were plastered with fake ice to assist their chum to 'fool the Customs'. The little thief had lent the real stones to the youngest of them all—a kid of seventeen—so that she could carry the can if there was any trouble. Or that was the idea. However, when mum made her entrance and picked out the real crook, she lost her nerve."

Luke glanced at his watch and drank up hastily. "And who shall blame her?" he inquired rhetorically. "Not Charles! Kitchen tiles to be laid tonight or else," he added briefly. "So long."

Sergeant Pockle in

SERGEANT POCKLE IN PARLIAMENT

William Fienburgh

Long before Jeremy Corbyn arrived on the scene, the Member of Parliament for Islington North was Wilfred Fienburgh, who was first elected in 1951 and held the seat until his death in a car crash involving the Rolls Royce he was driving, at the age of 38, in 1958. Born in Essex, he was brought up in Bradford, and served in the Army during the Second World War, taking part in the Normandy Landings. Fienburgh was gifted, if not universally popular even with political associates; the future Deputy Leader of the Labour Party Denis Healey said "his good looks and big brown eyes often led him astray". Yet he combined political achievement with literary success to a remarkable degree in such a short life and one can only speculate about what he might have achieved, had he lived. His posthumously published novel *No Love for Johnnie* (1959) was filmed starring Peter Finch as Johnnie, a disillusioned politician who may have had a good deal in common with his creator.

Fienburgh's detective stories had escaped my notice until, a couple of years ago, I read an article about them by Jamie Sturgeon in *CADS* 88. Fienburgh wrote no fewer than twenty-five short stories about Sergeant Pockle, all of which were published in the London *Evening Standard*, starting with "Sergeant Pockle at the Pub" on 17 February 1954 and concluding with "The Case of the Fractured Ankle" on 11 August 1956. Jamie noted that none of the stories have been published in anthologies or collected in book form, so it is a particular pleasure to reprint this story, with a setting that its author knew so well; it was first published on 26 March 1954.

S ERGEANT POCKLE, DCM, MM, CHELSEA PENSIONER, LOOKED round the Lords' Bar of the Palace of Westminster with distaste.

It was a bare room, much more austere than the average London pub. In one corner paint was peeling from the wall. Sergeant Pockle had been sold a pup. "Where's the perishin' peers?" he said to P-c Jones, who had asked him in for a drink.

"Their Lordships don't use this place," said P-c Jones. "Nobody knows why it is called the Lords' Bar. It is only used by us blokes when we're off duty, and a few MPs and journalists who want mild beer—it's the only bar in the building that sells mild beer."

"Bless my perishin' corn plasters," said Sergeant Pockle aggressively. "And 'ere's me, polished me brasses and me medals special for the occasion expectin' to see a few lords with robes and decorations 'avin' a quick one."

"Well, you were wrong for once, Grandad," said P-c Jones. "In any case you won't see a row of decorations like yours in this place. There's a rule that Members don't wear medals in the House of Commons."

"And what," said Sergeant Pockle, "is the perishin' use of 'avin' medals if you don't wear 'em?" And he looked down with becoming modesty at the ten medals on his own left breast.

A sergeant of police burst into the bar, round eyes popping beneath the brim of his helmet.

"Gawd almighty," he said, "there's been a murder. The Minister of Planning and Reconstruction has just been found in his office with his head bashed in. Outside blokes," he said to the three policemen in the bar, "back on duty."

They jumped to their feet. Sergeant Pockle finished his drink and, leaning heavily on his stick, followed them out of the bar and down several dingy corridors lined with prints and show cases of medals, until he came to a narrow opening down which a sign pointed: "Minister of Planning and Reconstruction."

Inspector Mars of the CID, who usually shared an evening pint with Sergeant Pockle at a pub off the King's Road, Chelsea, was just entering the Minister's office.

"What are you doing here?" he asked.

"I reckon you'll need my help," said Sergeant Pockle. And he followed the Inspector into the Minister's office.

It was a small room. There was a desk, a green leather couch—and the Minister sprawled face down over a mass of papers on the desk. There was a wound on the back of his head. The stand of a large metal desk lamp, bloodstained, lay on the floor by his feet.

A uniformed inspector of the House of Commons police closed the door behind them.

"What happened?" asked Det-inspector Mars.

"I dunno," said the police inspector. "I was called down here ten minutes ago by Mr. Bulrose, MP for Southshire. It seems he and a chap called Peckingham came to the Minister's room and found him here, dead. We asked Mr. Bulrose and Mr. Peckingham to wait in another room and phoned you."

"And who is this chap?" asked Mars, nodding towards a willowy young man by the mullioned window.

The young man, whose stiff collar was immaculate although his trousers needed pressing, answered for himself.

"I'm Renfrew," he said, "a civil servant, the Minister's private secretary. I was working late at the Ministry in Whitehall. I was sent for about five minutes ago."

"Can you tell me anything?" said Mars.

"Nothing," said Renfrew. "The Minister had a function earlier this evening. That is why he is in evening dress. He came back for the ten o'clock division and was then setting out to attend the last stages of a military reunion."

"It is only half-past ten now," said Mars. "What would his movements be between returning to the House and coming down here?"

"He'd leave his car in the Speaker's Court," said Renfrew, "come into his office through Star Chamber Court, leave his overcoat here, go up to the Chamber, sit on the front bench until the division, and he probably came back here for his overcoat on his way back to his car."

"And who is Mr. Bulrose?" asked Mars.

"He is member for Southshire, the Minister's Parliamentary Private Secretary." Then he paused, "… there is something," he added. "I do not know whether I should mention it or not, but there was a dreadful row at the Ministry this morning. I could hear it in the outer office.

"Mr. Bulrose was apparently on the mat. I heard the Minister say something about 'You will have to resign as my PPS, but that is not enough. You have gone too far this time. I shall have to speak to the Prime Minister about it in the morning.' Mr. Bulrose was very agitated when he left the Ministry a couple of minutes later."

"And what about Peckingham? Who is he?" asked Mars.

"He is chairman of a firm of contractors who have been doing some work for us. The Minister was not satisfied with them. He had a suspicion that there had been some corruption in bidding for contracts. I do not know much about it. The Minister had been handling it himself. But he did say today that he thought he had Peckingham at last."

"All right," said Mars, "perhaps you'd wait outside. We'll talk to the other chaps now. Let's take the M.P. first."

Sergeant Pockle had been sitting in a corner making himself as inconspicuous as possible, a little difficult in view of his bright red tunic. As they waited for Mr. Bulrose he caught Inspector Mars's eye.

"It's on a plate for you," he said. "Two perishin' motives in two perishin' minutes. All you have to do is choose which. 'Ave 'em in and do eeney meeney miney mo—and don't forget that private secretary. 'E seems a bit eager to land everybody else in the soup."

Before Mars could reply, the Member of Parliament for Southshire came in, very pompous, very suave. He looked everywhere but at the figure of his chief.

"What does this Parliamentary Private Secretary job of yours amount to, sir?" Mars asked.

"It's nothing much," said Bulrose. "Some people would call it the first rung of the ladder. Some people would say it is just a glorified errand-boy's job."

"Would it worry you that you were asked to resign this morning?" snapped Mars. Bulrose started.

"I suppose Renfrew told you that," he said. "Well, frankly I couldn't care less. I am a busy man. I would be able to strike out a bit more from the back benches if I were not tied to the Minister."

"Would it worry you if your Minister was going to report something to the Prime Minister?"

"What, for example?" asked Bulrose.

"Suppose you tell me," said Mars.

Bulrose was angry. "It was a purely private political matter. I have nothing to say. It was nothing important," he snapped.

Inspector Mars pondered. "We'll return to that later, sir. Perhaps we can see Mr. Peckingham now." Bulrose left.

"'E's a perishin' politician," cackled Sergeant Pockle "'E's probably lyin'. They all do."

Peckingham walked in with easy assurance. "Dreadful business," he said to the world at large. "Sad loss for the country. A great Minister."

"And what are you doing here?" asked Mars, cutting short the panegyric.

"I called at the House early this evening hoping to see him, but he was out, so I sat in the Strangers' Gallery and listened to the debate for a while. Then just before the division I saw the Minister come in and sit on the Front Bench. After the division he left the Chamber. I could see he was on his way to an engagement, so I thought I would try and catch him before he left."

"What made you think he was going to an engagement?" asked Mars.

"Well, he was all dolled up, tail coat, white tie, medals galore, best bib and tucker, so I shot down here as quickly as I could. I met Mr. Bulrose at the end of the corridor and we came in together and found him lying here."

"All right," said Mars, "that will do for now," and he showed Peckingham to the door.

Sergeant Pockle and Inspector Mars were left alone. "Do like I said," said Pockle. "Bring 'em in and do eeney meeney miney mo. And when you've done that you'd better arrest that perishin' Peckingham."

"And why?"

"'E lies worse than a politician," proffered Sergeant Pockle with a malicious chuckle. "When 'e met that Mr. Bulrose at the end of the corridor 'e was comin' away from this room, not goin' to it. 'E'd already seen the Minister."

"And how do you know that?" asked Mars tolerantly.

"Because 'e said 'e 'ad seen the Minister with medals on."

"So he had," said Mars, "saw him in the Chamber with them on."

"Oh no 'e didn't," said Pockle. "I've been learnin' about Parliamentary eticketty. These MPs 'ave some sort of rule they ain't allowed to wear their medals in the Chamber of the 'Ouse o' Commons. So this Minister bloke must 'ave come down to 'is room to pin 'em on. So if Peckingham saw any medals he saw 'em on this corpse just before it conked out. So 'e's lyin'.

"Perishin' daft idea not wearin' medals," he added. "What's the use of 'avin' 'em if you don't wear 'em?" And he looked down with becoming modesty at the ten medals on his own left breast.

Mark Raeburn in

MURDER IN ST. JAMES'S

Malcolm Gair

Malcolm Gair was a pseudonym of John Dick Scott (1917–1980), a Scot who studied at Edinburgh University, taking a degree in history. He worked as Assistant Principal at the Ministry of Aircraft Production in London during the Second World War before joining the Cabinet Office as an official war historian. He had a spell as literary editor of *The Spectator* in the mid-1950s, but in 1963 he moved to the United States in order to take up the editorship of the World Bank's periodical *Finance and Development*. That career change spelled the end of a diverse literary career which had yielded mainstream novels and detective fiction as well as the intimidatingly titled *The Administration of War Production*, co-authored with Richard Hughes.

No doubt the move made financial sense, but it was a pity in some respects, because under the name Malcolm Gair, Scott had created one of the more credible British private eyes, Mark Raeburn. Raeburn featured in six novels published by Collins Crime Club, as well as in a handful of short stories; they included this one, which first appeared in the *Evening Standard* on 7 September 1956.

"**I**S THAT MARK RAEBURN? THIS IS FRED LODER.*" THE VOICE OF Detective-sergeant Loder sounded both urgent and worried.

"Fred? Where are you speaking from?"

"A call-box outside Royal Masons' Yard. You heard about the old woman who was murdered here?"

"Take a grip on yourself," said Mark. "I read the papers, you know. In any case, it's within two hundred yards of my office. Of course I've heard about it." As he spoke, he squinted again at the evening paper which lay on his desk. Under the heading "London Woman Murdered," it described how an elderly woman had been found with "extensive head injuries" at the Masons' Cafe and Snack Bar, Royal Masons' Yard, St. James's, and had died on the way to hospital. She had been identified as Mrs. Nellie Parker, 67, proprietress of the cafe, who occupied a flat above it. "The police," said the report, "are anxious to trace Mr. Herbert Roper, fiancé of the dead woman's daughter, who they think may help them in their enquiries."

"I take it," said Mark, "that it was Mr. Herbert Roper who bashed his future mother-in-law?"

"That's what we think," said Loder, "but I wish you'd come along and look at it."

"Come along and look at it?" said Mark. He was completely astounded. It was an unheard of thing for a private detective to be brought into an official police job. "Who's in charge?"

"Werner is, but he wouldn't know. He's gone and left me to do some clearing-up jobs. He'll chew me up if I call him back unnecessarily. But that's nothing to what he'll do if I don't call him back when I should. Go on, Mark, come round for half an hour. You can afford to."

Mark made a Scots noise in his throat, hung up, and reached for his hat. He knew Royal Masons' Yard well, a narrow passage off Pall Mall, with a pub, a newsagent's, a grocer, an ironmonger, a tobacconist's, and two cafes.

Loder met him at the corner, inconspicuous in a raincoat and a black hat. He nodded without a word and led Mark quickly through the little knot of sightseers and the uniformed policeman at the door of The Masons' Cafe and Snack Bar.

Inside it was empty and quiet. Mark knew why. The body had been discovered at seven in the morning. It was after four. All the photographing and measuring, the putting of samples into envelopes, the searching and the preliminary interrogating had been done. Loder, a fair-haired man, rather short and slender for a policeman, began to explain rapidly.

"She was found here, by this door, with the side of her head busted… we've got the weapon, an iron bar with some cloth round it that was used for keeping the door open… no fingerprints. She probably died between midnight and one o'clock."

"And Roper?" Mark asked.

"Roper was engaged to her daughter, Annie. Apparently the old woman bullied them both. In fact she bullied everyone. She was a terror. She couldn't keep any ordinary staff, but she worked Annie and Roper like slaves. She wouldn't let them marry."

"And they stood for it?"

"Apparently. As a matter of fact, both Annie and Roper sound a bit weak in the head. Annie got ill, but it was months before the old woman got in a doctor. The doctor spotted TB at once and whipped her into hospital, Roper was heard saying that if Annie died, he'd do the old woman in."

"And did Annie die?"

"No. But she had an operation and was very ill. But the most damning piece of evidence is that just before the old woman died she came to for a moment and muttered: 'It was Nicky.'"

"But Roper is called Herbert."

"The old woman called all her assistants Nicky." Mark Raeburn thought for a moment.

"Well," he said. "The obvious thing is almost always right in our job. What's worrying you?"

"Come downstairs."

"Downstairs" turned out to be a small cellar-like room. It was half full of tea chests, spare china, tins of food, packing and odds and ends.

"If you were going to spend some time here," said Loder, "where would you lie down?" Mark indicated a row of boxes.

"There, if they'd stand thirteen stone."

"Sniff the wall at the end." Without comment, Mark bent and sniffed. Then he got down on his knees and sniffed carefully, and looked up sharply.

"Hair oil. Quite strong stuff. Someone *was* lying here."

"And recently. Or the smell would have faded."

"Probably last night," Mark said. "Was it Roper?"

"The neighbours say he has a crew-cut. Never puts anything on his hair. Not refined enough, one of the girls said."

"What would a stranger be here for," Mark asked, "that he might conceivably commit murder for if the old woman rumbled him? What's through that door?"

"That's what I was wondering," said Loder, and turning a key he opened it. They found themselves in a tiny yard surrounded by high walls and still higher buildings.

"Now wait," said Mark. "Let me think. This is my own neighbourhood. Let me work out what these buildings are… that's an insurance office, of course, so the next one must be Rolands, the fishing tackle people... then the Horse Guards Club—and then—of course—with that drain pipe, that's Pewsey." He glanced quickly at Loder.

"The antique jewellery people?"

"Yes. Up you go." In a moment both men were on top of the wall, examining it closely.

"No one was here," said Loder.

"No. He was disturbed before he got started. But look at that thing." At the end of the wall, so placed as to be invisible from the yard, but now strikingly obvious, was a grille with savage-looking down-pointing spokes. "No one could get past *that*," said Mark. "I wonder if we're right after all. Give me five minutes to poke about." At the end of ten minutes he rejoined Loder.

"Why did Mrs. Parker call all her assistants Nicky?" he asked. Loder looked surprised.

"I don't know. But two old neighbours have deposed that she did."

"Ask them why," said Mark. Loder was out of the cafe and back in a few minutes.

"I've just had a message from the Yard," he said. "Bert Roper's been found and brought in for questioning. The poor fool had her blood on his shoes. That tears everything."

"I don't know," said Mark. "Did you get the answer to my question?"

"I did, for what it's worth. The old woman once had a waiter who worked hard enough to satisfy even her. *He* was called Nicky. He seems to have made quite an impression."

"Was he a Cypriot?" asked Mark.

"Yes."

"I've found out that the one building you can get into from here is the Horse Guards Club. That thing sticking out at the back is a ventilation shaft. There's an inspection trap and steps up inside."

"But why should anyone want to get into the Horse Guards Club?"

"Well, if I were you I'd go and ask if Sir Vere Cunningham was sleeping there last night. He's here for talks with the Prime Minister, you know. The terrorists have sworn to get him. It might be worth investigating. Especially if the original Nicky was the political type."

Loder went out, and returned in five minutes. "Sir Vere *was* at the club. As for Nicky, the neighbours say he was an odd man who worked like a slave and hardly spoke. Only once in a while he'd make a speech about Cyprus and Greece."

"Some of this is guesswork," said Mark, "but I'd back it on essentials. When the terrorists learned that Sir Vere Cunningham was going to be in the Horse Guards Club they set Nicky to get into it. Perhaps he boasted that he could. He hid here until the club was all quiet. Then he moved. Mrs. Parker heard him. Perhaps she stood at the head of the stairs and began shouting. Nicky came up and killed her. He was in a panic. He may have thought the neighbourhood was aroused. He lost his nerve altogether and bolted. Poor old Roper came in the morning and waded into the blood before he saw what he was doing. Then *he* panicked. People panic quite easily. It's lucky for us… If I were Superintendent Werner I'd have the ports watched. With Nicky in a panic you might get him, with a bit of luck."

And with a bit of luck they did.

"The Chief Inspector" in

THE MOST HATED MAN IN LONDON

Patricia Moyes

Patricia Moyes (1923–2000) was born in Dublin, the daughter of a senior civil servant who eventually became a High Court judge in Madras. Educated in Northampton, she joined the WAAF in 1939, serving as a radar operator and flight officer. After the war she assisted Peter Ustinov on the film *School for Secrets*, continuing as the film star's PA for eight years. She had literary aspirations and became an assistant editor with London *Vogue*. During her time on the magazine, she translated a play by Jean Anouilh, which became known as *Time Remembered*; it was a hit on the London stage and also on Broadway. In 1960, she worked on the screenplay of the film *School for Scoundrels*; Ustinov made an uncredited contribution to the script.

Towards the end of the 1950s, she found a silver lining in a skiing accident, by starting to write her first novel, published as *Dead Men Don't Ski* (1959). The novel introduced her Scotland Yard cop Henry Tibbett, and his Dutch wife Emmy, who plays an important part in many of the stories. She drew on her life experiences in several books; for instance, *Murder a la Mode* (1963), which centres around the London fashion scene and a magazine called *Style* was based on her time at *Vogue*. This little story first appeared in London's *Evening News* in 1961.

" I T ISN'T OFTEN," SAID THE CHIEF INSPECTOR TO HIS CLASS OF trainee-detectives, "that you come across a case you can solve by pure logic; but the Max Scotland murder was a classic, and I'll give you a big hint. It was all a question of timing.

"If ever a man asked to be killed, Max did. He was officially a moneylender and unofficially a blackmailer. He conducted all his business, legitimate and otherwise, from an old-fashioned office in the City, where he made his 'clients' call in person to hand over their money. Not all of his victims were rich. Max was democratic. He'd exploit even five bob's worth of human misery.

"Since he was probably the most hated man in London, I wasn't at all surprised to hear, one Saturday, that he'd been found in his office with his head bashed in. The alarm had been raised just before noon by Alfred Lightfoot, a young clerk from a nearby shipping firm, who'd had an appointment with Max, and found him dead.

"Now, here's the interesting part. The suite of offices where Max worked—if you can call it that—was guarded by a doorkeeper. An old soldier, very reliable. There was no way in or out except past the cubicle where this character, George Potts, was sitting all the morning.

"Potts told us that Max had arrived at ten o'clock. Nobody else was in, it being Saturday, but during the morning Max had three visitors. Sure enough, we found his engagement book on his desk, but it didn't help us much, because Max had used code names for his victims. He fancied himself as a scholar and always gave the poor devils classical names. A Mr. Mars was expected at ten fifteen, and a

Mrs. Niobe at eleven o'clock. Mr. Hermes—alias Lightfoot—was down for eleven thirty, but the entry had been altered in Max's writing to twelve o'clock.

"From the names I guessed that Mr. Mars was involved with somebody else's wife, that Niobe's scandal had something to do with a child, and that young Alfred might have been better-named Lightfinger. Anyhow, it was obvious that each of them had a motive for murdering Max.

"George Potts knew Lightfoot and Niobe by sight. They were what he called 'regulars'—came at the same time, first Saturday of every month. He didn't know their names, but he described Niobe as young, beautiful, and rich—she wore a mink coat. As for Mr. Mars, he was a new client—middle-aged, stout, and extremely prosperous-looking.

"Mr. Mars, George said, had arrived at ten fifteen prompt and spent ten minutes in Max's office. Then he'd come striding out, apparently very agitated, slamming the door behind him. Niobe had only been in the office for a minute or two. When she came out, she was crying— but she always was, according to George. Lightfoot had arrived at five to twelve. It hadn't struck midday before he came running out of the office, shouting murder.

"The next thing I did was to look at the office. It was bleak enough— two chairs, a desk, a filing cabinet, and a safe. The safe was open, and it was empty. The only cheerful thing about the room was the coal fire, and from the look of the ashes all the papers from the safe had been burnt in it.

"Max was lying on the floor between the desk and the safe. His head had been smashed in from behind with a heavy iron poker. There was less blood than I'd expected—only a sluggish stream that had dried up just short of the doorway. There were no fingerprints except Max's, but there was a footprint. Just one, in the dried-up blood by the door. It was the print of a very fashionable ladies' shoe.

"We had one stroke of luck. Not all the papers in the grate were completely burnt, and we found several scraps with legible names on them—two of them women's. We got hold of photographs of these two ladies, and George Potts identified one of them as Niobe. She was Lady Elizabeth Carter-Johnson, daughter of an earl and wife of a rising politician. She was terribly distressed when I questioned her, begging me to keep her name out of the papers because of her husband's career. She didn't deny that she was being blackmailed, or that the footprint was hers. She'd arrived promptly at eleven, gone into the office and found Max lying there, dead. For a moment she'd been paralysed with horror. Then she'd run away and not raised the alarm, for fear of being involved.

"Alfred Lightfoot said he'd telephoned at twenty to eleven, spoken to Max personally, and arranged to postpone his appointment. This was confirmed by Lightfoot's colleagues in his office. When he got there at five to twelve, he had found Max dead. Well now..."

The Chief Inspector regarded his class quizzically. "How many suspects have you eliminated so far?" There was dead silence.

"The first person in the clear," the Chief Inspector went on, "was Lightfoot. If he'd been the murderer, Lady Elizabeth would have found Max alive, and couldn't have described to me just how the body was lying, as she did. Then, the lady was saved by her own footprint. The doctor confirmed it would have taken about ten minutes for the stream of blood to reach the door. If she'd killed Max, she couldn't have left a footprint where she did.

"It began to look black for Mr. Mars—in spite of the fact that Lightfoot's phone call apparently gave him a perfect alibi. You can imagine my surprise when Mr. Mars telephoned Scotland Yard that afternoon, before the murder was reported in the papers. He was a businessman named Dacres, and the first of Max's victims to have the guts to report to the police. He swore he'd left Max alive and well at twenty-five past ten. You see my dilemma? Apparently, all three were telling the truth. Yet somebody was lying, and somebody had killed Max.

"I went and checked again with Potts. He was positive he'd got all the times right. People were always punctual for Mr. Scotland, he said. Never kept *him* waiting. After that I went back to the Yard and thought it all out. And then I made my arrest."

"You mean, you broke Dacres' alibi, sir?"

"No."

"But—"

"The murderer," said the Chief Inspector, "was George Potts. I told you that Max didn't spurn the most humble of victims. After that second interrogation I knew Potts was lying. He insisted that all three visitors were punctual—but Lightfoot's usual appointment was for eleven thirty, and he didn't turn up until five to twelve. Potts must have known that the appointment had been changed—so he must have been *in Max's office* and seen the engagement book, after Lightfoot's phone call and *before* Lady Elizabeth arrived. And when Lady Elizabeth got there, Max had been dead for ten minutes. So, allowing three minutes for the phone call, George Potts must have killed him between seventeen and ten minutes to eleven. As I said, just a simple question of timing."

Inspector Robinson in

THE DEAD MAN CLIMBED UPSTAIRS

Raymond Postgate

Raymond William Postgate (1896–1971) came from a distinguished family with Yorkshire roots. His sister Margaret married the economist G. D. H. Cole, with whom she collaborated on a long series of detective novels. Raymond married Daisy Lansbury, daughter of the future Labour Party leader George, who edited the *Daily Herald*, for which Raymond worked as a journalist. His 1920 book *The Bolshevik Theory* prompted an improbable tribute: Lenin sent him a signed photograph, which he treasured for the rest of his life. He was a founder member of the British Communist Party but soon fell out with his colleagues, although he remained active in left-wing circles and at one point edited *Tribune*. He also founded *The Good Food Guide*, so perhaps he might be described as a caviar socialist.

His remarkable debut novel *Verdict of Twelve* (1940), which focuses on the jurors in a murder trial, reflected his political attitudes, but not in a crude or didactic fashion. This innovative story cast a cynical eye on British justice and has been reissued as a British Library Crime Classic, as has *Somebody at the Door* (1943), which focuses on a group of passengers travelling on a train from Euston. Postgate reviewed detective fiction from time to time and edited a strong anthology, *Detective Stories of To-day* (1940). His third crime novel, *The Ledger is Kept* (1953) contained interesting ingredients but was too downbeat to have much chance of success. It seemed as if Postgate's brief career in the genre had run out of steam and I wasn't aware that he'd written any short crime stories until Jamie Sturgeon drew my attention to this one, first published in the *Liverpool Daily Post* on 20 August 1963.

I F YOU ARE A RATHER TIRED TICKET-ISSUING CLERK, SITTING IN the booking hall of a London Tube station, very late at night, there is practically nothing to do but to watch the escalators and listen to them going *plak, plak, plak* all the time. That is what Gladys did every night and she was doing it this night too.

Late night duty was dreadfully dull. No company—not even passengers, for it was too late for theatregoers and too late even for drunks. There'd only been three people in the last twenty minutes, and it wasn't likely that there'd be many more, as there were only two trains still to run, one north and one south. Nothing to look at—the lights were turned out in the showcases, along the walls, the newspaper kiosk closed, and the brilliance of the overhead fluorescent lamps only made the place look even more desolate.

Gladys went to the head of the chattering escalators and looked down them. They went a long way, deep into the earth, and at the angle at which they were set she couldn't see the other end. As it always did, the upward escalator was bringing scraps of rubbish with it, and piling them up at the top against the brass rim where the escalator steps went under. How dirty people were! She looked disgustedly at the empty cigarette packets, ice cream cartons, matchboxes, envelopes, and torn newspapers.

They bobbed and jerked at the top, rather as if they had been flotsam brought up by the sea and thrown there by little waves. Nothing of any interest was ever among them anyway; the stairs just steadily went on clacking away and bringing up dirt.

She was turning listlessly away when a dark spot far down caught her eye. Something was coming up for once. Bigger than usual; looked like an overcoat. Well it would be up in a moment. She turned away and walked to the kiosk to stretch her legs; she was still not interested.

That was why she did not get a clear view of the bundle until it came right to the top of the stairs, rising suddenly and silently into her sight as if it had climbed up a cliff; and then she wished, and wished for many months to come, that she never had seen it. Because it was the most horrible thing that had ever come up the escalator: it was a dead man. Not a tall man, but a little grey hunched-up man, collapsed within a dusty brown coat. There was no doubt he was dead, for the impact of his body against the top of the escalator had thrown his head back, and Gladys couldn't help seeing the ghastly gash that had cut his throat. The motion of the escalator made his poor body twitch steadily as if he were still alive: his hand had fallen across a torn piece of newspaper and shook over it. His unseeing eyes were open and looked at her through rimless glasses. He jogged his head at her.

A minute may have passed. Gladys heard herself screaming like a siren, and found herself scrabbling at the telephone inside her ticket booth. She couldn't dial any number, though; all she could do was screech, and it was pure luck that help came quickly. Detective Inspector Charles Robinson walked in from the street merely because he had been working late and was going to take the last Tube train home.

Even he, hardened as he was, was momentarily stopped still by what he saw. It was several seconds before he moved. Then he rapidly shut the grille which closed the station off from the street, lifted Gladys away from the telephone and himself dialled a number. Next he drove his fist through the glass panel of the "Emergency Brake" sign at the head of the stairs, and pulled the lever to stop the escalator. It gave two more clanks and fell still: the body ceased from moving too.

From downstairs there came a diminishing murmur which showed that the last train had just gone. Gladys had fainted, and the silence under the glaring lights in a few seconds was total.

Later, there were three men only at the head of the escalator—three living men, that is: Inspector Robinson, the police doctor who was kneeling to examine the body, and a Mr. Hopkins from the London Transport Board who was worriedly waiting for permission to have the whole dreadful shambles cleaned up in time for the first morning train.

"I can't tell you the exact time of death. You ought to know that," the doctor was saying. "It's more difficult than ever with the artificial heat they have in these stations—keeps a body unnaturally warm. But he was killed a quarter of an hour or half an hour before you found him. He wasn't killed here, of course; there's nothing like enough effusion of blood. His throat was cut at one stroke with a very sharp knife—probably from behind, but that's a guess. Suicide is quite impossible. Anyway, there'd be a knife here. Aged about 57. Anything else will have to wait for a post mortem. You can take him away now."

"I will too," said Robinson, "as soon as the stretcher bearers come. Thank you very much, doctor. It's all clear now."

The doctor dusted his knees and looked at Robinson without admiration. "All clear, young man?" he said. "Solved it already, I suppose."

"I wouldn't say that," answered Robinson, false modesty shining from his face. "But I know who the man is, and why he was killed: I am fairly sure who did it and how he got him on the escalator. All I wanted was the times, and you've given me those." He almost rubbed his hands.

Mr. Hopkins intervened with his own preoccupation. "Can I call the cleaning women in, then?" he asked. "Everything must be ready by 5 a.m., for the first train, you see. It's a nasty mess too. I'll have to explain to them first."

"All right," said Robinson. "As soon as the body's been taken away. Rope this part off—don't let anyone else in—and tell the cleaners they're not to say a word about this to anyone. Not to anyone at all."

"Yes, sir."

When the two police officers were able to walk away, Robinson almost physically felt the doctor's disapproval of his boasting. "I wasn't showing off," he said to the silent man. "I just happened to know that the dead man was a tailor called Abram Kohn; lives in my district. I know all about his life; the only strange thing is that anybody wanted to kill so gentle and harmless a creature. And as for saying I know who killed him, that's more or less an accident, too. It just happened that way.

"Kohn is secretary of a Polish club called the New Poznania Social Club, and the chairman is a new man, a fairly nasty type called S. Wyman. Carries a razor. We get a report from an informer that they'd had a pretty fierce quarrel the other day. Of course that's not proof, not yet anyway, and I shouldn't have said so. But I do think I can tell you how it was done, if you'd be interested."

The doctor was elderly, Scotch, disappointed, and due to retire soon: he had no particular liking for confident young products of the Police College. However, there was still quite a way to go to Scotland Yard, and the time had got to be occupied somehow. "If you want to tell me, you will," he said grumpily, "and I canna stop you."

"Then I will gladly," said the younger man, taking off his hat and smoothing his hair. "Kohn's throat was cut somewhere else—we'll find the blood in due course. He had to be brought to the escalator. How was it done? Simple enough, at that time of night. Two friends—friends: God help us—supported him, one on either side, as if he were a drunk. A tight muffler or handkerchief wrapped round his throat hid the gash and absorbed any blood that might still ooze out. So they helped him out at the station, dragged him along, talking to him all the time, up to the foot of the escalator; and when they heard the other train coming in from the other way they dropped him on the escalator and walked on board it a few seconds later. Neat timing—that was all that was needed."

"Huh," said the doctor. "Where's the muffler? and the knife?"

"Probably on the railway line. We'll find them."

S. Wyman, chairman of the New Poznania Social Club, was sitting in the chair opposite Inspector Robinson. He seemed very much at his ease, very much indeed. He was about 5ft. 10ins., dressed in an expensive silver-grey suit, with smarmed down black hair, dark eyes and a long nose. He was only too anxious to help the police. Poor old Abie, his best friend!

Robinson had collected a little more information about him and his best friend. Kohn had been secretary of the club for twenty odd years, while it was a quiet group of old Poles who drank beer and played chess. Recently, when it had been near to expiring, Wyman had come in and revived it. Brought in some new members, mostly with police records, and from somewhere quite a bit of money.

As for his quarrel with Kohn, the police informer hadn't got near enough to hear what it was about, but Wyman had been nasty, very nasty, and had been threatening Kohn. Kohn had looked small and frightened, but had resisted with the sort of obstinacy that humble men sometimes show when they are required to do something they think wrong. Those weren't the nark's words, but they were what he meant.

Searching Kohn's room had been no help. Somebody had been there before, probably, for all the Club records were missing.

"Your best friend, Mr. Wyman?" said the inspector. "I thought you'd quarrelled."

"Me quarrel with old Abie? Why, we were like that, Mr. Robinson. Every time I could do him a good turn, I do it. Ebbsolutely." S. Wyman's accent was a curious mixture of genteel and foreign, though which "foreign" was not clear.

"You didn't sound like that on Thursday in Rider Street."

"Oh, that," S. Wyman smiled sunnily and tried to lean forward to grab the inspector's arm, but it was just out of reach. "You know what we Poles are. We get so excited over politics: it doesn't signify anything, but we've all suffered so we have to speak strongly. I better explain to you. Old Abie was a very good fellow; we all loved him; but he was *réactionnaire*—very backward. I am very advanced, like all my friends are. I am an old member of the Polish Social Democratish Party. But Abie is an Endek. You know what an Endek is?"

"You tell us."

"An Endek is a National Democrat, what they call themselves. It is a very old style party, full of colonels and army men. So Abie and I we argue about what will happen some day when Poland is free. And that is all. Nothing, nothing. You want to know why poor Abie was really killed?"

"Why?"

"Money, Mr. Robinson. Oh, you think Abie was a poor man, because he lived poor. But I tell you he had his savings, and maybe you find his room has been cleared out."

"Funny you should know that, Mr. Wyman. Funny, you should have been picked up just one station after Abie was killed. Funny, you should have blood on your tie. Wasn't it? There's a lot of funniness to be explained, Mr. Wyman." Robinson's tone had become suddenly very unfriendly.

"But I have explained." S. Wyman at last seemed disturbed. "I've told your assistant. I have explained. I got an alibi. I want my lawyer."

"Of course. You can have him. Take him away, Jones."…

"That man's a fake." Robinson went on when Constable Jones came back. "I mean he's phoney even as a Pole. Did you notice how he gave himself away by the way he spoke?"

"No, sir."

"He said he belonged to the Polish Social Democratic Party. There never was such a thing. It was called the Polish Socialist Party. He pronounced the 'c' in Social 'ts'—he called it 'Sozial-demokratisch'. He pronounced the last word 'Part-eye.' That's what a German would do. Then he said Abie was an 'Endek,' showing off to ignorant coppers. But we aren't as ignorant as all that. The National Democrats, the Endeks, were the anti-Semitic party. Jew-baiting was their fun. D'you see a man called Abram Kohn as one of their members? Not possible.

"But being a German won't do Mr. Wyman in. Something else will. The narcotics people have been on the phone. Heroin's being passed out through a social club in this area and there was a Mr. Abram Kohn who was going to see them this morning with some important information. He didn't turn up, and they want to know why. Well, I was able to tell them. It's going to be a mighty good alibi that'll save Mr. Bloody Wyman."

But it was a mighty good alibi. S. Wyman was able to prove that he had been outside the other Tube station for a full hour before the body appeared—all through the time the doctor said the murder must have been done. How did he prove it? Why, just like in the song, he wanted to know the time and he asked a policeman. His watch had broken down, and he was waiting for a friend who hadn't come. What friend? Why, his old friend Abie Kohn, by a curious coincidence. And then again later, only a few minutes after the body was found, he was still there. For he walked into a cruising taxi just then, bumped his nose so that it bled, and started a fight with the driver.

The alibi proved to be unbreakable. S. Wyman could be held for a day or two by the narcotics people, perhaps. But that would be all. Clever Mr. Robinson had failed. He hadn't even found a bloodstained muffler.

He would have stayed so—failed in his most important case so far—if it hadn't been that Mr. Hopkins of the London Transport Board liked to chatter. "I hope you never have another trouble for us like that escalator business, inspector," he said. "Such a trouble we had with the cleaners! They've been demanding quite ridiculous extra money, for extra work. And the union's taken it up now."

"Didn't seem much work to be done, to me," said Robinson, idly.

"Not much work! Not much work! Goodness me, you ought to have been there when they restarted the escalator. My God, there must have been buckets of blood underneath it. Great cakes of it dried on the stairs, and in the well it was even worse. Of course you couldn't see it from above. How the poor devil must have bled. But of course the escalator carried it all away underneath. If you'd not stopped the escalator it would have come back again and you'd have seen it. The women want five pounds each for doing the job and I'm afraid they'll have to have it."

But Robinson wasn't listening any more. The case against S. Wyman was on again. Abie hadn't been killed elsewhere, and not a quarter of an hour before. He had been killed at the foot of the escalator, just as the last train the other way was due. Wyman had been standing behind him and had sliced his throat open with a razor, let him drop on the stairs, and walked on to the train with no more than a few drops of blood on his tie. Back at the other station he had run up the old fixed stairs—nobody watches them now escalators have been installed. Then he hit a taxi driver.

All good liars tell as near the truth as they can. S. Wyman had been near the other tube station nearly all the evening. He did run into a taxi. He did have an appointment with Abie, but it was on the station platform. And after a while he had another appointment, this time with the hangman and in Pentonville gaol.

Late on the evening of the day when he kept it, Robinson and Hopkins happened to walk in from the street into the booking hall. The lights were blazing down on emptiness again, and Gladys was watching the escalators. She looked up and saw them. "Not you two again!" she said and let out a powerful wailing scream, the sort of penetrating howl which the old *Mauretania* made when she entered New York harbour.

Chief Inspector Hazlerigg in

BACK IN FIVE YEARS

Michael Gilbert

Michael Francis Gilbert (1912–2006) was born in Lincolnshire and lived for much of his life in Kent, but spent many years travelling to central London, where he worked as a solicitor with the firm Trower, Still and Keeling in Lincoln's Inn, with his main specialism being probate law. He wrote his books while commuting, and such was their quality and quantity that at least one prominent fellow author cast doubt on whether it was possible to write so much, so well, simply when going back and forth on the train. With characteristic urbanity, Gilbert replied that he only wrote on the outward journey; to write after a full day's work would be too exhausting. His understanding of the legal world around the Inns of Court gave a touch of authenticity to his wonderfully entertaining mystery novel *Smallbone Deceased* (1950), which along with *Death Has Deep Roots* (1951), partly set at a trial at the Old Bailey, and *Death in Captivity* (1952) has been reissued by the British Library as a Crime Classic.

Gilbert used a very wide range of settings for his books, but London often recurs, as in *Fear to Tread* (1953), in which a head teacher stumbles across the activities of a ruthless black-market gang operating in the city and in the many stories about his detective Patrick Petrella, notably the novel *Blood and Judgement* (1959) and the short story collection *Petrella at Q* (1977). The narrator in *Flash Point* (1977) works for the Law Society in Chancery Lane. This early story, featuring his first series character, Hazlerigg of Scotland Yard, first appeared in *John Bull* on 18 December 1948.

(As Told by Chief Inspector Hazlerigg)

I N THE EARLY THIRTIES, WHEN I WAS A JUNIOR INSPECTOR ATTACHED to the uniformed branch in a North London division, there were a number of known counterfeiters at work in London. I don't mean that we knew their names and addresses, for they tend to be shy people, but a surprising number of facts about them and their products were filed and tabulated at the Criminal Records Office and in the M-0 file.

There were forgers of Post Office Savings books, and there were those who specialised in passports and share certificates. But the kings of the trade were the forgers and utterers of banknotes. And the king of them all was a certain shy, unobtrusive genius who manufactured the "Beauties."

His identity was, of course, a mystery. He was known to us only by his £1 notes, finely etched and most scrupulously printed.

In a lot of ways they were a better product than the stuff being turned out by H.M. Mint. That young lady who sits up in an inset in the top left-hand corner (on the genuine pound notes she looks rather a pudding-faced young person)—well, in his productions she was a miracle of dignified beauty. That's why we called them "Beautiful Britannias," or "Beauties."

And you can take it from me that there wasn't a policeman in the Metropolis who wouldn't have given his belt and buttons for a chance to lay hands on the artist.

However, as it happens—and as it happens in most police work— it wasn't one man or even a few men who got on the track of the forger. When this happy event finally came to pass it was the result of a combination of luck and instinct backed up by the hard, slogging work of a great number of people.

We had regretfully decided that in the case of the Beauties we were up against one of those rarities in the field of crime—an entirely solitary and single-handed operator; a man with at least one godlike attribute, the strength which is said to come from loneliness.

He must have made his own plate—it may have taken him a year or more of patient trial and error, cutting, smoothing, and sizing. He even had a rotation system which enabled him to change the numbering.

But it was his method of distribution that put him at the top of the class.

Having printed a number of very excellent pound notes, he rationed himself to about twenty a week. These he would cash personally, going to shops and post offices all over London, and never to the same one twice. He would purchase some small object costing not more than a few pence or a shilling, pay with a pound note, and pocket the change. The system was laborious, but almost foolproof. And, but for one small thing, I really have my doubts whether we should have got on to him.

The thing was he had a weakness for pawnbrokers. Perhaps it was because pawnbrokers' shops are places which have a wide variety of things which you can pick up for a small sum; and they are usually rather dark and not very crowded and don't make difficulties about change. Anyway, it proved his undoing.

For pawnbrokers, as you may know, are people who like to work very closely with the police. There's nothing underhanded about it. It just happens to pay both sides. There's a Pawnbrokers' List of Stolen Articles which we publish at Scotland Yard, and most pawnbrokers make a practice of reporting anything suspicious to the local station. The local police, in return, keep a special eye on their shops, which are a tempting target to the light-fingered fraternity.

Well, over the months and years, reports piled up of these pound notes being received by pawnbrokers. So, just on the chance (that's a phrase which features pretty prominently in police work), a letter was sent round to all pawnbrokers saying that if they should happen to notice a man or woman coming into their shop who wasn't a regular customer, and who wanted to make a small purchase and proffered a brand-new pound note for it, then would they please make a careful note of his description, etc., etc.

After a time the descriptions started to add up. It was extraordinarily fascinating, sitting back in an office watching a living person being built up out of fractions, watching his features line themselves in, and his identity declare itself.

We got a picture of a man, middle-sized to small, plump, soft-spoken, with white, pudgy hands, strong black hair and weak, rather peering eyes. His clothes naturally varied from time to time and from place to place but the essentials were the same.

A very wide and elaborate net was then spread. I won't bore you with all the details, but you can gather the scope of it when I tell you it meant stationing policemen within call of almost every pawnshop which had not yet been visited and arranging a simple system of signals with the pawnbrokers themselves.

And that was how, at the beginning of June, 194–, the police at last caught sight of Mr. Mountjoy and followed him discreetly home to 14 Malpas Street. This proved to be a small shop in North London, with living quarters attached, and an independent flat over it.

Some further facts now came to light. All seemed to point to the one conclusion. To start with, Mr. Mountjoy's business was that of a one-man printer and typemaker; very suitable, we felt, allowing its owner to possess and operate various small machines and lathes without exciting suspicion. Then again, he was a solitary man, who, according to Mr. Crump, of 12 Malpas Street, his nearest neighbour,

310 METROPOLITAN MYSTERIES

spent much of his time out of his shop, apparently on journeys round London.

"Looking for commissions, I expect," said Mr. Crump. "Not that he seems to get much work. Manages to do very well for himself, none the less."

I was in charge of these local inquiries, and sensing a certain amount of rancour in that last remark, I guessed that there might be some trade rivalry. Mr. Crump was a newsagent and printer himself. However, he was unable to help me much, because he didn't know very much. But he did say that Mr. Mountjoy seemed to do a lot of work at night.

In some trepidation, because we didn't want to expose our hand too soon, I tried Mrs. Ireland, who lived in the flat over Mr. Mountjoy's shop. She was a middle-aged party, intensely respectable and slightly deaf. I visited her one morning in the well-worn disguise of an inspector of gas meters, and found her surprisingly willing to talk.

She, unlike Mr. Crump, had the very highest opinion of Mr. Mountjoy. Possibly he *was* one who kept himself to himself but there was no harm that she could see in that. Better that than clumping about sticking your nose into what didn't concern you. This, I gathered, was a back-hander at Mr. Crump, whom she didn't like. Unfortunately, her deafness prevented her from being able to corroborate the story of night work.

Well, there it was. You now know all that we knew at that point and you can see how we were fixed. I had no doubt in my mind. The description fitted. The setup was exactly what we had imagined. The printer's shop—the night work—the journeys round London.

There was only one thing to do—take a search warrant and chance the odds.

Accordingly, on Midsummer Day, 194–, just after four o'clock in the afternoon, I took Sergeant Husband with me and walked over to Malpas Street to put the matter to the test. And as I turned into the road the first thing that struck my eye was that damned notice and I realised that we had missed our man. How narrowly we had missed him became apparent as we pursued our inquiries.

The notice? It was pinned to the door of the shop. Written in a copperplate hand on a neat white card, it said: *BACK IN FIVE YEARS*.

No. 14 was the end house of a block of seven. It had the shop entrance in front, and an independent side entrance which led up to Mrs. Ireland's flat.

Now the curious thing was this. Five minutes before we had arrived, several people had seen Mr. Mountjoy come out and pin that notice on his door. But after that no one could say which way he had gone. This didn't all come out at once, but inquiries in the street, then and later, only deepened the mystery.

For instance, Mrs. Ireland had been sitting at her window, which overlooked the point where the side street joined the main. Although she might be deaf, she certainly wasn't short-sighted and she happened to have been keeping her eyes open for the postman. She was prepared to swear that Mr. Mountjoy had neither passed the end of the side road nor gone down it.

Suppose, therefore, he had turned to the left outside his front door? But Mr. Crump in No. 12 and the barber in No. 8 had both been in their shops the whole time and were positive that he had not gone past them. Had he gone back into his shop or the living room behind it? But these were most undeniably empty, and had, besides, the sort of "packed up" appearance of rooms whose owner has left them deliberately. The gas and electricity were turned off, the larder was empty.

There was a door leading into the garden, and this was locked. That, by itself, didn't prove anything, of course, but the garden was a dead end. There was a very high, glass bottle-topped wall on the street side, the blank elevation of another house at the end, and a garden full of little Crumps on the right.

Mr. Mountjoy, in fact, had walked into the street, pinned up his famous notice, and then dematerialised.

But, unlike the conjurer's lady assistant, he not only disappeared, he stayed disappeared. And that is not such an easy thing to do—not in this country, anyway, especially when the police are on the lookout for you and have your full description.

However, as with everything else, Mr. Mountjoy managed it competently enough.

The police force, like the Army, believes in moving its executives around, and it wasn't until well over four years later—nearly five—that I found myself back at the same North London police station, attached this time to the plain-clothes branch.

One of the first places I visited was Malpas Street, and there, still, was the notice: *BACK IN FIVE YEARS*.

In a district like that you'd have imagined that it would have been torn down long ago. But it hadn't.

I gathered, in fact, that it had become a sort of local tradition. Mr. Mountjoy had always been a mystery man to the neighbourhood, and his reputation had been nowise diminished by his dramatic disappearance and the interest of the police in his whereabouts.

There was a strong local feeling, amounting almost to an obsession, that five years after his disappearance (on the very day and at the very hour) Mr. Mountjoy would reappear and take that notice down again.

What would happen then no one could suggest.

I asked the station sergeant about the place. For instance, why hadn't it been re-let or taken over by the authorities? Mr. Mountjoy, I gathered, owned the building but the taxes must be mounting up and anyway it was a nice little shop and living quarters. We didn't talk about requisitioning in those days, but we had some powers. Apparently, however, all this had been foreseen by Mr. Mountjoy.

The day before he disappeared he had handed Mrs. Ireland a sum in notes (genuine ones this time) sufficient to deal with all foreseeable expenses *for exactly five years*. At the end of that time, he said, if he hadn't come back she could sell the house and keep the proceeds. And he had even executed a legal document enabling her to do this.

In short, she was to wait for him for five years, and at the end of that time, like the frog in the fairy story, she was to have her reward—unless the fairy prince had reappeared to claim his own.

It sounded pretty fantastic to me.

The next thing that happened, about three weeks later, was the arrival at the station of a badly worried Mr. Crump, with a tale that No. 14 was haunted.

He was so clear about it that we gave more attention to his story than the police usually accord to psychic manifestations. Also, of course, we were interested in that particular house.

"Scraping, cutting, and emery-papering," said Mr. Crump, his great red face moist but earnest. "Every night—about midnight or one o'clock. Just like he used to. I don't like it. Nor the wife don't like it. She's talking of moving if it isn't stopped."

"Did you go down and look in?" I asked. "Was there a light on in the shop?"

"Of course there wasn't no light on," said Mr. Crump. "Hasn't the electricity been cut off? I've told you, it's not yooman, this noise isn't."

When I suggested that it might be rats, I thought Mr. Crump was going to detonate, so I hurriedly promised him that we'd look into it and he departed.

We had the keys of the shop, so I let myself in that evening, going after dark to avoid causing any undue stir. I took a torch and made a thorough investigation. It was obvious no one had been there. The dust was inches thick over everything, and the place—well, it *smelt* deserted, if you know what I mean.

When I came out I found half Malpas Street gathered outside armed with sticks and bottles. Apparently a small boy had seen my torch flashing and the crowd were just summoning up courage to break in and lay the ghost when I stepped out.

After that, of course, there was no stopping the stories.

Mr. Crump appeared about a month later with an ultimatum.

Either the police "did something" or he was going to clear out himself. He couldn't stand it any longer. His wife had already gone on an indefinite visit to her married sister and trade was falling off. The sinister reputation of No. 14 was beginning to corrupt No. 12.

"All right," I said at last. "I'll come along myself tonight and we'll both listen."

When I came off duty at about half past ten that evening, I walked along to Malpas Street and Mr. Crump let me in. We sat in his parlour, which was on the first floor overlooking the street, and we drank beer and talked for a bit, and at midnight, at my suggestion, we turned the lights out and made ourselves comfortable in chairs near the window.

After a bit I must have dozed, because I woke up to feel Mr. Crump gripping my arm.

He said nothing, but I gathered from his breathing, which he was trying to control, that something had happened.

Then, in the stuffy blackness of the room I heard it, too. It was a thin intermittent burr, which sounded like a very sharp edge cutting across some tough substance. Then came the sound of scraping, and then the cutting started again.

I jumped up, leaped at the door, nearly broke my neck on the stairs, and three seconds later I was out in the street. I had my key at the ready and I snapped open the door of No. 14 and switched on my torch.

There was no one there. Nothing had been disturbed at all. There wasn't even the trace of a rat or mouse paw in the dust. I hadn't thought that there would be. There had been something indefinably human about that sound.

When I got back to Mr. Crump, I found he had turned on the light and poured out some more beer. He seemed much more cheerful. I think that half his trouble had been that no one believed his story.

Also, as we were finishing our beer, he said something which surprised me.

"Thanks be," he said. "I've only to put up with it for one more week."

"What do you mean?" I asked.

"Work it out for yourself," he said. "It's the seventeenth of June. Four years and 51 weeks ago he left. Said he'd be back in five years. Very methodical man was Mr. Mountjoy."

I could find no comment to make.

It was quite illogical and fantastic, and I felt that we were making fools of ourselves, but in the end I agreed, weakly, to post two sergeants to watch the back of the house while I kept an unobtrusive eye on the front.

If Mr. Mountjoy was going to maintain his reputation for punctuality he was due in the street at four o'clock in the afternoon. Accordingly, at five to four I turned the corner at the far end of the road and started strolling nonchalantly towards No. 14, stopping every now and then to look in at the various shop windows.

It was a true midsummer day, warm and windless, and the children were still in school, so that by Malpas Street standards it was almost quiet.

I looked at my watch and saw that it was just short of four o'clock. And Malpas Street was still most definitely empty.

At that moment, in the warm summer silence, I heard it again. I want to be quite clear about this. It was exactly and undeniably the same sound that I had heard that night when I sat up over Mr. Crump's shop. But it did not come from No. 14.

It was from the same side of the street but much lower down.

I moved cautiously along until I could locate it. It came from the barber's shop at No. 8, where Toni Etrillo, the barber, was shaving one of his swarthy compatriots. The burr and the rasp as the razor passed across the strong black stubble—these were unmistakable.

And in that moment the secret of Mr. Mountjoy's disappearance became as abundantly clear to me.

The first thing I did was purely symbolical. I took out my knife and levered out the tack which held up that notice. I was about to tear it up but thought better of it and dropped it in my pocket.

Conscious that a dozen pairs of eyes were watching from curtained windows, I went round into the side street and rang Mrs. Ireland's doorbell.

When she opened the door I didn't do anything dramatic; I just beckoned her out into the street and signalled to one of the sergeants to accompany us, and we all walked back to the police station.

For the greater part of the way we were silent, but I felt, in justice, that one thing had to be said.

"A marvellously well kept-up impersonation, Mr. Mountjoy. It's nothing new for a man to dress as a woman, and I have even heard of cases before where a landlord became his own lodger. But—it's a great mistake for any man to do his shaving last thing at night."

ALSO AVAILABLE

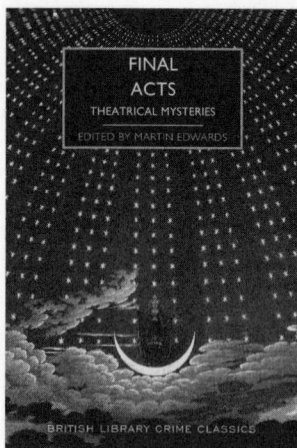

*"... and what a motive! Murder to save one's
artistic soul... who'd believe that?"*

Behind the stage lights and word-perfect soliloquies, sinister secrets are lurking in the wings. The mysteries in this collection reveal the dark side to theatre and performing arts: a world of backstage dealings, where unscrupulous actors risk everything to land a starring role, costumed figures lead to mistaken identities, and on-stage deaths begin to look a little too convincing. . .

This expertly curated thespian anthology features fourteen stories from giants of the classic crime genre such as Dorothy L. Sayers, Julian Symons and Ngaio Marsh, as well as firm favourites from the British Library Crime Classics series: Anthony Wynne, Christianna Brand, Bernard J. Farmer and many more.

Mysteries abound when a player's fate hangs on a single performance, and opening night may very well be their last.

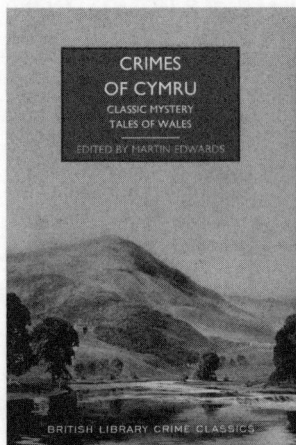

"Ahoy, my lad!" he bellowed back. "I didn't expect you so
early. Come for a dip! The water's fine. Everything is—"
Then it happened.

Mystery and murder run amok amidst ominous peaks and icy lakes. In hushed valleys, venom flows through villages harbouring grievances which span generations. The landscapes and locales of Wales ("Cymru", in the Welsh language) have fired the imagination of some of the greatest writers in the field of crime and mystery fiction.

Presenting fourteen stories ranging from 1909 through to the 1980s, this new anthology celebrates a selection of beloved Welsh-born authors such as Cardiff's Roald Dahl and Abergavenny's Ethel Lina White, as well as lesser-known yet highly skilled writers such as Cledwyn Hughes and Jack Griffith. Alongside these home-grown tales, this collection also includes a handful of gems inspired by, or set in, the cities and wilds of Wales by treasured British authors with an affinity for the country, such as Christianna Brand, Ianthe Jerrold and Michael Gilbert.

ALSO AVAILABLE
IN THE BRITISH LIBRARY
CRIME CLASSICS SERIES

Big Ben Strikes Eleven	DAVID MAGARSHACK
Death of an Author	E. C. R. LORAC
The Black Spectacles	JOHN DICKSON CARR
Death of a Bookseller	BERNARD J. FARMER
The Wheel Spins	ETHEL LINA WHITE
Someone from the Past	MARGOT BENNETT
Who Killed Father Christmas?	ED. MARTIN EDWARDS
Twice Round the Clock	BILLIE HOUSTON
The White Priory Murders	CARTER DICKSON
The Port of London Murders	JOSEPHINE BELL
Murder in the Basement	ANTHONY BERKELEY
Fear Stalks the Village	ETHEL LINA WHITE
The Cornish Coast Murder	JOHN BUDE
Suddenly at His Residence	CHRISTIANNA BRAND
The Edinburgh Mystery	ED. MARTIN EDWARDS
Checkmate to Murder	E. C. R. LORAC
The Spoilt Kill	MARY KELLY
Smallbone Deceased	MICHAEL GILBERT
The Story of Classic Crime in 100 Books	MARTIN EDWARDS
The Pocket Detective: 100+ Puzzles	KATE JACKSON
The Pocket Detective 2: 100+ More Puzzles	KATE JACKSON

Many of our titles are also available
in eBook, large print and audio editions